"Just a Minute," Colt Said. "We Haven't Finished Our Hand Yet. Besides, I Might Like Some of That Action Myself."

He nodded toward the pile of chips in the center of the table. "Now, you're going to finish out the game. And just to sweeten the pot, I think we ought to add the lady to the stakes. That should make the game even more interesting."

Cameron felt her heart stop. How could she have ever believed this man was a hero? She had deluded herself into believing that he was a wealthy, cultured gentleman. Now she saw him for what he really was. He was a gunfighter, a card shark, and infinitely more dangerous than any of the others at this table.

The man they called Colt gave an icy smile. No one moved. "Pick up your cards."

Dear Reader,

We, the editors of Tapestry Romances, are committed to bringing you two outstanding original romantic historical novels each and every month.

From Kentucky in the 1850s to the court of Louis XIII, from the deck of a pirate ship within sight of Gibraltar to a mining camp high in the Sierra Nevadas, our heroines experience life and love, romance and adventure.

Our aim is to give you the kind of historical romances that you want to read. We would enjoy hearing your thoughts about this book and all future Tapestry Romances. Please write to us at the address below.

The Editors
Tapestry Romances
POCKET BOOKS
1230 Avenue of the Americas
Box TAP
New York, N.Y. 10020

Nevada Nights

Ruth Ryan Langan

A TAPESTRY BOOK
PUBLISHED BY POCKET BOOKS NEW YORK

This novel is a work of historical fiction. Names, characters, places and incidents relating to non-historical figures are either the product of the author's imagination or are used fictitiously. Any resemblance of such non-historical incidents, places or figures to actual events or locales or persons, living or dead, is entirely coincidental.

An *Original* publication of TAPESTRY BOOKS

A Tapestry Book published by
POCKET BOOKS, a division of Simon & Schuster, Inc.
1230 Avenue of the Americas, New York, N.Y. 10020

ISBN: 0-671-54427-6

First Tapestry Books printing January, 1985

10 9 8 7 6 5 4 3 2 1

Printed in the U.S.A.

To my parents,
John Edward Ryan and Beatrice Curley Ryan,
with love

Author's Note

My childhood visits to my father's birthplace, Allumette Island, sparked a youthful imagination and a fascination for islands which continue even today. Although the characters in this novel are completely fictional, in my mind the gentle man I called Father will always be the adventurer, Michael Gray. And my beautiful, convent-bred mother, the fiery Cameron McCormick.

Nevada Nights

Prologue

December 12, 1856

> Diary, from the moment I first saw him, so handsome and proud, I was lost. When finally I learned who he was, it was too late. I had crossed the line of reason into a passion so intense it consumed me with its fire. I leave this world with but one regret. Never again will I feel the warmth of his strong embrace. The child born of our love will grow to be doubly strong, brave, proud—for the blood of two headstrong fools flows through her veins.

The glow from the fire flamed to a burnished copper the head bent over the diary. As the hauntingly beautiful young woman closed the leather-bound book and handed it to the servant, her eyes burned feverishly, two hot coals a glittering contrast to the fine, porcelain skin. Dark circles rimmed the green eyes. Weakly she leaned back against the soft feather mattress and stared at the newborn babe lying soundlessly in the cradle.

The servant removed a brick from the wall near the fireplace and shoved the diary inside. Then the brick was carefully replaced.

By the time the horse's hooves signaled the arrival of the man, the beautiful young woman lay near death, her breathing labored. With a tremendous effort, she roused herself for one last glimpse of the strongly chiseled features of his beloved face.

They clung wordlessly to each other until he felt the life feebly ebb from her slender body.

With tears coursing down his cheeks, he handed the tiny bundle to the servant and quickly wrote a note of instruction.

Long after the servant woman had left the tiny cottage to begin the first steps of the journey that would take her to a foreign shore, he sat huddled on the edge of the bed, cradling the lifeless form in his arms, his body racked with silent sobs.

Chapter One

1873

THE CLEAR, CRYSTAL CALL OF A BELL ANNOUNCED THE dawn.

Cameron McCormick awoke that perfect summer morning with no idea that, before the day ended, her life would be forever altered.

She stretched, yawned, then lay a moment listening to the familiar morning sounds. A dove cooed outside her window. The soft rustling of coarse, homespun skirts and petticoats indicated that one of the sisters was gliding along the dim, tiled hallway outside her room.

Cameron had lived her entire seventeen years at the Convent of the Sisters of Divine Charity. It was the only home she had ever known. The convent was located on Allumette Island, a tiny, crescent-shaped sliver of land only thirteen miles long and seven miles wide, in the Ottawa River in Quebec, Canada.

She scurried across the bare wood floor and washed

herself quickly in a round porcelain basin of water on her dressing table. Her mass of thick, red hair was brushed and deftly drawn into a neat knot at the nape of her neck. Pulling a prim cotton gown over her head, she tied the waist with a pale blue sash, smoothed the long skirts down about her ankles, picked up her missal, and headed downstairs toward the chapel.

At the door to the chapel, she stared in dismay. Old Father Edward was already at the altar, murmuring in Latin the opening prayers of the Mass. Without seeming to pause for a breath, he continued, "Mea culpa, mea culpa . . ."

"Through my fault, through my fault . . ." She sighed and lifted her pale blue veil over her head. As she expected, Mother Superior fixed her with a piercing look when she took her place beside the row of young women in long, coarse brown habits, each with head humbly bowed. Cameron bowed her head, then turned to wink at little Sister Adele. The corner of Sister Adele's mouth twitched, but she continued her concentration on the Mass.

Cameron glanced at old Father Edward. Each morning he arose at four o'clock, hitched his horse to his ancient rig, and rode across the island to say mass at the convent at five o'clock. On the ride back, the horse would pick his way over the familiar path while the old priest ate the breakfast prepared by Sister St. Francis de Sales. In her seventeen years, Cameron had never known Father Edward to be late. The only time he had ever failed to say Mass, he had been in bed for two weeks with pneumonia. Poor Father

Edward. The bishop considered Allumette Island too small and insignificant to spare a younger cleric to assist the old priest with the endless tasks of ministering to his flock.

After Mass, Cameron ate a quick breakfast, then laughed and chatted her way through chores and classes, all the while savoring the knowledge that the late afternoon hours would spell freedom. Since she was in the unique position of being neither novice nor sister, but simply boarding here, the afternoon hours which the novices and postulants spent studying theology and attending prayer sessions were Cameron's hours to spend as she chose, within limits, of course.

Reverend Mother Mary Claudius, Mother Superior, believed that it was her duty to broaden her young charge's horizons, despite the fact that Cameron lived within the convent walls. She knew she had to prepare Cameron for a life outside the convent. Therefore, the young woman was permitted to ride the horses, as long as she willingly helped the stable hands muck out the stalls. She was encouraged to assist at the birth of a foal or calf, since Reverend Mother believed that such experiences taught her about life. And once, Cameron was even allowed to work alongside the other residents of the island, helping with the harvest of a nearby wheat field when rains threatened to ruin the entire crop of a bedridden farmer.

Cameron relished any chance to escape the convent walls. Though she dearly loved the sisters, for they were the only family she had ever known, there was something in her which yearned for freedom.

She stood silently in Reverend Mother's tiny,

cramped office, watching a beam of light send rainbow prisms through a crystal paperweight on the corner of the desk.

"You wish to ride, do you, Cameron?"

"Yes, Reverend Mother."

The nun's sharp eyes scanned the sky outside her window, then slid over the slim girl before her. A mass of autumn hair spilled about her face. The green eyes danced with barely concealed energy.

"Well, it is a beautiful day." She studied the girl. "And I suppose when you're seventeen it's only natural to want to tear around the countryside on a spirited horse."

"Yes, Reverend Mother." She allowed the barest hint of a smile.

The Mother Superior pulled a list from her desk. "You can't ride alone. That wouldn't be proper. Let me see who is available." Her finger traced halfway down the list and stopped. "Sister Leona. She has the afternoon free." She glanced up at the girl. "You may ask her if she will accompany you."

Cameron was smiling broadly now. "Thank you, Reverend Mother."

"And Cameron . . ."

The girl paused in the doorway, anticipating the nun's next remark.

"Not too far," Mother Mary Claudius cautioned.

"Yes, Reverend Mother," she called over her shoulder. She pirouetted away before the nun had time to think of anything more.

Mother Superior stood smiling at the little whirlwind who had billowed off in pursuit of her pleasure. That child was such a joy. It was impossible to be in low spirits in her company. Just watching her made the older woman feel young and carefree again.

Cameron knew she would find Sister Leona in one of the outbuildings some distance from the convent proper. Sister spent most of her spare time helping with the farm animals, or tending the large vegetable garden.

Sister Leona was a tall, sturdy woman who had entered the convent late in life. She had spent half her life on her father's farm raising twelve younger brothers and sisters after their mother had died.

It seemed to Cameron that there was nothing Sister Leona couldn't do. It was she who had taught Cameron the value of being able to care for the horses, to raise her own crops, and who stressed the importance of being able to care for all her own needs.

As she suspected, Sister Leona was in the barn, lulling the cows in her softly accented French as she poured water in their trough.

"Reverend Mother said I may ride this afternoon, if you'll go with me," Cameron called.

Sister turned and smiled at the eager girl. Hanging the empty bucket on a peg, she rubbed her shoulder tenderly.

"Ah, *ma petite* Cammy. You know how I love riding with you. But my rheumatism is acting up today. Maybe tomorrow would be better."

"Oh, Sister Leona. It's so beautiful today. Please,"

she wheedled. "We'll ride very slowly. And the sun will be good for your stiff shoulder." That last had been added as a clever afterthought.

Sister Leona shook her head and smiled fondly. "You know you're going to win me over. You always do." She paused for a second. "All right. Change your clothes and I'll meet you at the stables in a few minutes."

"Oh, I knew you would! Thank you, Sister." Cameron's face was wreathed in smiles.

Sister Leona sighed in mock despair. "I didn't want to just sit around and baby myself anyway. Go on now, and change your clothes before I change my mind."

A short time later they left the convent walls and headed toward the green hills which ringed the island. They rarely rode near the small settlement, choosing instead to ride in the less populated area.

What an outrageous sight they presented to the occasional islander who came upon them.

Sister Leona refused to ride sidesaddle. She drew her voluminous skirt and petticoats up between her legs and cinched them with a cord, turning her drab habit into a kind of wide-legged pantaloon. Her stiffly starched wimple, framing her face, would often be soaked with perspiration by the time their ride ended, but true to tradition, Sister steadfastly refused to remove any vestige of her religious habit.

Cameron's entire wardrobe was supplied by a lawyer in the United States and arrived each year in a huge box on the ferry from the mainland. It consisted of simple wool and cotton dresses with matching pinafores. For special occasions there was always one elegant dress with matching coat and bonnet. The fact that everything always fit perfectly made her suspect that Reverend Mother kept the lawyer informed of her size.

Because of her limited wardrobe, Cameron had, out of necessity, rigged up a riding costume of sorts. From a discarded old wool dress stitched up the center of the skirt, Cameron produced a pair of ill-fitting britches. A thick, long-sleeved shirt made of rough homespun kept the sun from burning her pale skin, although the sun's rays still managed to filter through the fabric enough to turn her arms a soft bronze. Cameron traded her favorite book, Shakespeare's *Romeo and Juliet* to a stable hand for his faded peaked cap, into which she stuffed her long, tangled curls to keep her hair from blowing about her face as she rode. The front brim kept the sun from her face. She tucked her britches into the tall, cracked, leather boots she wore to muck out the stalls. This then was how she dressed whenever she rode.

As ridiculous as the two of them must have appeared to others, Sister Leona and Cameron rode about the countryside unselfconsciously, thoroughly enjoying their precious hours of freedom.

They had been out about an hour when Cameron gave her horse its head. He began cantering. As she crested a hill, she drew up short. Sister Leona wasn't following. Cameron retraced her trail and found Sister at the bottom of the hill.

"Sister Leona," she called breathlessly as she drew nearer. "What's wrong?"

Sister's face looked pale in the late afternoon sun, and tiny beads of moisture glistened on her upper lip.

"Nothing, Cameron, dear. Just my rheumatism. I believe I'll go up there." She pointed to a stand of maples to their right. "I'll rest in the shade while you get in a good run. Go on now," she urged as the girl hesitated.

Cameron watched as Sister turned her horse toward the shade. When the horse stopped, she wearily dropped the reins and waved the girl on. Cameron wheeled her horse, dug in her heels, and took off at a fast clip. Horse and rider crossed a flat stretch of meadow at a run. How good it was to feel the wind whipping her face. She loved the sense of freedom as she fairly flew across the field. She felt as if she could race a bird in flight. Tall grass parted beneath the pounding hooves of the chestnut gelding. Leaning forward in the saddle, Cameron flattened herself over the horse's neck, urging him even faster. When she felt his gait begin to falter, she eased up, sitting straighter in the saddle. The gelding instinctively slowed his pace, blowing and snorting after such powerful exertion.

Gradually her enthusiasm for the ride dimmed. This was no good. She knew she was being selfish. Sister Leona was hot and tired, and obviously hurting. It was time to go back. Cameron couldn't enjoy her pleasure at another's expense. Reluctantly, she turned her horse and cantered toward the cluster of trees.

What happened next came so suddenly there was no time to think, only to react. There was a flicker of movement in the tall grass by Sister's horse. The horse reared in panic, and Sister Leona was thrown roughly against the sharp tree branches. Cameron watched in horror as Sister clutched at her shoulder. Her hand came away dripping with blood. The horse reared again, crushing her against the tree trunk. When he dropped, Sister dazedly leaned far down over his neck in an attempt to reach the reins. They dangled tantalizingly just out of her reach. He reared again, then bolted. Sister Leona buried her hands in his mane and held on.

Cameron's horse, already tired from their run, was wheeling instinctively in their direction. She dug her heels in and urged the horse on.

Sister Leona was a very strong woman, but she had been badly stunned. How long, Cameron wondered, could she hold on? Also, the dangling reins could at any moment catch under the horse's hooves and trip him, breaking both the horse's and rider's necks.

Cameron had never ridden so hard or so fast in her life. She had to catch them, and quickly.

Miraculously, out of the corner of her eye, she saw a figure at the top of the hill. Assessing the situation, he was riding at an angle, hoping to intercept the runaway. Sister's horse, spooked by the stranger, veered sharply and sped on. Doggedly, Sister Leona hung on, although the pain in her shoulder by that time must have been unbearable.

Their paths converged, and the stranger came up alongside Cameron. For a few minutes, they rode even. Slowly, his horse, a huge black stallion, began to inch ahead.

Catching sight of her terrified eyes, he called, "Ride boy! Don't quit. Ride like the wind!" He urged his horse on even faster.

They raced through a thicket, the branches tearing the cap from Cameron's head and ripping away the sleeve of her shirt. Abruptly, they entered a clearing and saw, just ahead of them, Sister Leona's horse. He reared up his forelegs once again. Sister dropped to the ground, and the horse, now free of its burden, ran off.

The stranger dropped beside her and began fumbling with the stiff wimple, which had twisted sideways, nearly obscuring Sister's face. With a great ripping sound, he tore away the headdress, revealing short, gray hair matted with sweat. Next he began to rip the blood-stained fabric at her shoulder.

In a fit of outrage, Cameron leaped from her horse and attacked him, throwing all her weight against him, to force him away from the helpless form of Sister Leona. Caught by surprise, he twisted and rolled away from her flailing fists. With his massive size and strength he should have easily pinned her to the ground, but she was fighting like a wildcat, and he found himself breathless by the time he managed to restrain her. With the weight of his body pressing hers tightly to the ground and his hands securely holding her fists above her head, the only thing she could move was her head.

Wide-eyed, she faced him. Rage glittered in her eyes like hard emerald chips. To the stranger, she looked like some sort of wild creature, with her tangled hair spilling about her face and shoulders, her torn sleeve, still tightly fastened at the wrist, flapping loosely from wrist to shoulder and gaping open along one side.

"You keep your filthy hands off her! Don't you touch her again!" Cameron shrieked.

He stared at her in astonishment. "Are you crazy? She's bleeding! Can't you see? I've got to help her."

"You won't touch her! Don't put your hands on her. I'll take care of Sister," Cameron hissed.

He stared at her a moment longer, then loosened his grip on her wrists and rolled aside. Instantly she turned her back on him and knelt at Sister's side.

The front of Sister Leona's habit and the entire sleeve were soaked with blood. Her face was white from the pain. Gently, Cameron tore away the rest of her bodice and gasped at the huge purple welt which ran the length of her shoulder and arm. The jagged cut was deep and bleeding profusely. A sudden wave of sickness washed over Cameron.

The stranger walked up and knelt beside them. He was naked to the waist. He handed Cameron his shirt, and she realized he had soaked it in a nearby stream.

"Here," he said, more gently now. "Cleanse the wound the best way you can."

"Thank you."

He watched in silence, admiring the way the girl handled herself. He had noticed the pallor when she first caught sight of the wound. But she had control of herself now. She would be able to do what she had to. He understood her need to protect the nun's sense of modesty. If it weren't so serious, it would be laughable.

He stood and glanced down at the wild tangle of red-gold hair. When he had first spotted the slim figure on the horse, he had thought it was a young boy. Close up, despite the ill-fitting clothes, he realized she was an extraordinarily beautiful girl.

"We'll need a wagon," he said abruptly. "Where's the nearest place?"

Without looking up, she replied, "The convent." She motioned with her head. "Over the hill back there, and then head west for about five miles."

He left without another word. Cameron worked a long time cleaning the wounds. Tearing Sister Leona's heavy muslin petticoat into strips, she applied a tourniquet to stem the flow of blood.

Sister Leona's eyes fluttered open, and she moaned.

"You're going to be all right, Sister Leona," Cameron whispered. "A man has gone to the convent for the wagon. He should be here soon."

She offered a silent prayer that he would hurry. She couldn't bear to see Sister so deathly pale.

When at last she heard the creak of the wagon's wheels, relief flooded through her. As the stranger walked up, Cameron discreetly placed the remnants of torn petticoat across Sister's exposed skin. He bent and lifted her large frame as easily as though she were a feather. Running ahead of them, Cameron discovered layers of soft quilts and down pillows strewn in the back of the wagon. He set her down gently in the mounds of quilts and settled the pillows closely around her. As Cameron made a move to climb in with Sister, he clamped his hand tightly around her wrist, sending a spasm of shock through her.

"Do you know how to drive this thing, girl?" He watched her through narrowed eyes.

"Yes, but—"

Gruffly, he interrupted. "I know you don't want me tending her. But she may be bleeding inside. She can't be jarred. Now, if you drive slowly, I'll hold these pillows carefully about her so she isn't caused any more pain than is necessary."

He stared at the girl, who paused, undecided.

"Do you understand?"

"Yes," she said resolutely. She turned and climbed to the driver's seat. Picking up the reins, she called over her shoulder, "Tell me when you're ready."

"Just let me tie up these horses to the back of the wagon," he muttered.

In a few minutes he climbed in beside Sister Leona, wrapped her gently in the pillows, then said, "All right. Slow and easy."

Those few miles back to the convent were the longest Cameron had ever known.

Dear God, she prayed. *Please don't let her die. She is the dearest, sweetest sister. And all of this happened because I selfishly wanted to ride today. Please keep her safe.*

Several times Cameron turned and stared at the stranger. His naked torso glistened with sweat. His brows were drawn together in a frown, his mouth a thin, taut line of concentration. Though the heavy form of the nun wrapped in all those pillows must have sorely strained his muscles, he never relaxed his grip or flexed his arms for even a moment.

When at last the wagon entered the gates of the

convent walls, the late evening sun had cast long fingers of gold across the slate roofs and gleaming cross of the chapel.

A dozen sisters, with Mother Superior and the doctor from town in the lead, hurried toward the wagon. When the horse halted, the stranger eased his hold on the still form of Sister Leona, and stiffly, he climbed down. Cameron hurried to stand beside the wagon as the doctor knelt down next to Sister and began a brisk examination. He nodded in satisfaction and signaled for the stranger to carry her inside. The rest of the subdued crowd trailed behind.

The sisters, knowing they could do nothing for Sister Leona at the moment, moved off to find chores to occupy their minds until they could hear the doctor's verdict. Many of the sisters hurried to the chapel, where they would keep their silent, prayerful vigil.

Cameron couldn't tear herself away from the room. She stood just outside the door, watching as the stranger eased Sister gently onto her bed. By the time he had walked to the door, Reverend Mother and the doctor had moved to either side of the bed. The stranger closed the door softly and turned toward Cameron.

In a hushed voice, she asked, "Do you think she'll be all right?"

She didn't breathe as she waited for his reply.

He stared at her a long moment. Then he touched her arm and said, "You're bleeding. Did you know? This should be looked after."

The girl stared down at her arm in astonishment. Blood smeared her shirt and britches. She felt no pain, only warmth where his hand was touching her skin.

"It's nothing." She shrugged. "What about Sister Leona?"

"We'll know soon enough." He glanced around. "Where is the kitchen?"

She pointed behind her. "Down the hall."

He put his hands on her shoulders and turned her in that direction. "Come on."

Cameron was too exhausted to argue. In the kitchen, he filled a pan with hot water from the kettle and rummaged in drawers until he found a towel.

"Sit," he ordered.

She sat on a kitchen chair and watched dumbly as he began washing her bloody arm.

The man was tall—so tall she had to tip her head back to see his face. His hair was dark and thick and curled slightly around his forehead and neck. As he bent over her, it spilled across his forehead in a shaft of black silk. His eyes were dark, nearly black, with long sooty lashes. His jaw was firm, and he had an air of authority about him, as though he were accustomed to giving orders and having them followed without question.

Cameron had never been this close to a man before. She had lived all her life in a world of subdued, overly modest women. And this man was still naked to the waist. She stared fascinated at his powerful shoulders, the muscles of his arms flexing and unflexing as he moved. Her senses were assaulted by the strange, raw, masculine scent of him, which oddly stirred her blood.

What must it be like to be held in those arms? she wondered. Blushing furiously at her thoughts, she tore her gaze away from his arms.

She stared at his hands, so large that he could easily hold both of hers in one of his. Then she noticed the scar on his left wrist. It was large, knotted almost like a cord, and encircled the wrist like a bracelet. He must have nearly severed his hand to have sustained such a scar. Without realizing it, she reached out her hand to touch it.

"An old wound," he said, his voice so near her ear that she jumped.

He paused a moment, then continued washing her wounds. As he leaned across the table to reach a dry towel, his hand brushed her hair, causing a ripple of new sensations along her spine.

Her hair, he realized, smelled of bayberry soap. Her flawless skin glowed with health. Her cheeks were kissed by the sun.

She glanced up at him and found, to her dismay, that he was staring boldly down at her face. She lowered her eyes and felt the heat burning her cheeks. Her heart thudded painfully in her chest.

Recognizing her confusion, he began to speak softly to calm her.

"What is your name?"

"Cammy—short for Cameron," she said haltingly.

"Are you going to become a nun, Cammy, short for Cameron?" he asked teasingly.

She grinned at his humor. "No. I just live here."

"You live here. Why?"

"My father sent me here when I was born. For my safety, Reverend Mother says. And I've been here ever since."

He cocked his head to one side and regarded her. Was it her imagination, or had he stiffened slightly when she mentioned safety? There was a moment of awkward silence.

Then she asked, "And what is your name?"

"Michael. Michael Gray."

She licked her dry lips and wondered how much longer she could endure being so close to this overpowering man.

His deep voice forced her thoughts back to mundane things, and soon his simple questions had her caught up in an animated conversation.

"How did your island get its name?" The question was intended to soothe her tension.

She smiled, recalling the history lessons of her youth. "It's named for the reeds growing in the area, which are used for matches. *Allumette* means match in French."

His lips quirked in a half-smile, as if he may have already known this.

"And did you know that Champlain actually traveled as far as Allumette Island in 1613?"

He nodded. "Interesting." All the while, his gaze roamed appreciatively over her animated features.

At ease now, she prattled on. "Did you know we're in the path of the ice age? Reverend Mother said that upstream from Pembroke and below Des Joachims is one of the few remaining valleys resulting from the stresses of that era. She saw a plateau of granite which juts hundreds of feet above the valley floor. She said it's—spectacular." She hesitated, realizing how silly she must sound to this stranger.

"Yes. I've seen it. And it is spectacular." His lazy smile caused her heart to tumble wildly in her chest. "Haven't you seen it?"

Cameron shook her head, causing her silken hair to drift softly about her neck and shoulders. "I've never left this island," she admitted softly.

"Never? This little strip of land is all you've seen?" He studied her intently, loving the color which flooded her cheeks at his scrutiny. "There's a big world out there to explore someday."

"Someday," she echoed wistfully.

Reverend Mother scurried into the kitchen and skidded to a stop at the sight of the two of them. Then she held up a rough, homespun shirt, which she had obviously borrowed from one of the stable hands.

"This will have to do for now, Mr. Gray. If you will accept our hospitality for the night, we will have your own clothes in order by tomorrow."

"Thank you," he said. "This is fine."

Cameron watched in fascination as he slipped on the shirt and stretched it over the taut muscles of his shoulders and chest, quickly tucking it into the waistband of his pants. When Cameron saw Reverend Mother's narrowed eyes boring into hers, she forced herself to look away.

"The doctor is finished with Sister Leona," Reverend Mother said. "She would like to see both of you before the sedative he gave her takes effect."

Reverend Mother walked to the doorway, and Cameron and Michael quickly followed. Walking behind Reverend Mother into Sister Leona's room, Cameron stopped abruptly. Sister Leona had always been the strongest woman in the convent. Her erect carriage and solid, sturdy build gave the impression of a person completely in control. This stranger lying in the bed frightened Cameron. The removal of her headdress, revealing short, gray hair curling slightly about a pale face, made her appear older and more vulnerable, more human. Her breathing was even, as though she were asleep. Her arm was swathed in thick dressings.

"Sister Leona, Cameron and the young man are here," whispered Reverend Mother.

Turning to Cameron, Reverend Mother admonished, "You have only a few minutes with her. She needs her rest." Turning, she softly closed the door as she left.

Sister Leona's eyelids fluttered open, and she turned a weak smile on Cameron.

Relief and guilt flooded through Cameron. She flung herself on her knees at the bedside.

"Oh, Sister Leona! I'm so sorry. Please forgive me," she sobbed.

"Here, here, child. Whatever are you sorry for?"

"For coaxing you to ride with me. I knew you weren't up to it. It was so selfish of me." A tear coursed down her cheek as she pressed her hand over Sister Leona's.

"Cameron, stop that. Do you hear? It wasn't your fault my horse bolted. It was a snake, I believe. And you did just fine, child. Why, you and this man saved my life."

As Cameron wiped her eyes, Sister Leona stared up at him. "Reverend Mother tells me your name is Michael Gray," she said slowly.

"Yes, Sister."

"Michael, do you believe that the hand of God directs all our lives?" Sister's voice was thick and muffled from the sedative.

"It's not something I've given a lot of thought to, Sister. But I'd say yes, I believe that," he replied seriously.

"Good. Good." She seemed to be speaking to herself. Then louder, to both of them, she added, "I don't know how you happened to be on Allumette Island today, Michael, but I do know that God required both you and Cameron to work together to save my life. Neither of you alone could have done what you did together." Her words were slurred, as though talking had become a great effort. "God bless you, Michael Gray. You will be in my prayers always."

Cameron leaned down and kissed her cheek and followed Michael Gray from the room.

Before they had left the room Sister Leona was asleep.

As they descended the stairs, the wonderful aroma of cooking reached them from the kitchen.

Little Sister Adele smiled shyly at Michael and said, "Reverend Mother wants both of you to come and eat." Putting her arm around Cameron's shoulders, she murmured, "Dear Cameron. You must be exhausted."

Cameron smiled at her and allowed herself to be led once more to the kitchen. There were only two places set at the table, and Cameron realized with some apprehension that she would have to sit and face Michael Gray over dinner. He held out a chair for her, and she averted her eyes as she sat down. Several of the sisters were busy washing up pots and pans, making tea, and hunting up any other chores that would keep them in the kitchen to hear what Mother Superior would have to say to the stranger.

Reverend Mother entered the kitchen, and Michael rose to his feet. He held her chair, then moved back to his place at the table.

"Will you be staying long on our island, Mr. Gray?" she asked.

"No. I was leaving today, when"—and he turned a smile on them both—"I found myself detained. I'll be leaving tomorrow."

Cameron's heart sank.

"We are most grateful, Mr. Gray. Sister Leona believed that you and Cameron behaved most heroically today."

Michael glanced at Cameron with a bemused expression. Her cheeks burning, she lowered her eyes and moved the food around her plate. It was very warm in the kitchen. Warm and safe. If only she could rest her head for a moment. As the voice of Reverend Mother and the deeper timbre of Michael's voice washed over her, she set down her fork and propped her head on her hand. The steamy warmth of the room comforted her. The familiar kitchen sounds were lulling her. Her eyelids fluttered, then closed. The next thing she was aware of was a sensation of being lifted in strong arms. She was floating. There were distant voices, and she thought she heard Reverend Mother say, "Her room is up here."

Cameron brought her arms up around a rough shirt and buried her face in warm flesh. She could feel a pulse beat against her lips. She sighed contentedly and heard a deep, throaty chuckle.

Under her warm quilt, she slept soundly.

Chapter Two

CAMERON AWOKE AT FIRST LIGHT AND MOVED STIFFLY. Her arm and shoulder ached. She tried to remember coming up to bed the night before. Then memories began to flood her mind, and she groaned and covered her face with her hands.

She had fallen asleep at the table, right in front of Michael Gray. She had probably buried her nose in her food. And Michael had seen her.

Michael. He was here somewhere, sleeping under the same roof. She jumped from her bed, oblivious to the pain and stiffness. Stealing a glance in the small oval mirror over her wash basin, a moan escaped her lips. She looked horrible. Her hair was all tangled, her face smudged.

It took Cameron more than an hour to repair the damage of the day before. By the time she came downstairs to chapel for morning Mass, she was scrubbed fresh, her hair washed and arranged in a neat knot at the back of her neck. She wore a fresh green cotton dress which Sister Adele had once said gave her green eyes a warm glow that put emeralds to shame.

Her arm throbbed painfully, and she found that it was less painful if she kept it bent slightly in front of her. Carrying her prayerbook in her other hand, she entered the chapel.

Cameron knew the exact moment when Michael entered the chapel. Mass was nearly over when he walked in. She forced herself to stare at the words in her prayerbook. He entered the pew across from her. She knew without looking that his gaze was on her. She would not look at him. She could not. But with a will of their own, her eyes betrayed her. They moved up, over, and then she was meeting his steady gaze. He smiled, and she allowed herself a demure smile, feeling a swift rush of heat stain her cheeks, before forcing herself to stare once more at the book in her hand.

When Mass ended, she remained in her pew until Michael stood and began to leave. Walking out behind him, she gazed in fascination at the width of his shoulders. His clothes had been carefully cleaned and pressed. She realized that his jacket was beautifully tailored, and the collar of the shirt, which yesterday had been soaked in a stream and used to bathe Sister Leona's wounds, was of the finest linen and intricately embroidered with his initials.

Breakfast was a festive affair, held in the huge

refectory. Except for the bishop, who visited the convent once every five years, they rarely had a visitor. Reverend Mother sat at the head of the long table, with Michael Gray at the other end. The sisters and Cameron sat along the sides.

Cameron listened as the sisters asked Michael endless questions about where his travels had taken him and discovered that he had seen most of the United States and Canada. She said nothing, hoping no one would call attention to her. Every time she thought about last night, falling asleep at the table, probably with her face in her plate, she wanted to hide. How foolish she must have looked to a man like Michael. How childish.

Sister Marie was telling Michael something about her home. Cameron stole a quick glance at his face. His eyes caught and held hers. He winked wickedly, and she felt the flame once more burn her cheeks.

Too soon breakfast was finished, and the sisters were walking Michael to the door. Cameron followed, wondering what she could possibly say to him in front of all of them.

His horse was saddled and waiting in the courtyard. Cameron stared at the hand-tooled leather and the exquisite silver gleaming in the sunlight. This was further proof, she knew, that Michael was a man of wealth and breeding.

The sisters gathered around him to bid him their goodbyes. Reverend Mother made the sign of the cross over him with her right hand, offering her blessing for his safe journey. Each of the sisters shook his hand, thanked him for his help, and promised to pray for him. Cameron was the only one who had not spoken.

He moved forward and stared down at her. "Cameron," he said gently. "You are a woman of many surprises."

A woman! She had never been called that before. She felt herself blushing right down to her toes.

"And that arm of yours is giving you much pain," he added.

"Oh!" she gasped. "How did you know?"

"I just know," he whispered. Then, looking over her head, he said aloud to Reverend Mother, "When the doctor comes today to check Sister Leona, have him look at Cameron's arm." Glancing down at her once more, he said, "Goodbye, Cammy, short for Cameron. Stay well."

He lifted both her hands to his lips and kissed them lightly.

He turned, mounted his horse, saluted them all, and rode smartly away.

No one moved until he was out of sight. It was as though none of them wanted this to end. Michael Gray's visit had been an extraordinary event in their tranquil lives.

Chapter Three

A WEEK LATER, AN ATTENDANT FROM THE FERRY ARRIVED at the convent bearing a huge gift box. It was addressed simply to "Cameron" at the Convent of the Sisters of Divine Charity.

Sister Adele, holding her skirts above the rows of vegetables, came scurrying to the garden to find her.

"Come quickly, Cameron. Reverend Mother wants you in her office."

Cameron followed the little nun to the office, only to find most of the sisters already clustered around Reverend Mother's desk. Cameron stared at the mysterious box. Except for the clothes from her father's lawyer each year, she had never received a gift.

Slowly, she lifted the lid on the box. Inside, wrapped in layers of tissue, she discovered a pair of fawn-colored suede jodhpurs, a beautifully tailored black velvet riding jacket, a matching black derby, and a soft ivory shirt with a high neckline and mother-of-pearl buttons. At the very bottom of the box was a pair of hand-tooled leather boots. The box bore the name of a very exclusive ladies' shop in Ottawa. A tiny handwritten card was tucked into the folds of the jacket. It read simply "Michael."

Cameron held up the jodhpurs. They were the right length. She slipped on the jacket and buttoned it. It fit. She slipped off one shoe and slid a dainty foot into the soft, glove leather boot. It fit as though it had been made just for her.

She shook her head in wonder. "How could he have guessed my size?" she asked shyly. She looked at Reverend Mother. "May I keep them?"

Reverend Mother, whose face registered her amazement, studied his card, then nodded affirmatively. Setting down his card, she said dryly, "I see no return address for our Mr. Gray. I think you have no choice but to keep them, Cameron."

The slim young woman hugged Reverend Mother and carried the box of clothes to the privacy of her room. She wanted to wear them always, and to read and reread his name, written in his own hand. Michael. *Oh, Michael!* she thought. *How did you know my exact size?*

Cameron stared at her reflection in the mirror. Had

he studied her that carefully? Her pulse raced at the thought.

Just thinking of Michael Gray, of his dark eyes, of his muscled strength, of the deep timbre of his voice when he spoke her name, would carry her dreamlike through the long, bitter winter on her island in the Ottawa River.

Chapter Four

AFTER MICHAEL'S VISIT, MOTHER SUPERIOR BECAME aware of a gradual transformation in Cameron. The green eyes would soften and take on a dreamy, faraway look. Although she still rushed headlong around the convent and grounds, Reverend Mother noted that Cameron occasionally slowed her pace, moving in a fluid walk, her hips unconsciously swaying with natural feline grace. The child was there still, but she was becoming submerged in the woman.

Alarmed at hearing nothing decisive from Cameron's father in all these years, Mother Superior decided that she must take steps to ensure the future of her young charge.

Reverend Mother assigned Cameron to assist with the small, one-room schoolhouse at the French settlement of Chapeau on the north shore of the island.

There is a special look about children who are denied love and affection. They have a hungry, yearning look about them. Cameron discovered that she could always spot a child who needed special attention. It seemed strange that she, who knew no family except the sisters in the convent, never grew up feeling deprived of love. She could feel affection emanating from all the women who surrounded her. She was a sort of special bonus to them. They had embraced this lifestyle believing they would never know the satisfaction of raising a family. They had turned their backs on marriage and family life to dedicate themselves in a special way to God's work. Suddenly, they found this noisy, inquisitive little girl growing up in their midst. Although there were times when they yearned for peace from the constant rush of a whirling, wild little tomboy, still, she brought a special joy to their lives, and they showered her with love and affection. She grew up feeling very secure.

After some weeks of teaching, Reverend Mother asked Cameron to her office for a serious conversation.

"Sit down, Cameron." The old nun paused, clearing her throat. "Mr. Bassette was here earlier today to ask me about you."

The two Bassette children attended the island school. Since their mother's death several years earlier, they had become shy and withdrawn, unable to recite aloud in class. Cameron's heart had gone out to them. She had been working patiently with them, encouraging them, offering praise whenever they did especially notable work. She had even mentioned to their father not long ago that she felt they were responding well to her encouragement.

"Have I done something wrong, Reverend Mother?"

"No, Cameron. Mr. Bassette was here to ask some—personal questions."

"Personal. I don't understand."

"He particularly wanted to know your status—whether or not you contemplated becoming a sister. You are, after all, an object of some curiosity here on the island."

Cameron sat for a moment, letting this sink in. Then, suddenly realizing what this was leading to, she let out a gasp. "Oh! Reverend Mother! What did you tell him?"

"I told him the truth, Cameron. That you grew up here—that you have a father somewhere in the United States. That you are an excellent teacher. Apart from that, there is nothing more to say. If you wish Mr. Bassette to pay you court . . ." She shrugged, staring intently at the young woman.

Cameron's mouth dropped open as she stared at the nun. A man was seeing her as a woman he wished to court. She thought of the thin farmer, shy to the point of being barely able to speak to strangers, and of his two sweet children, who needed the love and attention of a mother. Cameron's heart went out to all of them. And her heart soared at the knowledge that a man could see her as a potential wife. But marriage to him! Mother to them!

Her eyes softened as she stared into space, and

another picture sprang unbidden to her mind: a tall, compelling figure on a black stallion, whose mere touch caused her skin to burn. As long as there existed such a man in this world, she could never consent to be a shy farmer's wife.

She looked up to see Reverend Mother staring thoughtfully at her, and she wondered how much had been revealed on her face. Instantly, she glanced at the floor, allowing her thick lashes to veil her thoughts from the astute woman across the desk.

"No, Reverend Mother. I couldn't even consider it." Her strong voice spoke her conviction. "My father shall send for me one day, and I must be free to go to him." Lifting her head proudly, she faced the nun. "Shall I tell Mr. Bassette myself?"

Reverend Mother smiled gently. "I suspect Mr. Bassette would run to the far side of the island if you dared to speak to him about such a personal thing as courtship. I will tell him for you."

"Thank you, Reverend Mother."

As Cameron walked from the room, the old nun watched her with a sigh. For too long this young woman had lived on the fragile thread of hope that her father would send for her. She whispered a silent prayer that Cameron's faith in him was justified.

Even during the harshest part of the winter, Cameron invented ways to escape the boredom of her confinement. She had mastered snowshoes and skiing, although all of the sisters steadfastly refused to attempt to ski with her. She rode horseback whenever she could, and though Reverend Mother still disapproved of her going anywhere without a chaperone, she occasionally permitted Cameron to go out alone, especially during the bitter days of the winter.

On these solitary outings, her eyes would scan the frozen landscape, remembering that perfect summer day. She could remember everything about Michael Gray—his eyes, dark and probing, his strongly chiseled features, his mouth, firm, inviting, and the touch of his hand on hers. Her heart would forever recall the smell of him, the touch, even the way his warm voice and laughter trickled over her senses like warm butter.

Whenever she spotted a figure in the distance, her heart would hammer in her chest, until drawing nearer, an islander would wave or call. Momentary disappointment would wash over her, and she would chide herself for entertaining such romantic notions.

It had been an especially harsh winter in a land that was accustomed to hard winters. Allumette Island, exposed on all sides to the raw elements, took a battering from the ice-choked waters of the Ottawa River. Several feet of ice had piled up on the northern tip of the island, and the ferry had been unable to run from the mainland for over a month.

It was mid-morning on a Saturday, and Cameron was enjoying helping Sister Leona feed and water the stock in the barn. Sister's arm and shoulder had healed satisfactorily after her accident, but her rheumatism seemed to cause her more severe pain with each change of season. Not that she complained. No one ever heard Sister Leona mention it. But Cameron noticed that she carried her arm stiffly at times, and her face often wore that pinched look of pain.

Young Sister Marie shoved the huge barn door open, causing the snowflakes to swirl in on a gust of wind. Her eyes, normally downcast, were bright with excitement.

"Cameron! Come quickly! Reverend Mother is waiting for you in her office with a stranger!"

Cameron glanced wordlessly at Sister Leona, then dumped the rest of the feed in a trough and hurried after the young messenger.

The wind tore at them as they crossed the flat stretch of land between the barn and convent. As they braced the door against the cold blast of wind, Cameron asked, "How ever did a stranger get to our island in this weather?"

Sister Marie whispered, "I heard that he hired the ferry just to bring him across. He was the only passenger. Can you imagine!" she added in wonder.

Cameron couldn't imagine. It was unthinkable that the ferry would travel from Pembroke to their little island for just one passenger, especially during the treacherous winter. He must be very important.

Cameron hurried to Reverend Mother's office, unmindful of the fact that the wind had whipped her unruly hair about her face and that the mounds of snow on the ground had thoroughly soaked her stockings and the hem of her skirt.

She knocked.

"Come in," Reverend Mother called.

Cameron stared at the short, balding man seated

across from the desk. He was staring at Cameron with keen interest.

"Cameron, this is Mr. Georges Bouchet, a representative from the Canadian office of your father's attorney."

The man rose and took her hand.

"Miss McCormick," he said in heavily French-accented English. "I have been instructed to take you to your father."

Once, when Cameron was eleven, she had come flying down the darkened hall of the convent, rounded a corner, and had all her breath knocked from her lungs as she had hurled all her young weight against an ancient vault which workmen had removed from the bowels of the cellar. Falling backward, she had nearly blacked out from the impact. Struggling for breath, she had sat, stunned, lightheaded from the blow.

She felt that same way now. She stared at this stranger. There were no words to speak.

For as long as she could remember, she had dreamed of this day. But in her daydreams her father had come in person to fetch her, a tall, handsome man who wrapped her in his warm embrace and declared his undying love for his daughter. The sun was a brilliant globe in a summer sky. The day was like no other. Trumpets sounded. The whole world stopped.

Why now? On this drab, dreary day, like so many other days, why had she been summoned? And why had her father not come himself? Her heart stuck in her throat. Was he too old or ill? Worse—dying? Was the danger that had threatened her safety all these years now threatening him? Was she so unimportant in his life that he would not come to her himself?

Pulling herself together, she angrily brushed these thoughts from her mind and grasped the only important fact. Her father wanted her. He had sent this stranger to fetch her home. Her mind whirled. Her father must be very wealthy. Hadn't the ferry been dispatched for just this one courier? No. For her. Her very wealthy, very powerful, very important father wanted her. Whatever danger had been hanging over her was now removed. She was finally free to go to him.

Frantically trying to scramble through the maze of thoughts that raced through her mind, she glanced helplessly at Reverend Mother. The nun's usually placid face was wrinkled in a frown, the lower lip trembling. Cameron's eyes widened in horror as she realized that Reverend Mother was fighting for control.

Please, God, don't let her cry, prayed Cameron. If Reverend Mother cried, she would lose her composure and cry also. And she didn't want any tears to mar this joyous news. She was going home. Her father had sent for her.

"When?" she asked softly, hearing the tremor in her voice.

The bald man smiled at her apparent confusion. "Why, now, Miss McCormick," he said casually. "As soon as you can get your things together. They're holding the ferry for us. But we must leave before dark. The ice is treacherous in places, and the captain will attempt the crossing only during daylight hours."

Cameron didn't move. She continued to stare at the stranger. She couldn't just pack up all the eighteen years of her life in a few minutes. He acted as though she were leaving after a week's visit. What right did he have to disrupt her life so completely and expect her to meekly follow him to some strange new place? She glanced in fury at Mother Superior. She would understand and demand more time.

Reverend Mother turned her back on them, pretending to be busy searching through her files. Over her shoulder she ordered, "Go up to your room, Cameron, and pack your trunk."

"But the children, Reverend Mother. I have to be at the schoolhouse Monday. Who will teach them?"

Mother Superior was in control again. Taking a deep breath, she said calmly, "We have always known this day would arrive, haven't we, Cameron?" Turning slowly, her sharp eyes met and held the young woman's. "Go now, and pack. Your father is waiting for you."

Turning to the lawyer, Reverend Mother asked dryly, "Would you prefer tea or hot cocoa, Mr. Bouchet?"

Cameron, realizing that she had been dismissed, turned stiffly away.

Up in her room, Cameron slumped on the edge of her bed as warring emotions battled within her. She had begun a new life this year, teaching the island children. She had discovered hidden talents within herself. There was a sense of satisfaction in the work she was doing. Now it was being snatched from her. Why was her father sending for her at this time? Was he punishing her for making an attempt at independence? She dismissed that thought almost immediately. There had to be a purpose for this. It had to be more than the fact that her father wanted finally to see her. He'd had nearly eighteen years to want to get to know her.

The danger. Somehow this was connected with the danger. She was sure of it. Whatever threat of harm had been hanging over her life had now been removed. Cameron clenched her hands tightly in her lap. It would have been so wonderful if her father had come for her himself. She had always pictured him as tall, and handsome, and dashing, a knight on a white horse—someone strong who would carry her from this tiny island into the world of excitement beyond. Lifting her head higher, her chin thrust defiantly, she seized a new thought.

Her father was far too busy, his duties too demanding, to allow him to come for her. That was why he was sending an emissary. Her busy, important father would be waiting impatiently, counting the hours until he could be united with his daughter. She mustn't keep him waiting. And a new thought sent her rushing to pack. Somewhere beyond this island was Michael Gray. She had known by looking at him that he belonged to the wider world beyond her shores. Now there would be a chance of their paths crossing. It didn't matter that that was a big unexplored world out there. Somehow, she and Michael were fated to meet. With that thought to lift her spirits, she began methodically packing her trunk.

Giving one last look around the bare room,

Cameron picked up her heavy cloak and dragged the huge trunk along the hallway.

Downstairs the sisters had assembled in the main parlor. Cameron noted with a smile of relief that Mr. Georges Bouchet was waiting on a rough bench in the hallway. Obviously, Reverend Mother wanted their last goodbye to be personal. Cameron took a deep breath and drank in the faces of the dear sisters who had been with her all of her life.

Reverend Mother walked forward and handed Cameron a small tin box. "This contains all the documents which were given me when you were brought to us as an infant. When you have some time alone, you will want to go over them." She sighed sadly. "I'm afraid they hold no answers. They are woefully inadequate. But soon you will have all the answers you seek. You are going to your father, Cameron. And all of us here wish you well. I will not worry about you. You have a great well of strength within you. I am confident that we have taught you well." She embraced the girl and said firmly, "Go with God, Cameron McCormick. You are a fine woman now. Do us proud." Wistfully, she added, "Perhaps someday you will come back to visit us."

Cameron swallowed the lump which threatened to choke her. Through a mist of tears she saw Mr. Bouchet waiting impatiently for her in the doorway. With a flourish of quick embraces, she followed him through the entrance and down the wide stone steps to a waiting carriage.

As they clattered off, Cameron turned and waved to the darkened figures massed in the doorway. She couldn't see their faces in the shadows, yet she knew each one clearly.

The captain of the ferry was pacing furiously on the deck when they arrived. As soon as they had stowed Cameron's trunk, he shoved off from the frozen shore. Mr. Bouchet bustled her into the warm cabin section of the boat. As he settled himself on one of the benches, Cameron pressed her face to the glass and stared at the receding land.

Ignoring the freezing temperature, Cameron suddenly bolted out on deck to watch as her beloved island seemed to drop away from her. Her gaze scanned the white frosted landscape, searching all the dear, familiar places of her childhood.

In the distance she could see the roof of the one-room schoolhouse where only recently she had begun to teach the island children. She watched the slate roofs of the convent buildings, the thin winter sun glinting on the gold of the cross. Even the frigid air couldn't drive her away from the rail of the ferry. She had to see her beloved Allumette Island until there was nothing left to see.

Home! She was going home! But this dear place was her home. And oh, how she would miss it. Silent tears began to course down her cheeks. She realized that she was watching her childhood recede along with her island. Oh, Sister Leona. Who will help you feed and water the stock and tend the vegetable gardens? Reverend Mother, who will sorely try your patience now that I've gone? How can I leave you? What will I do without all of you to scold me, to urge me to try harder, to calm me down when I'm high-strung, to love me?

The tears froze on her cheeks, glistening like diamonds in the light reflected from the warm cabin of the boat. Still, Cameron huddled in the biting wind, unable to leave the deck, unable to tear her gaze from her beloved island. Finally, there was nothing left to see but a dim white haze in the distance, glimmering in the frozen waters.

But, she told herself, she wasn't leaving it all behind. She would carry her island with her, locked in her heart. She could close her eyes and see the water of the Ottawa River lapping gently on the shore of Allumette, or hurling itself in a frenzy of foam after a storm. She could see the jagged ice floes inching along the channel and piling up on the frozen beach, tearing away great chunks of earth as they grated one against the other to hug the shore until they became one with the land, a vast, ice-encrusted still life. No matter how far her voyage took her, Cameron would carry this tiny island, its smell and taste, and the wonderful people who were its pulse, with her always.

Chapter Five

A NARROW BEAM OF SUNLIGHT FILTERED THROUGH A jagged tear in the heavy draperies. In the bed the figure curled like a kitten, dozing in the circle of warmth. Cameron lay quietly, on the fine edge of half-wakefulness, unwilling to rouse herself and experience the now familiar aching of her body. After enduring nearly two weeks of both train and stagecoach, spending unending days jostled between perspiring strangers, feeling every hole and rut in the trail, her body screamed in protest. The slightest movement awakened an array of stiff, creaking muscles.

Yanked from her orderly, peaceful life on the island, she had watched in fascination as a whole new world of color and sound had greeted her in one swiftly moving, dizzying tableau. From the windows of the train and stagecoach she had seen dazzling, snow-covered mountain peaks wreathed in gauzy clouds and had slowly slipped from the biting cold that blanketed her familiar world of winter to barren, rock-strewn desert and a relentless sun that scorched everything in its path. Fascinated, she had watched a continuous parade of mankind, from simple farmers in Ohio to mule skinners in Colorado Territory, and from gaudy street women in Kansas to prim Mormon families moving west to Utah Territory.

Gingerly stretching out one leg, Cameron marveled at the strange sounds she was beginning to identify. Wheels clattered along the street below. Cowboy boots, with spurs jingling, beat a steady tattoo on the wooden walkway as the town of Virginia City, Nevada, awakened to another day. Hotel doors slammed. People shouted and muffled words erupted into laughter. Somewhere below someone was clattering pots and pans. So much noise! At the convent, on her remote island, the sounds had not run together in such a chorus. Each laugh, each peal of a bell or chirp of a bird, could be enjoyed for itself. But here . . . Cameron shrugged. She would have to get used to this. She stretched the other leg and winced as her cramped muscles protested the movement. If a broken axle hadn't delayed the stagecoach, she would be at her father's home by now. When they had finally rolled into the town of Virginia City around dawn, the driver had refused to go any farther, and she had been forced to spend the night, or what was left of it, here in the hotel. The driver had promised to contact her father's lawyer, whose office was at the end of the main street, as soon as he had a chance to catch some sleep.

An explosion of sound shattered her thoughts. Gunshot! Cameron leaped from the bed, ignoring the spasm of pain in her lower back. Pushing aside the drape, she stared at the scene in the street below. A man sprawled on his back in the dust. Blood oozed and mingled with the dirt to flow in a mottled, red pool. Near his outstretched hand lay a gun. A man, his back to her, moved with catlike grace toward the fallen man. He stooped, touched the other's wrist, then strode lazily toward the swinging doors of the saloon. Cameron's gaze was riveted on the moving man. Michael Gray! Her glance took in the ripple of muscle beneath the exquisitely tailored jacket, the loose, easy stride of a leopard, the glint of sunlight on dark hair. The door swung shut behind him, and still she stared at the empty spot where he had stood.

Pressing her palms to her feverish cheeks, she played over in her mind the scene she had just witnessed. A man lay dead in the street. Another man had just shot him. And in her tired, confused state, she had thought she was seeing Michael. Impossible. She closed her eyes, forcing herself to recall the image she had carried with her since that long-ago summer day. She relaxed. The man she secretly worshiped was noble, a hero. Michael could never shoot a man in cold blood. Opening her eyes, she stared at the still swinging doors. She wouldn't move until the gunfighter came through that doorway. Then she would prove to herself that he wasn't Michael.

At an insistent knock, she turned from the window. Pulling her cloak about her for modesty, she opened the door and stared at a man whose fist was poised to knock a second time. She was nearly eye level with him, standing only an inch or so shorter than this gray-haired man in beautifully tailored dark pants and cutaway coat. A gold chain stretched across his vest, adding to his look of importance. His dark eyes were openly studying her.

"Miss McCormick?"

"Yes."

"My name is Harold Sturgiss. I'm your father's lawyer."

Cameron extended her hand, holding the cloak with her other hand.

"I'm sorry, I haven't dressed yet. I can't invite you inside."

"Quite all right. Why don't you get yourself ready, and meet me downstairs? I understand your coach was delayed for several hours last night."

She nodded.

"Then I suggest we eat breakfast before I take you to your father's house. It's just outside the town. I have a rig." He glanced at the watch attached to the gold chain. "Is half an hour enough time?"

"Yes. That's fine."

Cameron closed the door, then, remembering the gunfight, hurried across the room to stare at the saloon door. The movement of the door warned her that someone had just passed through it. Her gaze swept the dusty street until she spotted the figure striding toward the stables at the far end of town.

Something familiar about his walk caused a pulse to flutter deep inside her.

With a sigh of frustration, she tore herself from the window and dressed quickly. What need had she of seeing the gunfighter? He couldn't be Michael. And today was the glorious day for which she had waited a lifetime. Today she would meet her father. Today, she would discover herself.

Mother Superior had not exaggerated the inadequacy of the documents. When Cameron had found a quiet time to examine the contents of the metal box, she had found only a scrap of paper documenting the time and place of her birth and the name of her father. Her mother's name had been torn from the page. The only other item in the box was a snip of red hair wrapped in a silk handkerchief.

Soon she would have her answers.

By the time the unrelenting sun had climbed high overhead, Cameron and Harold Sturgiss were seated in his handsome rig, rolling through the dust-choked streets of Virginia City toward the huge, three-story house high on a hill overlooking the entire town.

The horse pulled the carriage effortlessly up the steep incline and stopped at the wide porch that encircled the front and sides of the wooden structure. Cameron blinked in the brilliant sunlight and stared across at the lawyer. He stepped out and offered her his hand.

"Welcome home, Miss McCormick," he said formally.

Cameron caught her breath, stepped from the carriage, and stared at the huge double doors opening before them at the top of the porch. A servant woman stood slightly back from the doorway, watching them without expression.

"We're here to see Mr. McCormick," Mr. Sturgiss said briskly.

She nodded, stepped aside, then closed the door behind them. Cameron could hear a babble of voices from a room off the foyer. Mr. Sturgiss walked into the room, which appeared to be a large parlor. Cameron paused in the doorway. Several heads turned to examine the intruders.

A tall, frowning man walked toward the lawyer. "Sturgiss," he said, in a puzzled tone. "What brings you here today?" He was addressing the lawyer but staring beyond him to study Cameron.

All the chatter had stopped. There was no sound in the room until the lawyer's voice broke the stillness.

"Good day, Alex," Sturgiss said. "I'm here on John's orders. He instructed me to bring his daughter to him the minute she arrived."

Cameron could feel all the eyes in the room examining her.

"His daughter!" Alex's exclamation sliced the silence.

The lawyer abruptly turned his back on the occupants of the room. "I'm afraid explanations and introductions will have to wait. Right now we're going up to see her father. Come along, Miss McCormick," he said briskly.

Taking her arm firmly, he led her to a broad staircase, and they walked to the second floor. The lawyer led the way along a wide, dimly lit hallway to the door at the far end. He knocked and opened the door without waiting for a reply from within.

Cameron paused in the doorway, and as her eyes grew accustomed to the dimness, she saw a servant girl holding a glass to the lips of a man lying in a huge bed. The man's gaze fastened on her. He motioned the servant aside.

In a contrite voice Mr. Sturgiss said, "I'm sorry it took so long, John. The journey has been treacherous."

The man nodded and waved his hand feebly. "Leave us."

The lawyer followed the servant from the room, closing the door behind them with a soft click.

"Cameron." The word was one long sigh, as though wrenched from his soul.

He held out his palm, and she moved closer to take his hand in hers. It was big, engulfing her fingers, but the grip was surprisingly weak. He could barely squeeze her hand.

Cameron's heart was hammering wildly against her chest. "Father." She said the word aloud, tasting it, savoring the sound of it on her lips.

The man's eyes drank in the sight of her, lingering on the cloud of red-gold hair, the emerald eyes, the proud tilt of her chin.

"Oh, you are so like her," he breathed.

Her heartbeat quickened. Her mother. Now she would have all her answers.

"Sit here," he said, patting the edge of the bed.

Cameron sat, still holding his hand in hers. She studied his handsome Irish face. The skin was pale, almost translucent, with blue veins about the temples. Thick hair, steel gray, stuck to moist skin. She had not inherited his hair. It looked as though it had once been very dark. Blue eyes studied her. The bluest eyes she had ever seen. There were crinkles at the corners of his eyes, as though he were squinting against a bright light. He must look wonderful when he smiled.

"I named you for my father," he said. "Cameron McCormick. A fine name."

"And my mother? Please tell me about my mother."

He tried to squeeze her hand. She heard a sigh, from deep inside his chest. "God, how I loved her. She was the only woman I ever loved."

"Then why did you remove all trace of her?" Cameron asked plaintively. "Why is her name torn from my birth documents?"

"I had to protect her, Cameron. And you," he whispered. "It was selfish of me to send for you. I've placed you in grave danger."

At his words, a sliver of ice inched along her spine. So, she had been wrong. The danger, whatever it was, still threatened.

He looked away, then his eyes came back to stare into hers. "But I had to see you. I had to."

"I don't care about the danger." She spoke the words with a vengeance, as if to assuage her own fears as well as his. "I'm your daughter. I belong here with you." She softened her words with a smile. "And the two of us together can take care of ourselves." She watched the creases of his face as he smiled. "Can't we?"

"Of course we can," he said. "Now that you're here, I'll fight this thing. I'll grow stronger. Big John McCormick and his daughter, Cameron. We'll be a formidable team."

"Father," she whispered. "Please tell me now about my mother."

"I will, Cammy my love. I'll answer all your questions." He covered the hand holding his with his other hand. "I have so much to tell you." He sighed. "Oh, Cammy. I've made so many mistakes. Hurt so many people. If only we could live our lives over."

On an impulse, she leaned over and kissed his cheek. "Don't dwell on what was before. Think about what we'll do together."

"Together," he murmured. "It's all I've ever wanted."

His eyes closed, then fluttered open. "I knew the sisters would do well by you. Did Sister Mary Claudius tell you she once saved my life?"

"Reverend Mother?"

"Reverend Mother now, is she?" He chuckled. "When I was very young, barely more than a boy really, I was tossed off a ship for cheating at cards. Funny thing is, that time I really hadn't cheated." His blue eyes opened wide, dancing as he remembered. "I often cheated. Most of my life, in fact. But that time the cards were good to me. I just couldn't lose. But I was accused of cheating by one of the men who had lost heavily, and an angry crowd of sailors beat and stabbed me, then threw me overboard in the dark. In the morning a very compassionate, very young Sister Mary Claudius found me on the beach near death and took me back to the convent. When my wounds healed, I stayed on, sleeping in the stables, helping out with farm chores, until I was strong enough to leave. It seemed a long time before I was completely mended in body and soul." He turned a solemn gaze on the young woman beside him. "When you were born and the whole world seemed against us, I thought of those good sisters and knew they would do right by you." His eyes glittered feverishly. "Has it been a hard life in the convent, Cammy girl?"

"A hard life? No—Father." Strange, how easy it was to call this big man Father. "It was a good life. They loved me. They were very kind." In a breaking voice, she whispered, "I miss them."

His eyes were closed, his breathing unsteady. She watched the rise and fall of his massive chest beneath the covers. Somehow she had known her father would be a big, powerful man. She studied his wide shoulders, the muscled arms. He must have cut a fine figure in his youth.

Cameron leaned down and brushed her lips over his damp brow. "You sleep now, Father. We have all our days together now. And we'll talk and talk and talk."

She stood and smoothed the blankets, gently tucking his arms beneath. She watched his slow, labored breathing for a few minutes longer, searching for something familiar. Did she resemble him, perhaps about the eyes or chin? Would she have recognized him across a room crowded with people? Her father! After all these years, she had found her father. And now that she was here, no matter what the dangers, she was never going to leave him. She had come from foreign shores, clear across this land. She was home. And she was home to stay.

Moving quietly across the room, she let herself out. On a bench, Harold Sturgiss sat waiting for her. He looked up as she approached.

"My father's asleep," she said. "We'll have a nice long visit tomorrow."

The lawyer nodded and said, "Now we'd better face your reception below. Are you ready?"

Cameron squared her shoulders and unconsciously lifted her chin in a gesture of defiance. "Yes. I'm ready."

Chapter Six

VERY FORMALLY, HAROLD STURGISS TUCKED HER SMALL hand into the crook of his arm and escorted her down the stairs and once more into the parlor. The sound of voices stopped abruptly, and all heads swiveled to study the slim girl standing hesitantly in the doorway.

The man who had confronted them earlier now rose and stormed toward them. His imposing figure cut off Cameron's view of the others. He made no effort to conceal his hostility. With hands on hips, he stared down at the girl who was the object of his anger.

"Cameron McCormick," the lawyer said, "this is your stepbrother, Alex Bannion."

"A stepsister!" The words were spit from between clenched teeth. "Just what this family needed." He folded his arms across his chest and regarded her coldly. "And what did you think of Big John McCormick?" he asked sarcastically.

"I found him very tired," she replied. "We'll have a nice long visit tomorrow."

He spat out a cruel laugh and turned toward the others in the room. "Well, don't just sit there. Come and meet Big John's latest surprise."

Cameron surreptitiously studied the burly, black-tempered Alex. His hands were big, work-roughened. His eyes, as black as his hair, as black as his mood, were narrowed in contempt. His lips were thin, cruel, curled in a sneer. He looked to Cameron like every picture she had ever seen of the devil himself. He frightened her. She made a mental note to keep far away from Alex.

The lawyer led her across the room. "Miss McCormick, this is Alex's brother, Jarret."

Brothers. Cameron stared at the smaller, paler version of Alex. Jarret was staring at her with wide, almost colorless eyes beneath light hair. His features were bland, registering no emotion. Suddenly he offered his hand, and his mouth split into an imitation of a smile. Cameron expelled the breath she had been unconsciously holding. At least he was being civil, maybe even friendly. Returning the smile, she accepted his handshake.

"Jarret. How nice to meet you."

"Alex, she's beautiful," Jarret said over her head in a burst of almost childish enthusiasm.

Cameron felt herself blushing. She removed her hand from his and turned away, but not before Alex gave a chilling, calculated smile. His brother's comment gave him an idea for some fun with this intruder. He'd find the proper time for it.

Sturgiss led Cameron to a long sofa, where a young girl sat covered with a velvet lap robe.

"Miss McCormick, this is your half-sister, Miriam McCormick."

Cameron stared at the pale, blond girl whose eyes were the same deep blue as the man upstairs. Yes. This was John McCormick's daughter. But a half-sister. That meant that they had different mothers.

Cameron extended her hand, smiling brightly. "Miriam. It's so nice to discover I have a sister. I'm eighteen. How old are you?"

The hand she took was as cold as ice. The girl said nothing, but Cameron noted the narrowing of her eyes, the hard line of her mouth. She wasn't even trying to disguise her dislike of Cameron.

A cruel laugh from Alex startled her. "Eighteen. Why she's the same age as you, Miriam. Big John certainly spread himself around. What a sly old tomcat."

Cameron winced at the remark and started to turn away from Miriam's accusing eyes.

A foreign-looking man said solemnly, "Miss McCormick, my name is Ti. I am the brother of Nina." He indicated an unsmiling, darkly beautiful woman seated across the room. There was a musical lilt to his carefully cultured English voice. Though he, too, was unsmiling, there was a softness about his mouth and eyes.

In a tall wing chair sat the exotic Nina. She looked alien, with coffee-colored skin gleaming in the sunlight and huge dark eyes staring thoughtfully at the newcomer. Jet black hair was pulled into a tight knot at the back of her head. Large gold hoops dangled through her ear lobes. She was dressed in a black gown with a heavy black shawl draped tightly about her shoulders.

Cameron approached her, extending her hand. "Nina."

"Cameron. Welcome." Her tone of voice, the expression on her face, said otherwise.

A servant entered the room leading a small, dark-haired, dark-eyed little boy. Cameron turned and studied him, knowing that he had to be the son of this mysterious woman. He could belong to no one else. The eyes were the same. The same thick, black hair.

He moved solemnly to Alex, whose eyes were still fixed on Cameron with a look of pure hatred.

"Good afternoon, Father. Anna says I have to take a nap."

The man turned, becoming aware for the first time of the arrival of his child. Alex shook his hand formally. No loving kiss for him, thought Cameron.

"Alexander, meet Cameron McCormick," Harold Sturgiss said. "Cameron, this is Alexander Bannion."

The child crossed the room and formally extended his hand. "You have the same last name as Grandfather."

"Yes, I'm his daughter. And I'm very happy to meet you," Cameron said smiling. "How old are you?"

"Four and a half." He returned the smile, then ran to the dark woman seated by the window.

"Will you come up and read to me, Mama?"

She took his hand in hers. Nodding at Cameron,

she glanced around the room and said to all, "Excuse me." The voice had the same musical lilt as Ti's. It was an accent Cameron had never heard. With the most graceful walk Cameron had ever seen, her hips swaying sensually, she moved fluidly across the floor.

Before his wife and child could leave the room, Alex boomed, "And just where did Big John keep you hidden all these years?"

The others in the room watched Cameron's face. They all shared Alex's curiosity about this young mysterious woman.

"I was raised in the Convent of the Sisters of Divine Charity, in Canada," Cameron replied.

"A convent!" With a grunt of derisive laughter, Alex added, "Now, that's perfect. Who would have ever looked for a daughter of that old thief in a convent?"

Cameron drew herself up to her full height and faced his scorn. Around the room she could feel the heightened interest. From their attentive expressions she knew they were secretly enjoying this confrontation.

Alex crossed to a cabinet and lifted a crystal decanter. "Would you care for a glass of sherry?" Smiling mirthlessly, he added, "Since you are my little sister"—and he made a mocking bow—" I'll forget the formality and call you Cameron."

The sunlight cast its glow on the ruby liquid held aloft in Alex's hand.

"No, thank you."

Mr. Sturgiss interrupted. "I think some tea might revive you, Miss McCormick."

"Tea is for Englishmen and nuns," scoffed Alex.

Cameron turned to a servant girl. "Please bring me some tea." It gave her a small sense of satisfaction to duel with this arrogant man.

She kept her hands steady as she accepted the cup. Tipping the scalding liquid to her lips, she felt its warmth seep through her veins, renewing her determination. She used this time to pull her thoughts together.

Mr. Sturgiss sat in a comfortable chair, sipping his sherry and observing the scene. *Good girl,* he thought. She was doing just fine. If she showed the least bit of reluctance to face up to Alex, he would back her into a corner like an attacking dog. But this girl had spunk. Even after the tedious trip, she wasn't whimpering.

"I wish to go to my room." Miriam's high-pitched wail arrested Cameron's attention.

Almost instantly, Ti hurried to the hall, then returned with a wooden chair mounted on wheels. With great care for her comfort, he lifted Miriam from the sofa and settled her gently in the chair, careful to replace the lap robe and drape it over the length of her thin legs.

Cameron's shock registered on her face.

Miriam laughed contemptuously. "What's wrong? Haven't you ever seen a cripple before?"

"I'm—sorry." There was nothing more she could think to say.

"Excuse me," Ti said formally, before pushing the wheeled chair from the room.

Miriam never looked back.

Alex obviously thought of himself as the person in charge here. Cameron addressed herself to him. She was determined to keep her voice calm. After all, she had every right to be here. This was her father's house. He had summoned her. And for his sake she would not back down.

"It has been an exhausting journey. If you don't mind," Cameron said firmly, "I should like to go to my room now."

Taking a long gulp of the wine, Mr. Sturgiss stood and offered her his arm.

"Where is Miss McCormick's room?" he asked the servant.

The woman looked questioningly at Alex.

Scowling, he said, "Give her the room at the far end of the hall." A smile suddenly turned up the corners of his lips. "Since we weren't expecting anyone, it may be a bit musty. I'm sure you'll forgive us, won't you, Cameron?"

Nodding stiffly, Cameron took the lawyer's proffered arm. Keeping her back erect, she moved slowly from the room and up the stairs. At the end of a long hall, at the opposite end from her father's room, the servant opened the door to a large suite of rooms. Cameron stood just inside the doorway and surveyed the scene. Mr. Sturgiss wrinkled his nose at the dust, which had settled on everything. Even the huge bed looked moldy, as though the linens hadn't been changed for a year.

With a wan smile, Cameron squeezed his arm. "It's quite all right, Mr. Sturgiss. I'm so exhausted I could sleep anywhere. Later I'll set about cleaning this."

She walked back downstairs with him. At the front door, he paused. "I must remind you, Miss McCormick. You are not back at the convent now. You are the daughter of a wealthy man. You are not expected to clean your own room. That work is for the servants."

At her look of protest, he said firmly, "In the parlor, you handled yourself admirably. You must keep reminding yourself that you are in control of your own life. Never let them think that you will take orders from any of them. And the servants must be expected to do your bidding. If you lose their respect, you will lose valuable allies. Do you understand me?"

Cameron nodded. "Yes. Thank you, Mr. Sturgiss. Will you be back tomorrow?"

"I'll be back when your father summons me," he said, smiling gently at her downcast eyes. Quietly, so as not to be overheard by the others, he added, "I know you need a friend, Miss McCormick. But take your time sorting things out. Then you will discover who is your friend and who is not."

Cameron thought about the people she had met. Could any one of them truly be her friend?

"Thank you, Mr. Sturgiss, for everything. Good day."

He accepted her handshake and smiled. "Good day, Miss McCormick. Stay well."

She stood alone on the porch and waved as his carriage moved away. Shielding the sun from her eyes, she blinked at the figure on horseback watching from a nearby hill. Something about the horse and rider made her heart turn over. Clutching the railing, she stared harder, willing herself to make out the face from so great a distance. The figure remained unmoving for long moments, then wheeled and disappeared below the crest.

Cameron chided herself, recalling all the times she thought she had seen Michael on her island. She must stop this foolish nonsense. It was time to grow up. When would she stop seeing him in every stranger? Picking up her skirts, she hurried to the privacy of her room, where she could be free to relive again every moment of the brief but precious time she had spent on her island with Michael Gray. Those wonderful memories would help her forget, for a little while at least, the unexpected hostility she had encountered in her new home.

Chapter Seven

CAMERON SURVEYED THE DISMAL ROOM, THEN SIGHED IN resignation and began methodically removing her clothes. Now that the journey had come to an end and she had met the father she had dreamed of, along with an assortment of family members who seemed to run together in one long, unrelenting, unforgiving blur, she felt exhausted beyond belief.

Despite the moldy bedclothes, she would rest awhile before facing that hostile band below. She would need all her wits about her to deal with them.

Drawing the dusty drapes tightly over the windows, she pulled down the coverlet and crawled between the sheets. In an hour or two she would be ready to face what was to come.

Her last conscious thought was of her father, tall and handsome, astride a white horse, drawing nearer and nearer, holding out his arms in welcome. The figure became younger; the horse, a black stallion. Caught up in a fierce embrace, she felt warm, and safe, and loved.

Something disturbed the still figure in the bed. Something, some sound perhaps, had roused her. She opened her eyes in the darkened room and tried to recall where she was. Her father's house. The musty room, smelling of years of neglect. The hostile family who hated her just for being alive.

A door slammed somewhere down the hall. She heard raised voices. From somewhere below a shrill laugh sounded. The bedroom door was abruptly thrown open and Ti hurried across the room.

Cameron sat up, tucking the quilts discreetly about her chin.

"What are you doing here?" she demanded.

"I'm going to try to find the doctor. He could be anywhere. Your father is dead," he announced without emotion.

"My father—" She blinked once, twice. Her eyes grew round, trying to take in what he had said. Her father couldn't be dead. She had just met him—was it an hour ago? He had said they would have a long talk. He would tell her about her mother, about herself. They would have a lifetime together. A lifetime.

Pushing the quilts aside, Cameron forgot about modesty and swung her legs to the floor. As she stood, everything seemed to go black. She would have fallen, but Ti caught her in his arms and shook her roughly.

"Get hold of yourself. Stand still and it will pass."

"Yes. I—I'm fine now," she said, pushing herself free of his grasp.

He handed her a shawl from the foot of the bed. "If you'd like to see him before the doctor gets here," he said softly, "the room is empty of servants now."

"Thank you." She draped the shawl about herself and moved numbly toward the door. With her hand on the knob she turned and said, "Please send for a priest as well."

"A priest?" Ti looked puzzled. "No priest will come to this house."

"I said a priest, Ti." She spoke each word deliberately, then walked away without waiting for further argument.

The hallway was empty, as was her father's room. Empty, except for the figure of her father in the huge bed. She moved closer and stared at him, trying to memorize his face.

You were going to tell me about my mother. You said I look like her. Was her hair red? Were her eyes green? Why didn't you marry her? Hesitantly, she moved closer and reached out to touch his face. She expected him to open his eyes and smile at her. She stared at his chest, anticipating the rise and fall of steady breathing. *How could you die now? You had no right, do you hear me? No right to send for me, holding out all that sweet promise of hope, and then snatching it from me.* Taking his large hand in hers, she knelt beside the bed. *Please, Father, wake up. Please open your eyes and talk to me. There was so much you were going to tell me.*

Dry-eyed, she studied his face, then automatically

began to whisper the words of the Act of Contrition, in case he had forgotten his childhood lessons. "Oh my God, I am sorry for having offended Thee. . . ." When the words were said, she bent to kiss his forehead. One last goodbye, although they had barely said hello.

She paused, bent over the lifeless form. There was an odor, strange yet familiar. She moved closer. Yes. A bittersweet smell. She couldn't place it, but she had smelled it before. Perhaps some medicinal herb used at the convent.

Cameron started at the single knock on the door. Nina stood just outside the doorway, as though afraid to enter a room touched by death.

"The servants will not attend—the body—until they have orders from Alex," she said without expression.

"Then I'll speak to Alex."

"He isn't here. He and Jarret are in town."

Exasperated, Cameron said briskly, "Then I'll go to town."

As she brushed past the woman, Nina looked startled. Trailing Cameron to her room, she paused in the doorway, watching as Cameron began pulling on a prim cotton gown.

"Are you aware that it is dark outside?"

Cameron glanced at the heavily draped window. She had thought it was still afternoon. Had she slept away the entire day? She shrugged. "It doesn't matter. I'll still go."

"There is no one here to hitch a horse to a rig." Nina twisted her hands nervously.

Why was this woman giving her silly, useless arguments now, when her father lay dead in the other room?

Impatiently, Cameron turned and met her troubled gaze. "Nina, I can sit a horse. Now tell me where I can find Alex."

The woman paused, undecided. Then, "In the Delta Saloon. He and Jarret play cards there almost every night."

Gritting her teeth, Cameron rushed headlong down the stairs and out into the blackness of the night.

In the stable, she swung a saddle across the back of a gray gelding. She would be eternally grateful to Sister Leona for the years she had forced Cameron to see to her own needs. She scorned these helpless women who wrung their hands and waited for their men to return to take care of things.

As she headed the horse for the lights of town, she seethed. Alex Bannion. Would he now assume her father's position as head of the McCormick house?

As Cameron tied her horse, the tinny sounds of a piano filtered through the night air. She stood for a moment outside the doors of the saloon, bracing herself for the unknown. She had never been inside a place like this before. She had no idea what to expect.

Squaring her shoulders, she pushed the swinging doors and strode inside, then halted abruptly at the burst of raucous laughter from a table in the corner. For one brief moment, no one noticed her. Then, as if a signal had been given, all eyes turned to the slim woman standing just inside the doors. The rumble of voices grew silent. Even the piano player turned toward the object of everyone's interest, then abruptly stopped, his hands still poised above the keys. From the table in the center of the room, a voice intoned a vulgar comment, then laughter erupted.

Her cheeks flaming, Cameron stared about the room until she located Alex and Jarret seated at a corner table. Lifting her skirts, she moved toward them, trying not to meet the eyes of the leering men around her. The room reeked of sweat and stale tobacco and cheap whiskey. Cameron fought down the panic rising inside her, aware that she was dangerously out of her element in this place.

As she approached, Alex scraped back his chair and, scowling, turned to face her.

"What the hell are you doing here?"

"You're needed at home, Alex. My father—"

Swaying, he caught her shoulders in a painful grip. "Hellfire, boys, isn't this sweet? My little sister's come to join the party."

She flinched. "You're drunk."

"Not nearly as drunk as I intend to be." With his hand digging into the flesh of her shoulder, he turned her toward the group. "You haven't met the newest addition to our family, have you? This is Big John's best-kept secret, his daughter, Cameron McCormick."

A man at the table stood and gripped the back of his chair, gaping at her as if he had just seen a ghost.

"Little sister, that's Quenton Lampton. He's the neighbor whose house faces ours across the hill. And don't you mind the way he's weaving and staring at you. Quenton's the town drunk. He always looks like this by nightfall."

Cameron couldn't tear her gaze from the man's face. It had gone chalk white. Rusty hair, liberally sprinkled with gray, added to his pallor. With jerking movements he stumbled toward the bar, drank down two tumblers of whiskey, then leaned heavily against the bar and studied her again before lurching across the room and out the door.

The others involved in the card game had remained seated, staring with detached interest at the scene. As Alex continued the introductions, Cameron became aware of one man at the table who hadn't moved a muscle since her arrival. Now she turned to study him, noting the obviously expensive shirt beneath a perfectly tailored black coat. One hand holding the cards rested casually on the table. The other hand was out of sight beneath the table, and she sensed, rather than saw, that it was holding a gun. Her gaze traveled slowly upward to a wide-brimmed hat that tilted rakishly low over his forehead, casting his face in shadows. But even though his features were obscured she knew him. His image was indelibly imprinted on her mind. Her heart leaped into her throat. Her mouth rounded in surprise. Although no words came out, her lips clearly formed his name. Michael. But even as she was mouthing the word, Alex was introducing him. She noted the respect in his tone.

"And this is Colt. He's been known to do deadly things with that widow maker he carries."

Cameron stared helplessly at the one man whose memory she had carried in her heart for so long.

With the tips of his cards he pushed the hat back, allowing the lamp hanging above the table to illuminate his face. His gaze raked her insolently, and then, as if dismissing her, he asked, "Mind if we finish the hand now?"

She went deathly still. It was as if he had taken a whip to her. For long moments she stood transfixed.

"Please, Alex," Cameron finally managed to whisper, tearing her gaze from Michael's face. "You have to come home with me. My father has died."

His hands gripped her upper arms so tightly she thought she would cry out from the pain.

"He's dead? You're sure?"

She nodded, feeling her throat tighten. "Ti has gone for the doctor. The servants won't touch—his body—until you give the word. Please come home."

She watched his eyes narrow. Slowly, a sinister smile played on his lips. He released her, throwing back his head in a roar of laughter.

"Another bottle for this table. In fact, drinks all around. We're going to drink one for Big John McCormick."

One of the saloon girls sidled up to Alex and brought her arms around his waist. He seemed about to ignore her, then seeing Cameron's look of disgust, he grinned wickedly and drew her closer to him. Planting a wet kiss on the girl's painted mouth, he leered at Cameron.

"My little sister spent a lifetime locked away in a convent. She's probably never had a man kiss her. Or"—and he grunted in delight—"had any kind of fun, if you know what I mean. Take a look at her face, boys. The little lady's scandalized." He stared meaningfully at his brother. "What a waste. Don't you agree, Jarret?"

Giving him a hateful look, Cameron whirled, intent on running from this evil place. In one swift motion, Jarret snaked out a hand and held her fast. She was stunned by the strength he possessed, despite his slight appearance. His bland face, so like a child's, broke into an artless smile.

"She's so pretty, Alex. It doesn't seem fair that Cameron's never had any fun. Can I have fun with her, Alex? Can I?"

The faces of the men around the table grew grim, watching Alex Bannion. Cameron's heart seemed to stop for a full minute before beginning a painful hammering in her breast. He couldn't mean this. Jarret was her stepbrother. They were family. He wouldn't, couldn't mean what she thought he meant. Then she stared closely at his eyes, those gray, nearly colorless eyes, and realized they were vacant. Jarret had the simple-mindedness of a child. One word from Alex, one nod of approval, and Jarret would believe he had every right to do with Cameron as he pleased. He wouldn't even see the wrong of it. Like any child, he was selfishly interested only in his own gratification.

The sound of Alex's laughter brought ice to her veins. This wicked, hateful man was thoroughly enjoying her terror. And he intended to use his power over his weak-minded brother to torment her.

Alex shrugged, then spread his hands expansively, as if he were a monarch, granting a very special favor.

"I don't see why not, Jarret. Might as well keep it all in the family. Cameron will probably enjoy it and be most grateful."

Jarret's grip on her arm tightened. With his free hand, he caught at the pins that held her hair in a neat chignon. Waves of amber cornsilk drifted about her face and shoulders. Several men at the table caught their breath at the sight of her. With his fingers entwined in the thick mass of hair, Jarret pulled her head back with a rough jerk.

"So pretty," he muttered. "Cameron, you're so pretty."

She bit her lip to keep from crying out. Swallowing, she whispered, "Please, Jarret. Don't do this. Let me go home."

"It'll be fun, little sister. You'll see. I know all about men and women. Alex takes me to Rose's every week or so. I know all kinds of things to show you."

Shame washed over her, and she fought down a rising panic as his fingers fumbled with the pearl buttons which ran from her throat to her waist.

"Stop this, Jarret." Through clenched teeth, she appealed to the others. "Won't any of you stop him?"

One of the men, a big, burly miner, squirmed in agitation. "I stay out of family fights, ma'am. It just ain't my concern."

Feeling Michael's dark gaze riveted on her, she flushed and hung her head as the bodice of her dress was pulled open by work-roughened hands to reveal the swell of her breasts.

Laughing, Alex sat down at the table, yanking the saloon girl to his lap. With his face buried in her hair, he said, "If you'd like a little privacy, Jarret, Charley can give you a room upstairs."

"Good." Dragging Cameron along by the wrist, Jarret began walking toward the bar.

Before he had taken three steps, Michael's voice stopped him in his tracks. His tone was so cold, Cameron barely recognized it.

"Just a minute. We haven't finished our hand yet. Besides, I might like some of that action myself."

Several men at the other tables looked up at the commanding tone. A quiet murmur of excitement rippled through the crowded saloon.

Alex scowled. He hadn't counted on this.

Jarret returned to the table, hauling Cameron behind him.

"Now listen, Colt—"

"No. You listen. The hand was dealt. Each of you drew your cards." He nodded toward the pile of chips in the center of the table. "Now, unless you want to forfeit a whole lot of money to me, you're going to finish out the game." He flashed a malicious smile in Jarret's direction. "And just to sweeten the pot, I think we ought to add the lady to the stakes. That should make the game even more interesting."

Jarret appealed to Alex. "You promised, Alex. You said I could have her. Don't let him get away with this." His voice whined like a pouting child.

"Shut up." Alex roughly thrust the saloon girl from him and studied the man who sat so calmly, one hand holding the cards, the other hand still out of sight beneath the table.

Like a mongrel, the saloon girl crept up behind

Michael and began running her hand along his shoulder.

"Why fight over a skinny thing like her? Let him have her, Colt. You can have me instead."

One menacing look from him sent her scurrying away to join the others near the bar.

"What if we say no?" Alex began to rise from his chair.

The man they called Colt gave an icy smile, and Cameron felt her heart stop. How could she have ever believed this man was a hero? She had deluded herself into believing that he was a wealthy, cultured gentleman. Now she saw him for what he really was. The expensive saddle, the flashy clothes. He was a gunfighter, a card shark, and infinitely more dangerous than any of the others at this table. Their fear of him was obvious in their downcast eyes.

"You have no say in this. I've already decided." At the chilling words, Alex slumped back down in his chair. No one moved.

"Pick up your cards." Not once did Michael glance in Cameron's direction.

Each man around the table nervously picked up the hand that had been dealt.

Cameron, still held fast by Jarret, watched in horror as he reached for his cards, spread each one carefully with his thumb, then set them back down. She didn't understand the game.

Alex grinned at her, obviously pleased with the hand he had been dealt. "This is draw poker, little sister."

Every person in the room had crowded around to

watch the outcome of the game. The piano player climbed on the piano stool for a better view. The room grew so silent, Cameron was afraid they could all hear the pounding of her heart.

"Let's see them." Cameron was only dimly aware of Michael's clipped words.

"It's impossible to beat these." Alex tossed down his hand, revealing a king, queen, jack, ten, nine of diamonds.

"A straight flush," he said triumphantly.

Around the table, each man in turn spread his cards, then pushed them to one side, indicating they couldn't even come close to Alex's hand.

Alex turned to his brother. "Well, now, I give her to you, Jarret, with my compliments." He bowed grandly.

"Not so fast." Colt's icy words brought Alex's head around with a jerk.

"You can't beat 'em, Colt!"

Casually tossing the cards in the center of the table, the gunfighter watched their faces.

"Colt drew a straight flush, too," one of the miners said with a trace of awe. "With ace high."

Cameron stared at the hand: ace, king, queen, jack, ten of hearts.

The murmur of excitement grew to a fever of cursed exclamations.

The gunman stood, scraping back his chair, and unwinding his frame with surprising, catlike grace. In his hand gleamed the Colt, reminding all of them of his claim to fame.

"Guess we'll be going now, gentlemen. Got some

rather—pressing business to attend to. But it's been a real pleasure."

With a snap of his fingers he summoned the grizzled bartender, who scurried toward the table. Quickly he tallied the chips, counted out some bills, and handed them with a great show of deference to the man they called Colt.

He pocketed the money, nodded to them, then bowed solemnly before Cameron, whose hand clutched with unspoken dignity at the front of her gown.

"I believe you've just become my property, ma'am," he said.

The crowd erupted into laughter.

Taking her hand from Jarret's grasp, he yanked her harshly away. The dress once again gaped open. Cameron's face went scarlet in rage and humiliation.

Stumbling, she finally had to resort to running to keep up with his long strides. She gasped as he shoved her ahead of him through the swinging doors of the saloon. The roar of jeering laughter trailed after them.

He untied the black stallion, then mounted before reaching down, lifting her easily in his arms, and planting her squarely in front of him.

She wanted to scream, to let the whole town know that she was being taken against her will. But the terror had risen like a great lump in her throat, threatening to choke her.

Chapter Eight

THE HORSE'S HOOVES THUNDERED ALONG THE DUSTY road of the town, then continued the driving pace into the hills that ringed Virginia City. Cameron held herself stiffly in the oversize leather saddle, achingly aware of every part of the body pressed tightly behind her. One hand encircled her waist, holding her firmly in place, while the other hand rested near her hip, loosely holding the reins.

The breeze created by the movement of the horse seeped through her open bodice, thoroughly chilling her. Her body, already battered from the torturous journey of the past weeks, protested every movement she was forced to endure.

The rich cloud of hair danced in the wind, flaying the cheeks of the man who held her against his length. Finally putting a safe distance between them and the town, he allowed his thoughts to return to her. Damn fool woman looking at him so helplessly, with her heart in her eyes! It nearly tore his guts out to watch this child-woman being pawed by that animal. It had taken every ounce of his willpower to keep from killing Jarret Bannion on the spot. His finger had actually trembled on the trigger. More than anything, he had wanted to squeeze, to watch the look of surprise on that brutish face gradually turn to horror as he realized he'd just been shot. He wanted to empty the gun into that lout until he lay lifeless on the floor for the whole town to see.

Luckily the cards had come up the way he had planned them. Of course, if they hadn't he had been prepared to shoot his way out of that place and take her with him.

That knowledge rankled. The feelings that had nearly overpowered him tonight in the saloon were dangerous for a man in his position. The last thing he needed right now was to feel protective, to feel anything at all, toward one of the McCormicks.

McCormick. Who would have ever believed her name would be Cameron McCormick? He'd have to remember that, brand it into his brain, in order to fuel the hatred. Because it was absolutely necessary that he hate her. This was war. And you didn't take the enemy into your camp.

She shivered, and the hand around her waist tightened its grip, drawing her even closer to him. His hand traveled upward, finding the torn, gaping bodice. He drew both arms tightly about her, hunching over her slightly to ward off the wind. His face was buried in her hair, inhaling the wonderful woman scent of her. He was drowning in the smell of her. He fought to steel himself against it.

On the crest of hill overlooking the McCormick house he halted his horse and dismounted. Reaching up, he hauled her roughly from the saddle and, without releasing her, stared down into her upturned face.

Rage glittered in her eyes, and he was reminded of the last time he tangled with her, on her island, where she attacked him. He could still recall the shock that had registered when the flying, flailing she-cat had finally been pinned beneath his body on the damp ground. She had been soft as only a woman can be.

"This morning you killed a man in the street."

If he was startled at her outburst it didn't show. He remained silent.

"I saw you. Then you calmly walked to the saloon."

When he spoke, his voice was dangerously quiet. "Yes. He drew first. I had no choice. Kill or be killed. And the sheriff was in the saloon."

Her eyes blazed. "And of course, being a good citizen, you wanted to be sure you made a complete report to the sheriff."

"That's right."

"Take your filthy hands off me, Michael Gray."

"Still the little wildcat, I see." His look hardened. "Lesson number one, Cameron McCormick. Don't ever call me Michael again. Here in Virginia City, the name is Colt."

"Michael, I—"

He caught her roughly by the shoulders and nearly

lifted her off the ground. Her hair fell forward, swirling about her cheeks.

Through clenched teeth, he snarled, "The name is Colt. Say it."

He watched her eyes narrow with hatred.

"Damn it, Cameron. Say it. My name is Colt."

He raised his hand as if to strike her. He saw her flinch. Still she kept her mouth firmly clamped shut. He recognized the tiny amber flames of defiance that leaped into her eyes.

"Say it, Cammy, or I'll have to hurt you."

He watched the tears well up, then spill over, coursing down her face. He swore viciously. He wanted to kiss them away. He wanted to fold her in his arms, to murmur into a tangle of hair that he was sorry. He wanted to rock her in his arms like a child. He wiped away her tears, cursing himself with a fury that astounded him. Catching her by the shoulders, he wasn't even aware that he had tightened his grip on her until she cried out in pain.

She shuddered, then looked down at her feet, feeling the tension within them both about to erupt.

"All right. Why not? Maybe Michael Gray never existed at all. Maybe he was just someone I made up, someone I dreamed of on long, winter nights."

His voice softened. "That's right. Now you keep on thinking that way." He tipped up her chin. "Say my name."

He watched her eyes narrow. "Say it!"

She could no longer fight the demand in his voice. "Your name is Colt." She spit each word with venom.

"Don't you ever forget it. If you ever slip and call me Michael . . ." He paused for emphasis. "I'll have to kill you."

"Why, Michael?"

It seemed a reflex. He shook her almost violently. For one shocked moment, they simply stared at each other, too stunned to react.

Suddenly, it was all too much for Cameron. Tears of pain and rage spilled over, staining her cheeks.

"I can't take any more. I can't. Don't you understand? My father has just died. I've traveled clear across the country to be with him, and he's dead. And the family I've always dreamed of has become a nightmare. And now you're not Michael anymore. You're a—a gunfighter named Colt. Look at you, in your fancy clothes and shiny gun." She laughed contemptuously. "And I once thought you were some noble gentleman. I'll never trust another man. Never! They let you down. They lie and cheat and take from you. Liars! All of you. Liars!"

Without thinking, Michael let his hand drop lightly to her shoulder. "Don't judge all men by your father. Or me, little Cammy."

With an anguished cry, she tried to push away from him.

"Don't touch me. You have no right to touch me."

"I won that right, remember ma'am?" A bleak smile curved his lips as he reached up to brush away her tears with his thumbs. The touch was gentle, a reminder of another time, another place. Both of them seemed to sense a subtle change. Suddenly afraid, aware of her vulnerability, Cameron clutched at the gaping bodice of her dress with both hands, anxious to keep a barrier between them.

Michael caught her hands. His voice was a raw whisper. "Don't. Please. At least let me look at you."

A shaft of moonlight spilled through the leaves of a tree, showering them in golden light. Her cloud of hair shimmered in the haze. Her breasts were nearly exposed beneath the open dress. Defiantly she tossed her head, causing her hair to drift like a halo, before fluttering down around her cheeks and shoulders.

She was so lovely, she took his breath away. Clean, untouched, a breath of air in this hellhole. Desire ripped through him, and he fought the growing need.

"Please, Michael. Don't—look at me like that."

He froze. "What did you call me?"

"Colt." She licked her dry lips. "Colt, please."

"Please what?"

"Please, just let me go."

He could sense, knew instinctively, what she was fearing. She had the look of a mustang that had been run to ground and held fast by a dozen ropes. A wild thing cornered. He knew he must never let himself spoil what she was. Still . . .

Reluctantly, his hands dropped to his sides. She felt a sudden chill. They stood, almost touching, staring into each other's eyes.

"Cammy, little Cammy," he murmured.

He paused for long moments, watching the heaving of her shoulders as she fought to calm herself. His eyes narrowed. "Promise me something." His voice dropped to nearly a whisper. "Promise me you'll go back to your convent."

She blinked in surprise.

"You don't belong here, Cammy. This town teems with the scum that has been forced to leave other towns. This is a place for drifters and cons. And your family is a pack of curs. They'll rip you apart. A girl like you doesn't stand a chance."

He studied her face. Slowly, that look was returning. He could see the growing anger, as she prepared to fight back. Forgotten now was the fear and frustration of a few minutes ago. As much as he admired her spirit, he was honestly worried about her. She didn't stand a chance against these odds.

"Will you go back?"

Her chin lifted. "My father sent for me. I'm staying, and no—gunfighter named Colt can change my mind." She spit his name from between clenched teeth.

He expelled a savage breath. "You damn little fool!"

Without thinking, he caught her roughly by the shoulders. He was shaking from wanting her. The seething drive he fought to control was fighting to control him, longing for release. If he had half a brain he would take her here and now. It was what everyone back at the saloon expected. And from her trembling response he knew it was within his grasp. God, how he wanted her.

Desire was shattering his cool control. Desire made his body ache for hers. He knew he should be tender with her. This innocent deserved a gentle lover. But his control had slipped completely. There was no time to think, to be slow, to be easy. There was only this driving need that grew and grew.

His mouth covered hers savagely. The kiss was hot, hungry.

He felt her stiffen in his arms, holding herself rigidly in control. He had no way of knowing how devastating the kiss was for Cameron.

She was losing herself. Her world was rocking, teetering on an abyss. And then she was slipping, drowning in waves of feelings she never even knew lay within her.

Something hot flamed deep within her, coursing through her veins, searing even her skin.

Struggling with his own raging passion, Colt moved his lips over hers, until, ever so slowly, he felt her resolve begin to slip. Now, lightly, his mouth moved over hers, tasting, allowing her time to taste him as well.

"I knew your skin would be creamy," he breathed against her mouth. "And I knew it would be like the underside of a rose petal to the touch." Gently he ran his fingertips along the smooth, velvet skin of her throat and shoulders. "And I knew you would taste like this," he muttered thickly, letting his lips follow the trail of his fingertips.

She trembled violently. Both of them sensed the primitive stirrings of passion taking over their control.

For a man who had known many different women, the depth of the emotion that suddenly gripped him was a puzzle. He wanted her. God, how he wanted her. But despite the passions that surged through him, he couldn't bear the thought of hurting her. He felt a raging need to protect her, while at the same time he longed to lay in the grass with her, to feed on her sweetness, the warmth of her.

For Cameron, this kiss was cataclysmic. It was the very first time she had ever known such feelings. Dazed, confused, she tried to push away from his embrace. With her palms against his chest, she pushed with all her might. Colt's strength was too overpowering. He simply tightened his grasp on her, thrilling to the provocative movement in his arms. Cameron was stunned to feel the drumming of his heartbeat. It was as thunderous as her own.

Now his lips moved gently over hers, with the barest whisper of a touch. He inhaled the scent of bayberry soap and knew that for the rest of his life he would never be able to smell that delicate fragrance without thinking of her. Caught up in the sweetness of her, the kiss gentled like a fine mist after a summer storm.

For Cameron, shock soon turned to pleasure. Her lips parted slightly, allowing his tongue to invade the sweet, intimate recesses of her mouth. Tiny curls of pleasure skittered along her spine, making her knees weak. Almost with a will of their own, her hands crawled up his chest, then moved along his muscled shoulders, clinging to his strength.

She felt a core of heat and weakness from deep within her begin to radiate all the way to her fingertips. It was unlike anything she had ever experienced.

For a moment, Colt stopped and held her a little

away from him, needing to see her face, needing to confirm what they had both felt. Wide, luminous eyes stared back at him. Her lips, moist and swollen from his kiss, pursed into a rounded mew of surprise. With a sudden intake of breath, he cupped her face between his hands, then buried his fingers in her mane of honey hair. Pulling her firmly against him, his lips took hers again, this time with a fierce longing that rocked her. She was instantly caught up in the kiss. His hands trailed down her body to her hips, drawing her tightly to him, making her aware of how perfectly they fit together. She wrapped her arms around his waist, needing to cling to him. Her knees were growing weak, her limbs heavy. His arousal made her achingly aware of her own sudden, shocking desire.

Pressed to him, she was no longer cold. Not only the heat of his body but his very being seemed to merge with hers, demanding that she give as well as take. There was hunger in his kiss, and possession.

Something raw and primal seemed to take over her control. She was no longer Cameron McCormick, the proper, convent-bred young woman, but a mass of nerve endings, a hungry, trembling wanton.

"Oh God, Cammy." He spoke the words inside her mouth, unwilling to break the contact. "How I want you. Now. Now."

In one last burst of sanity, she pushed away.

"I can't think." She pressed her hands to burning cheeks. Her breathing was shallow. "This can't be right. You're Colt—a gunfighter. And my father has just died. How can I feel such things just hours after his death? What kind of person am I? What can I be thinking of?"

She turned away from him, close to tears. His hand gently stroked the silken tangles.

"Yes. I know, Cammy. I understand. That independent girl I met in the convent would need to know why and how. You have a right to question what's happening in your life. And you have a right to control your destiny. It's just—" His voice tightened. "Be warned. I want you. And I won't be the only man in this town who will."

With a sob choking her, she covered her face and turned away.

"Little Cammy—"

"Don't. Don't touch me again. Ever!"

Gently, he turned her toward him. "Look at me," he commanded.

When she looked up, he saw the glimmer of tears on her lashes.

There was a long silence. Then, in an ominously tight voice, he snapped, "You can walk back from here. I can't go any closer to the McCormick house."

She blinked. "You're not going to . . . force me?"

He gave her a grim smile. "I don't think force would be the proper term for it now, do you?"

His fingers traced the tiny trail of tears along her cheek. She stood very still, fighting the desire to move like a kitten against his hand, almost regretting it when he finally broke the contact.

He swore in frustration, then turned and swung into the saddle before saying gruffly, "Think about what I said. Go back to your convent, Cammy. You don't belong in Virginia City, or in the McCormick house."

She was back in control and feeling the sting of humiliation as she realized just how easily she had succumbed to his persuasions.

"It's my house too—Colt," she hissed.

She pivoted away. Without looking back at him, she began to run toward the lights of the house—her father's house. No. Her father was dead now.

She slowed. Tears stung her eyelids. She seemed to have shed more tears this night than she had in a lifetime. There would be no more. Angrily she brushed them away with the back of her hand before stumbling blindly on.

Now it was Alex's house. *And mine,* she thought fiercely. *Mine.*

She shuddered and, drawing the remnants of her dress tightly about her, wondered how she could survive this savage world, her bitter, unforgiving family, and above all, the new, terrifying passions this man had unleashed.

Chapter Nine

WELL, WELL. OUT MEETING THE CHARMING MEN OF Virginia City."

Cameron whirled at the shrill voice coming from the darkened parlor. Taking a candle from the hallway, she entered the room. Near the window, Miriam sat in her wooden chair. The smug look on her face faded as she took in Cameron's torn dress, her loosened hair streaming about her face and shoulders.

Pulling the wheels with trembling hands, she glided nearer.

"Were you . . . Are you—hurt?"

Her real concern wasn't lost on the trembling young woman. At least it was a start toward friendship. Cameron lifted her head. "No. I'm—fine."

The look of concern was instantly erased. The voice hardened. "I've heard that the citizens of Virginia City are a tough lot. That's one of the things I won't ever have to worry about. And you wouldn't either if you didn't go about the countryside alone."

"Thank you, Miriam. I'll remember that in the future." Cameron kept her voice even. "And now, if you'll excuse me, I'm afraid I've had all I can deal with tonight."

As she walked from the room, Cameron could feel her half-sister's gaze leveled at her.

She was painfully aware of their contrast. Miriam's fine, cornsilk hair was perfumed and curled, perfectly arranged in a mass of ringlets and tied back with pale blue ribbons to match her blue gown trimmed with blue velvet bows at the neckline. A pale blue shawl fell softly about her lap, to hide her withered limbs.

Cameron's wind-tossed mane fell in tangles about her face and shoulders. The once demure gown hung in tatters, the hem torn and spattered with dirt. She looked like a creature from the wild.

She held herself erect, though, refusing to give in to the utter weariness that enveloped her until she was safely alone in her room.

For the first time in her life, Cameron felt the need to lock her door. Shoving a heavy dresser across the floor, she positioned it so that it was impossible for anyone to open her door from the outside. Too exhausted even to undress, she fell across the bed and slept fitfully.

Cameron sat in the library with the other family members. She had wanted to avoid this, but Mr. Sturgiss insisted she be present when her father's will was read.

The funeral that morning had been almost primitive. At her insistence, Jarret drove the rig to town for a priest. Both Jarret and Alex acted as if nothing had happened the night before. For the moment, Cameron was willing to go along with the charade. There were more important issues to deal with. But even as they stood on opposite sides of the pine coffin, Cameron could feel the hairs on the back of her neck bristle as she recalled the terrifying scene at the saloon. Would she ever be able to wash away the feeling of Jarret's hands on her skin?

The shriveled old cleric, who looked as if all his juices had been sapped by the relentless sun, went through the motions of a funeral in a trance. After saying a few prayers over the casket, the priest turned and cupped her chin in his gnarled hand. Cameron waited, expecting to hear him utter his sympathy, needing some familiar words of comfort. Instead, he broke into a fit of coughing and, pressing a soiled handkerchief to his lips, turned away without a word. The other members of the family followed him. As the carriage carrying him back to his rectory clattered along the road, they disappeared inside the house.

Cameron stood alone on the windswept hillside as two old men lowered the casket into the ground and began silently shoveling red sand into the cavity. At her direction, one of the men hammered a simple wooden cross into the mound of earth. Long after they left, she stood, staring at a spot on the ground. The finality of it all overwhelmed her. Her father was really gone. Forever. And with him went all the answers she was seeking. She had lived her whole life on promises that someday, somewhere, someone would tell her who she was. She had lived for the day when she would receive that wonderful summons to come and share her father's life. A few days ago, she had been on top of the world. Now, that whole world had come crashing down around her. And all because she had let herself believe that one man would make everything all right.

She fingered the lovely gold locket about her neck, a parting gift from Sister Adele, whose lover's broken promise had sent her to the convent for solace. The beautiful young sister's words echoed. "Oh, Cammy, don't ever pin your hopes and dreams on a man. For he'll be a thief and steal your most precious possession of all—your hopes, your dreams, your very future. Remember, Cammy, don't ever trust your life to the whims of a man."

Tears squeezed from beneath lowered lids and trickled down her cheeks. A sob caught in her throat, and she swallowed it and turned away from the grave abruptly.

Surrounded now by family members, she felt more alone than at any time in her life.

Fool! What a silly, childish fool she had been! She had forgotten all the words of caution and had counted on someone else. Her father. Michael. No one could be counted on to change her life. Only herself. Cameron resolved to heed the betrayed nun's warning or she would be doomed to repeat the mistakes forever.

She came to a decision. She would heed Michael's . . . Colt's advice. This wasn't her world. When the will was read, she would go back to the convent where she belonged.

Sitting alone, to one side of the room, Cameron could see the tense profiles as Harold Sturgiss removed a document from his case and began to read.

"To my daughter Miriam."

Cameron studied the young woman seated stiffly in her wooden wheelchair. Her gaze was locked on the lawyer's face, as if willing him to read what was in her mind. She seemed to be hardly daring to breathe.

"I leave this house in which she was born and all the furnishings therein."

A slow gleam of triumph spread across Miriam's face. Her eyes narrowed as she turned to stare at Alex and Jarret.

The lawyer cleared his throat.

"To the twin sons of my dead wife, Salina."

Cameron nearly gasped in surprise. Twins. She studied the profiles of the two men. Where Alex was tall and muscular, with fierce, hard features and dark, swarthy coloring, Jarret seemed slighter of build, with pale skin and bland, vacant eyes. Yet his blandness was deceptive. She knew from the bruises on her wrist where he had gripped her last night that he was a powerful man.

The lawyer's voice intoned, "I leave two hundred fifty acres of the southernmost section of land and any building thereon. Fifty percent of all profits from this land shall be held in trust for young Alexander. That money, plus the interest accrued, shall go to Alexander on his twenty-first birthday, or be split equally among my heirs in the event of his death. The other fifty percent of the profits shall be shared equally among all my heirs."

Cameron noted that her father never referred to them as his stepsons. He obviously didn't wish to refer to them in any familiar way. She watched as the two exchanged glances. Alex seemed about to speak, but the lawyer cleared his throat and continued.

"To my daughter Cameron."

Everyone in the room turned to stare sullenly at her.

"I leave the two hundred fifty acres which adjoin the Lampton property and any buildings thereon. I have every confidence that she will put this land to good use."

Cameron sat in stunned silence.

Harold Sturgiss gathered his papers and stuffed them into a briefcase.

Alex bounded to his feet, his eyes blazing.

"Big John McCormick was a double-dealing gambler all his life. I should have realized he'd hide a trump card up his sleeve."

He towered menacingly over Cameron. "So this is why he kept your existence a secret from us all these years. Even in death he was determined to cheat us. He promised our mother that all this would be ours. That was the only reason she agreed to marry him. In return for her being mistress of his fine house, he agreed to secure the future of her fatherless twin sons. That was the agreement they made. It was the only way for a helpless widow to survive."

Cameron found herself wondering about the woman who could have raised such villainous men. A helpless widow? Though Big John McCormick was hardly a saint, judging by the things she had already heard, it looked like he may have struck a bargain with a she-devil.

Alex's voice thundered. "And now this! You've been brought here to take what's ours. But then, Big John always cheated. He beat old Lampton out of all this years ago. And now he's cheated us out of our rightful inheritance." He lowered his voice to a chilling whisper as he caught her arm. "You will live to regret this, little sister."

All heads snapped to attention as Cameron's unwavering voice stopped him.

"Take your hand off me, Alex. Don't you ever touch me again."

His eyes widened in surprise, then narrowed in fury. "No little nun can tell—"

"I said, don't ever touch me again. Do you understand?"

His fists clenched at his sides. Not now, but very soon, he would make her regret this humiliation.

Cameron stared around the room, allowing her gaze to linger for a brief moment on each family member. Then, regally lifting her skirts, she spun and hurried to her room, leaving behind her a stunned silence.

A short time later there was a knock on her door. She opened it to admit the lawyer.

"Mr. Sturgiss, why did my father do this?" She paced the center of the room, clearly agitated.

"I'm sure he had his reasons, Miss McCormick."

"But I didn't want their inheritance, Mr. Sturgiss." She turned to face him. "You saw their reactions. They all resent me. They think I came here to steal from them what is rightfully theirs."

"Theirs, Miss McCormick? All of this belonged to Big John. He had the right to leave it to whomever he pleased. And it pleased him tremendously to give you that land."

"But he expected me to stay here, to make my home here on his land." Her voice lowered. "I can't possibly stay here with these people, with all this bitterness."

"I suppose not," the lawyer said dryly. "I would guess it is tempting to think about the simple life in the convent. I'm sure your life there was serene. All your needs were taken care of. Of course, it may be a bit stifling for a spirited woman like you, but at least it's safe." He paused. "Well then, leave, Miss McCormick, and ask Alex to manage your estate." He leveled his gaze on her. "Is that what you wish?"

Cameron walked to the window and stood silently, staring down at the barren landscape. She had promised her father they would be a team. She had promised herself she would be strong enough to control her own destiny. Was this land her birthright? What did she want—security, or a chance to taste life?

Should she stay long enough at least to put up a fight for what was hers?

The lawyer stood quietly, watching as she suddenly clenched her fists at her side.

She turned to face him. "I can't imagine Alex managing my—estate."

"You will be staying then, Miss McCormick?" he asked gently.

"Yes. For the time being anyway, Mr. Sturgiss, I'll be staying."

A flicker of a smile softened his professional bearing. "I'll see myself out. Good day, Miss McCormick."

Cameron tied her horse at the railing and entered the general store. Several pair of eyes studied her intently. She realized glumly that many of the men of this town had probably witnessed her humiliating experience at the saloon.

"Yes, miss. What can I get you?"

She lowered her voice, hoping to keep her business a secret from the curious bystanders.

"I wish to purchase a hand gun."

If the shopkeeper felt surprised at her request, he didn't show it. With barely a pause he said, "Over here."

She followed the storekeeper to a locked case. Taking a key from his pocket, he set three guns on a countertop.

"I don't know anything about these things," she muttered. "Which one do you recommend?"

"Depends." He looked her over, noting her short stature and slender figure. "You going for distance or close range?"

She frowned. "Fairly close range, I think."

"You going to wear it on your hip or conceal it on your person?"

A good question. She hadn't thought about that. But it was obvious that she had no intention of going about the town wearing a gunbelt. "I believe I'd like to conceal it."

His hand paused at a little derringer, then moved on. "This little Remington would fit in a pocket, or even the waistband of a petticoat, begging your pardon, miss."

Cameron bestowed a smile on him, instantly approving of his manners. Gingerly she cradled the pistol in her hand.

"Will you show me how to load it and use it?"

The shopkeeper ran his hands across his shirt front, considering. "I'll show you how to load it, miss. But using it's another thing. It'll take a lot of time and practice to comfortably shoot a pistol. The best way is to go out back behind a barn and keep on shooting till you can hit a target every time." He smiled gently. "Just keep in mind that some folks never get the hang of it."

She met his look. "I intend to get the hang of it." She handed him the Remington. "If you'll be good enough to show me how to load it then."

"Yes, miss." He took a box of bullets from the cabinet and demonstrated the proper way to load.

Then he handed the gun back to her and watched as she followed his lead.

Satisfied, he nodded. "You're a clever little lady. You might just learn how to shoot this thing like you said."

As she sauntered from the store, the man watched her with obvious approval. The curious bystanders were left to mutter among themselves, speculating on the strange behavior of Big John's daughter.

Chapter Ten

CAMERON STOOD AT THE WINDOW. DAWN SOFTENED THE darkened hills that littered the barren landscape. In the silent hours while the world slept, she had allowed her mind to travel the miles back to her beloved Allumette Island. There she rode wild and free, the hooves of her horse flattening the grass as he broke into a run. From a crest above her, a mysterious rider on a black stallion moved effortlessly toward her until their paths converged. Strong arms lifted her from her saddle and settled her firmly against a body corded with muscles, which complemented her soft curves. She melted into an embrace that spoke of tenderness, and unending love, and endless delights. She actually blushed at some of the images that flitted through her mind, as she wondered what it would be like to be loved completely by her dream lover.

Renewed by her fantasy visit to that gentler place,

she crossed to the door, safely barricaded by the dresser. Shoving the barrier aside, she hurried out to escape to the hills before the rest of the brooding household awoke.

In the secret hours of night, resolutions are easily made. But in the harsh light of day, the reality of her situation came back to grip her.

She was no longer that child of her memory. She would never again feel completely secure. Here, in this hostile land, there were vipers coiled to strike. Who among these could be counted on as friend?

When the horse had carried her a safe distance, Cameron tethered him in a shady spot and pulled the Remington from the folds of her gown. Loading it as the shopkeeper had instructed, she held it in shaking hands and squeezed the trigger. The bullet ricocheted off a nearby rock, whistling through the air, and imbedded itself in the trunk of the tree directly beside her.

"Damn little fool! A couple of inches more and it could have killed you!"

Cameron whirled at the sound of Colt's voice.

"You! What are you doing here? Did you follow me?"

"Don't flatter yourself. I have better things to do than make camp outside your door all night."

"And I have better things to do than stand here wasting my time with a gunfighter."

He saw the flash of fire in her eyes and smiled thinly. "Who better to teach you how to handle this thing?" Taking the pistol from her hand, he examined it carefully before returning it to her.

"By now, everyone in Virginia City knows that the newest member of the McCormick clan bought herself a gun."

He studied her intently, noting the eyes rimmed from lack of sleep, the overly bright color to her cheeks. He cursed silently at the faint bruises on her wrists.

"So you've decided to throw in with that pack?" He watched her lips thin. "Then you'd better become an expert with this gun, little Cammy. Mad dogs have been known to turn on their own if they spot any weakness."

"What makes you think I didn't buy this to use on you, Colt?"

He saw the glitter of hard emeralds before she lowered her lashes.

After a silent pause, he murmured, "All right, Cammy. Fair enough. But it wouldn't even be a contest unless you learn how to handle this first. And I'm the expert on guns."

He caught her by the shoulders and twisted her around. Surprised, she tried to resist as his arms encircled her from behind and came up under her arms to clutch the gun. Positioning her fingers around the pistol, he lifted it to eye level. His lips grazed her ear.

"Think of this as part of your hand. Hold it, fondle it, until you're so familiar with this little piece of metal that you know every groove, every angle, every edge."

"You make it sound like a lover."

She heard his sudden intake of breath. Ignoring her

taunt, he tightened his grip over her hands. "Close your eyes. Feel it with your fingertips. Balance it in your palm. Know it, Cammy, so that you can be comfortable with it even in the dark."

She obeyed, dropping her lids, letting the warmth of his voice flow over her. She felt a tingle curl itself along her spine as his lips continued to brush her temple and cheek. It was so easy, with her eyes closed, to forget about Colt; to remember only Michael, the lover of her dreams. In his strong arms she felt safe and warm. His voice commanded, lulled, softened, until she wanted only to turn and bury her face in the warm flesh she would always remember. More than anything in the world, she wanted to feel his pulsebeat against her lips.

He felt the change in her as she relaxed against him, and he swore softly, berating himself for the swift surge of desire he had to fight to resist.

Cameron kept her eyes closed, to lock out the reality around her. If only she could stay here on this hill, cradled in his arms. If only she didn't have to go back to that house, to be a member of that hostile band. If only he didn't have to go back to a life of drifting, and card playing, and gunfighting. If, if, if! She forced herself to concentrate on the lesson rather than the teacher.

"Pick out a target." His voice caressed beside her ear.

"That tumbleweed by the rock."

"All right." He continued to cover her hands with his. "Line up your target, looking just about here." He rested a finger along the top of the gun. "This is your sight. When it's perfectly lined up, squeeze off your shot."

Cameron did as she was told. As the gun fired, her hands flew up, then back, startling her.

"What happened?"

"That's just the reflex from the release of the bullet. After a while, you'll learn to allow for it. You won't even have to think. It will all become one smooth motion."

Cameron watched in dismay as the bullet spewed dust several feet beyond the tumbleweed.

"Adjust your distance and try again."

Gradually she became so absorbed in the instruction she began to forget the man whose voice coaxed beside her temple.

"Over a bit more. Good. Shoot."

Again and again she squeezed the trigger, loading the small Remington each time she emptied the chamber. For over an hour they stood, his arms at first wrapped around her, guiding her through the lesson. Gradually he withdrew until, seemingly unaware, she continued on her own, aiming at targets, squeezing, correcting her own inaccuracies.

Colt leaned against a rock, watching her with a mixture of grimness and admiration. She had spirit. Maybe, just maybe, she'd be able to protect herself.

His gaze slid over the slim figure, looking incongruous in the prim pink gown, boldly aiming the pistol. There was a familiar look of resolution on her face. The wind had pried loose little tendrils, which glinted flame in the rising sun. He thought fleetingly of Jarret's hands soiling her beauty, and a knot of rage tightened within him. Even with a gun, what chance could she possibly have against all the dangers he knew she was facing?

"I hit it!"

He found himself smiling at her childlike enthusiasm.

"So you hit the target once. Tumbleweeds can't shoot back. If it were a man, you'd be dead by now. Don't gloat until you can hit any target in your sight at least ten times in a row without missing."

"Ten times. That will take forever."

"You don't have forever, Cammy. Keep thinking about Jarret and that scene in the Delta Saloon. That ought to be enough to make you work harder."

Instantly, he saw her blanch. Why had he reminded her of her humiliation? His hands clenched into fists. He wanted to tell her he was sorry. He wanted to erase those ugly memories from her mind for all time.

She turned away, the smile replaced by a look of grim determination.

Without warning the gun was yanked from her hand and dropped to the sand at her feet. His hands caught at her shoulders, turning her toward him.

His lips covered hers, stifling her little gasp. The kiss was intense, smoldering. There was anger in his kiss, as his lips took hers. Anger, and a fierce protectiveness.

Her reaction to his kiss shocked her. After the first moment of sudden stillness, she swayed against him, parting her lips for his deeper exploration. She fit so perfectly in the circle of his embrace. Their hearts kept perfect rhythm. It seemed the most natural thing in the world, to be standing beneath a shimmering sun, lost in the delights of this newly discovered passion.

"Ummm, you taste so good," he muttered against her lips. "Like cool water on a hot afternoon."

"I do?" She lifted her gaze to his dark eyes and smiled as she saw herself reflected there.

"If I didn't know better, Miss McCormick, I'd think you were flirting with your teacher."

A delighted laugh escaped her. "Do you know, Colt, this is the first time I've ever flirted with a man. The very first time."

He caught a stray wisp of hair and lifted it. His eyes narrowed as the fiery strands sifted through his fingers.

"Then you're very good at it, Miss McCormick. This being your first time."

"Am I?" She pressed against him and felt his fingers suddenly grasp her shoulders, pulling her even closer.

Lifting her face to his, she stood on tiptoe to bring her lips to his. For one heart-stopping moment he paused, his lips hovering a fraction above hers. Then, with a sigh, he wrapped her in his arms and brought his mouth to hers. The kiss was demanding, seething with undercurrents of restrained passion.

With a little moan, she moved in his arms, wanting to give in a way she had never before experienced.

His hands moved along the small of her back, pinning her firmly against him. Slowly he moved his hands up along her sides, allowing his thumbs to graze the soft swell of her breasts.

With a sudden gasp, she tried to pull away. His hands lowered, pulling her close, caressing her back. She relaxed in his embrace and tentatively allowed her tongue to explore his mouth. She heard his moan of impatience before his lips closed over hers once more, devouring, seducing, demanding.

Colt caught her by the shoulders, suddenly holding her at arm's length. Through narrowed eyes he studied her, an unreadable expression on his face.

Abruptly he strode to where his horse stood tethered beside hers. Swinging into the saddle, he caught up the reins and stared down at her.

"If any other man was thinking what I'm thinking about you right now, I'd kill him."

Without a backward glance, he rode away.

Chapter Eleven

CAMERON TURNED THE DUST-STREAKED HORSE OVER TO A scowling Alex without a word, then strode to the house. As she climbed the steps, she saw the corner of the curtain flutter.

In the parlor, Miriam sat in her wheelchair, watching the doorway. Cameron was aware of the eager, questioning look, which Miriam instantly tried to hide with a scowl.

Reverend Mother had once said there was a way to reach each person's heart. The problem was, some people put up barriers, and others were afraid to cross them. The wise ones learned to look beyond the image, to discover the person hidden within.

Maybe Miriam had been hurt too often in the past. Could she be so afraid of rejection that she hid behind a wall of anger? Cameron determined to risk Miriam's wrath.

"I rode over some of our land today."

Miriam frowned. "You mean 'your' land."

Cameron chatted easily. "It's beautiful, Miriam. Have you ever seen it?"

Another frown. "Yes. I wasn't always a cripple." Her tone hardened. "Before my—fall, I used to play out there. I hate it! It's ugly. Scarred with deep mine shafts."

Cameron moistened her lips and plunged on. "Is that how you . . . Is that what happened to you?"

"I—fell down a shaft when I was six."

Cameron couldn't hold back the gasp. "How terrible. Who found you?"

"My father. Alex and Jarret brought him. He had to lower himself on a rope, strap me to his back, then climb back out."

Cameron could imagine a child's terror in the blackness of a deserted shaft. "You must have suffered great pain."

Miriam was silent for long moments. Her expression was closed. "I don't remember."

Cameron let that comment pass, knowing that it must have been so horrible that Miriam had locked it all away, to keep from remembering. "Have you ever been out of this house since?"

"No." She bit the single word off.

Cameron took a deep breath. "Oh, Miriam, there's so much beauty in the world. Each day, when I return from my ride, I'll describe everything and everyone I saw. It will be just as if you've been there with me."

Blue eyes lit with life, then abruptly dimmed. "Why would you want to do that?"

"Because we're sisters. I'll be your legs, Miriam."

Suspicion was replaced by a steady, narrowed look. "Huh. Maybe."

Cameron expelled the breath she had been holding. It wasn't friendship. It wasn't much of anything yet. But it was a start.

The day was warm. Almost too warm. Removing her shawl, Cameron draped it across the saddle and lifted her heavy hair from her neck, shaking it loose. As her horse crested a hill, she reined him in abruptly.

Standing on the side of the grassy knoll, staring at her, was the man who had rushed out of the saloon on that night—a night Cameron would forever think of as her "night of humiliation."

"Your name is Quenton, I believe."

He continued to stare until Cameron felt her temper flare.

Some of the fire was evident in her haughty tone. "My name is Cameron McCormick."

He smiled. It was a gentle smile that softened all his features.

"Forgive me." He walked closer and stared up at her, shielding the sun with his hand. "It's just that you're so beautiful. I can't help staring. You see, I'm an artist, and it isn't often I see someone so lovely. Would you ever consent to allow me to paint your portrait?"

Now it was Cameron's turn to stare. Beyond him she could see the easel and paints.

Dismounting, she led her horse along the knoll.

The canvas on the easel was blank. Disappointment showed on her face.

"I'd hoped to see some of your work." She turned to him with a look of anticipation. "I've never met an artist before."

"Then we're even. I've never met a vision before. And, Miss McCormick, you're a vision of loveliness." He brightened. "I'll make you a proposition. If you'll sit for me, you'll have a chance to watch an artist work. And I'll have the most beautiful portrait model in the country. What do you say?"

Cameron barely hesitated. His offer was too tempting. Besides, she liked this shy man's smile and his gentle manners.

"All right. When do we start?"

"Now, Miss McCormick," he said eagerly. "Right now."

He helped her dismount, then lifted the saddle and blanket from the horse, tethering him in the shade. Spreading the blanket on the grass, he took her hand and led her to sit down, positioning her face upward to catch the sun. Her windblown hair fell in a cascade of soft curls about her face and shoulders.

Standing by the easel, he studied her for long moments, frowning in deep concentration. He stared at her for so long, Cameron began to think he had actually forgotten her.

Slowly, he picked up some charcoal and began to sketch.

"Can you talk to me while you work?" she asked tentatively.

He smiled. "Yes. What would you like to hear?"

She shrugged. "Tell me about yourself."

He seemed almost shy. "There's not much to tell. My name is Quenton Lampton. I live in the house on that hill which faces the McCormick land."

"Do you live alone?"

"No. I live with my father. He's very old, and infirm. He rarely leaves his bed now."

"I'm sorry. Is there someone besides you to care for him?"

"There's an old housekeeper. Rose. She's been with us since before I was born."

"Such a big house for so few people," she mused. "It must seem empty."

"Yes. Of course, there's . . ." He paused, then leaned quickly to his work. "We have a boarder. But he's gone for long periods of time."

Cameron watched as his hands moved quickly, sketching, pausing, then bending once more to the canvas. "How did you learn to paint?"

"I've always been drawing and sketching. Ever since I was a lad. For my fourth birthday my sister bought me every book about artists and painting that she could find. I suppose that changed my life. I've always known I wanted to be an artist."

"That's wonderful. Your family must be very proud."

She saw the look of pain in his eyes, before he composed himself.

"My sister is—gone. And my father has never approved. He thinks it's—unmanly."

Cameron felt a surge of sympathy for this shy man. How painful, to desire the approval of the one person who could never give it.

He saw the green eyes darken. "Well, I think it's a wonderful, God-given talent that you should be proud of. Reverend Mother said we must all use the talents God gave us."

"Reverend Mother?"

Cameron blinked. She had forgotten for a moment that this man was a complete stranger. Sitting here in the sun, watching the movement of his soft hands on the canvas, she felt completely at ease with him. It was as if she had always known Quenton Lampton.

"I was raised in a convent, in Canada."

He studied her, then turned his attention once more to his work. "Were you happy there?"

"Oh yes." A dreamy smile crossed her face. "It was a very orderly life, but a simple one as well. I suppose it was like a smooth road. No hills or valleys, just one continuous line." She was speaking more to herself than to Quenton. Her tone became softer, almost wistful. "I'm still not sure I like climbing these hills, or racing down the valleys, but I'm slowly discovering that the view is certainly more exciting than one long smooth road."

The artist smiled at her words. She had revealed much more about herself than she realized.

"Have you ever left Virginia City?" Cameron asked on an impulse.

He nodded without looking up from the canvas.

"Once. For nearly a year. I served with the Texas Rangers."

Surprise showed on her face. "I've heard they're rugged, tough men who'll go to any lengths to capture men outside the law."

"I'd say that's pretty accurate."

She studied his features, wondering how a gentle man like Quenton could have found the courage to ride with the Texas Rangers.

He glanced up and, seeing her expression, smiled gently.

"Maybe I thought I would prove to my father that I was a man. Or maybe I needed to prove it to myself. At any rate, I served for a year." He shrugged and bent once more to his task.

"And did you prove anything?"

She watched the breeze ruffle the rusty hair. The sun revealed a sprinkle of silver strands. "I think so. At least I didn't run from danger. I think I did my company proud. And I came home, thankful for the beauty around me."

He stood back. "I think you've endured the sun for long enough today, Miss McCormick. Will you sit for me again?"

"Oh yes." She stood, brushing down her skirts. "May I see what you've done?"

He paused. "I'd really prefer to wait until it's completed. Would you mind?"

She was eager to see what he had done. But she understood his unwillingness to share an incomplete work.

"All right. I'll practice patience, Quenton. When would you like to meet again?"

"How about the day after tomorrow? Come to my house. I have a gown I'd like you to try on. I think it would be perfect with your hair and those eyes. Would you mind?"

The thought of a new adventure exhilarated her. "Not at all. I'd love to."

Pounding hoofbeats startled them. A black stallion appeared over the ridge and, astride him, the brooding Colt.

Cameron felt a shiver pass through her at the sight of him. Quenton stared from Cameron to Colt. No one spoke.

"Why don't you come at noon." Quenton gave her a warm smile. "If my father is awake, you can meet him and take your meal with us."

He quickly saddled her horse, then helped her mount. He took her hand.

"Thank you, Miss McCormick."

She smiled. "Call me Cameron. And the pleasure is mine."

She gave a hurried glance at Colt, who sat in frosty silence, watching them. "Will you be all right?"

Quenton squeezed her hand. "Don't worry about me, Cameron. I'll be fine."

"Are you sure? I—have a gun."

His eyes widened for a fraction. His smile deepened. "Thank you. But I can manage." He stepped back. "Go now."

She gave one last glance at Colt, and the mere sight

of him caused her heart to lodge in her throat. With a touch of her heels, the horse turned and broke into a canter.

Each day, Cameron continued to ride off at first light, determined to examine every inch of land willed to her. Always she carried the gun, and as soon as she was safely away from prying eyes, she practiced loading and shooting, until she was satisfied that she could hit a target.

True to her promise, as soon as she returned she would settle herself at Miriam's knees and describe everything. At first Miriam sat quietly, the perpetual frown occasionally replaced by one of bland indifference. But Cameron's enthusiasm was contagious. Soon Miriam was caught up in the narrative, her laughter joining Cameron's with girlish abandon.

"Today I rode to the highest peak. See?" Cameron pointed out the window, and Miriam's gaze followed her direction. "You can see for miles. Far below, I saw deserted mines, rusted wagon wheels, and mining machinery. There was a mare and foal on the next ridge. They seemed to be heading for a line of trees in the distance, where a stallion stood waiting for them. They looked so wild and free. I envied them."

Miriam's eyes sparked with life. "You're wild and free like them."

"Me? No, Miriam. No matter how far I wander, I have to come back here by nightfall. Where else would I go?"

Miriam nodded thoughtfully. "I never thought of

that. I guess none of us is really free. We all have a different prison. I have this chair." She frowned. "And Nina has Alex."

"Oh, Miriam. What are you saying?" Cameron's heartbeat quickened. This was the first time Miriam had ever volunteered any information.

The pale young woman shrugged. "Ask Nina sometime."

As Cameron began to leave the room, Miriam said haltingly, "Thank you, Cameron."

"For what?"

"For keeping your promise. I like having you be my legs. And . . . I'd like to be your ears in return."

Cameron hurried back to Miriam's side. In hushed tones she said, "You'd do that for me?"

Cool blue eyes appraised her. "Yes. I hear a lot in this house. I have little else to do but listen. If I hear anything you should know, I'll tell you."

Cameron hesitated, then leaned down and kissed Miriam's cheek before hurrying away, unaware of the look of surprise in the startled eyes or the dreamy smile as she touched a hand to her pale cheek.

On her daily expeditions, Cameron discovered a crumbling cottage which stood on land that bordered the McCormick land and the adjoining Lampton property. Nearly hidden behind a stand of ancient spruce, the cottage offered a cool shelter after a hot, dusty trek.

Hesitantly, Cameron pushed open the door, then surveyed the single room. One wall had begun to crumble, and the roof sagged. A wooden bed frame still stood in one corner. A tattered, hand-stitched quilt covered matted straw. Against a wall leaned a wooden rocking chair. A broken water pitcher lay in a porcelain basin. Through a shattered window a rose bush had thrust its branch, like a flower-bedecked arm, lending its fragrance to blend with the pungent scent of the earthen floor.

There was nothing outstanding about her surroundings, yet Cameron was drawn further into the room. Sitting down in the chair, she rocked for long moments, pleased that it was still sturdy enough to hold her. A feeling of peace pervaded the room. There had been love here. She could sense it. After the hostility in the big McCormick house, this decaying cottage, with its memories and ghosts of happier times, was a soothing balm.

Cameron moved about the room, touching the faded quilt, fitting the jagged pieces of the pitcher together to study the lovely floral design. Lifting a brick that lay on the floor, she reached up to fit it back into the wall. Something white gleamed in the hole. Reaching deeper, Cameron removed a pile of yellowed pages. They had long ago pulled loose from their binding, and most were curled, the strong, neat handwriting smeared from the moisture of years.

She moved to the light from the broken window and began to read. It was a diary. Her heart leaped. She might be able to decipher some of these pages and get to know the people whose love was still so strongly felt in this place.

Pulling the old rocker beneath the window,

Cameron began to sort through the yellowed pages, reading bits and pieces of someone's life.

September 6, 1855

Father has been in a black temper for days. He lost five hundred acres of land to a drifter in a card game. He says the gambler cheated him. But I've heard rumors. Father got drunk and wouldn't quit until he had lost too heavily.

I can escape his fury by riding across the hills for hours until he is calmer. But poor baby brother must bear the brunt of it. Such a shy, sweet dreamer. He will never please father. Sad to say, I should have been his son. Sadder still, we all three know it.

A girl! This diary was penned by a girl.

A cloud passed over the sun, plunging the room into shadow. Startled, Cameron wondered how long she had been here, lost in another time. Carefully stuffing the pages back into the hole in the wall, she replaced the brick. If the diary had remained here undiscovered all these years, it would be safer here than in her room back at the house.

With a last glance around, Cameron pulled the door shut and surveyed the land around her. This cottage stood on her land. Her father had said in the will that he felt certain she would make use of it. If nothing else, this tiny building would become her haven from the simmering anger around her.

As she mounted and rode down the barren hillside,

she had the sensation she was being watched. Scanning the distance, she saw no one. Yet during the entire ride back the feeling persisted.

On her way home, Cameron came to a decision. Although she had faithfully described to an eager Miriam everything she saw and did on her daily rides, including sitting for a portrait for Quenton Lampton, she would not mention the cottage or the diary. These were her secrets. She wasn't yet ready to share them with anyone. She would hug them to her heart, and when the world around her became too harsh, she would hurry to her secret place to renew herself.

Chapter Twelve

CAMERON COULD HARDLY CONTAIN HER EXCITEMENT AT the chance to sit again for Quenton. She was curious about his house that faced the McCormick house across the hills. And even more curious about the two men who shared that home.

As she saddled her horse, she felt the dark, brooding gaze of Alex fixed on her. They rarely spoke. She forced herself to show no emotions, neither fear nor anger, in his presence. She lifted her head in a challenge, mounted, and rode away without a backward glance.

Behind her, Alex stood with fists clenched at his sides. The thought of her gnawed at his mind. She had already begun to act as if all of this were really hers.

Patience, he cautioned himself. The lust for revenge that was growing like a cancer inside him would be all the sweeter, knowing he had to go slowly, until the time was right. Cameron McCormick would serve a useful purpose in his plot. And she would taste the bitter gall of defeat.

As Cameron approached the Lampton land, its disuse was evident. All around her she noted the rotting fenceposts, the shabby outbuildings.

The house was even worse than she had imagined from a distance. The porch was sagging. The roof showed patches and holes.

Quenton was watching for her.

"Cameron." He took her hand as she mounted the steps. "I've told my father about you. He's eager to meet you."

As she stepped inside, a cheery parlor greeted her. The furniture, though old, had once been obviously expensive and well kept. Heavy drapes were tied back to allow a cool breeze to sweep through the room.

Quenton took her shawl, then led her toward the stairs.

"Would you mind taking your meal upstairs with my father and me?"

"I'd like that." She smiled at an elderly woman who stood at the top of the stairs, studying her closely.

"Rose. This is Cameron McCormick." Quenton kept his hand beneath her elbow as he assisted her up the stairs.

"Hello, Rose." Cameron stopped and offered her hand.

The old woman grasped her hand in both of hers and peered so closely Cameron felt as if she were staring through the very pores of her skin.

"Cameron. Oh, you're as lovely as Quenton said."

"Thank you." Cameron glanced at Quenton. Why this great curiosity about her?

He was watching them both. "Come on. My father is probably growing impatient."

They entered a corner bedroom. In a large, oak, four-poster bed lay the compelling figure of an old man. Several down pillows had been placed beneath his head, propping him in a half-sitting position. His hair, steel gray, still showed strands of black. The eyes were alert, jet black, like the eyes of a crow, watching her as she crossed the room.

"Cameron, this is my father, William Lampton. Father, this is Cameron McCormick."

His gaze moved slowly over her, as if memorizing her features. His eyes narrowed as she removed her bonnet, revealing a cloud of rich, red gold.

"Hello, Mr. Lampton." She took his gnarled hand, noting the blue veins that stood out against the pale skin.

"I invited Cameron to take her meal up here with us."

The old man continued to stare at her. His eyes glittered with a brightness that animated his features. Still he didn't speak.

Two chairs had been pulled up beside the bed. Between them stood a small, round table. Quenton indicated the chair nearest the bed.

"Here, Cameron. Make yourself comfortable."

"Thank you."

She sat, all the while smiling at the older man. He reached out his hand, and she again took it in hers.

While Quenton and Rose set up a tray of hot soup and bread still warm from the oven, along with a pot of tea and hot biscuits with jelly, Cameron continued to sit quietly, the old man's hand resting in hers.

"Cameron grew up in a convent, Father."

Rose poured the tea and studied the young visitor's face.

"Would you like to hear about it?"

The old man nodded to his son, while continuing to look at Cameron.

She smiled. "Well, I'm afraid it isn't a very exciting story, Mr. Lampton. I grew up in the Convent of the Sisters of Divine Charity, on Allumette Island. That's in Canada." The old man nodded when she paused. "And I lived there until recently, when my father, John McCormick, sent for me."

She saw the look of fury that crossed the older man's face at the mention of her father's name. Ignoring it, she continued. "That's about all I know. My father died just after I arrived. I had hoped he would tell me about myself, who my mother was. After his sudden death, I thought about returning to the convent, but I was left some of the McCormick property in his will. I decided to stay a while longer."

She felt the old man's grip tighten.

"Which part of the land is yours?"

She was surprised at the deep, resonant voice. It wasn't at all the voice of a frail old man.

"The two hundred fifty acres that adjoin your land."

She felt his grip gradually relax. She thought she detected a slight tremor.

Rose and Quenton stood on either side of the bed and together lifted the old man to a full sitting position. Quickly tucking the pillows behind him, Rose tied a napkin around his neck and handed him a steaming cup of tea.

Staring at her over the rim of the cup, he said, "I bear a lifelong grudge against Big John McCormick. I've never permitted his name to be mentioned in my house."

Cameron glanced at Quenton. His gaze was riveted on his father's face.

Cameron stood. Her sudden, blazing anger was reflected in her eyes. "Then I'll leave you to feed your hatred, Mr. Lampton. I am my father's daughter. And a grudge against him is against me as well."

The old man's hand shot out, clutching her sleeve. For long moments they faced each other.

At last, he broke the silence.

"Forgive me, Miss McCormick. Please stay."

Her gaze didn't soften. "I can't promise not to mention my father, Mr. Lampton."

"I won't ask that of you."

She nodded slightly, satisfied. Quenton and the ancient housekeeper seemed to heave a sigh of relief.

While they ate, Rose hovered, filling their cups, pouring fresh water in glasses. When she wasn't busy, she sat across the room staring at Cameron as if she, too, had a need to memorize her features.

"I think it's wonderful that your son is an artist, Mr. Lampton." Cameron cast a warm smile at Quenton.

"Do you?" The old man finished his soup and waited until Rose took the bowl from him.

"Don't you?" There was ice in her words. She seemed to be issuing a challenge.

He glanced at his son. "I suppose I'm resigned to it now. It's obvious that he'll never work this land."

"But he has a wonderful gift. I think you should be proud."

"Do you?" The bright, birdlike stare fixed upon Cameron. "And are you proud of your family?"

She flushed. Immediately his hand reached out for hers.

"Excuse an old fool's outburst. I'll—contain myself."

Quenton, silently watching, now interrupted. He wanted to distract these two from growing hostility.

"Cameron, would you like to try on the gown now?"

She smiled, as if aware of his clumsy attempts to assuage her temper.

"All right."

He turned to Rose. "I'd like Cameron to pose in the green satin gown. You know the one."

The old woman led Cameron to another room. A hand-stitched quilt of embroidered roses covered the canopy bed. Sheer curtains hung at windows shut tightly against the cool breeze. The room had the musty smell of age and disuse.

"Whose room is this?"

The old woman sighed. "This was Elizabeth's room. William Lampton's daughter."

"Quenton said she has gone. Where did she go?"

The old woman's face seemed to crumple. "Elizabeth is dead."

"How long has she been dead?"

The old woman turned. "Eighteen years."

Eighteen years. And still Quenton couldn't speak of her death.

Going to a closet, Rose brought out a beautiful gown of green satin. Setting it on the bed, she opened a jewelry box and removed a black velvet ribbon on which was pinned an exquisite emerald broach.

"Shall I help you into the dress?" she asked.

Cameron nodded. Slipping out of the prim cotton gown, she raised her arms and felt Rose slide the satin gown over her head. Behind her, the old woman's stiff fingers fumbled with the hooks that ran from her shoulders to below the waist.

Next Rose fastened the velvet ribbon, while Cameron lifted her heavy mane of hair.

"Oh, look at you." Rose's voice was hushed, almost reverent.

Cameron turned to study her reflection in the dressing mirror. The woman staring back at her was a stranger.

The dress was cut very low in front, dipping to reveal the swell of her breasts. The gown was fitted to show off her tiny waist. The skirt fell in soft folds to the floor.

The emerald at her throat caught the sun's rays, gleaming vividly, perfectly matching her eyes.

If Cameron believed in magic, she would believe it was in this dress. It transformed her. She found herself standing taller, her chin thrust proudly. She tossed her head, sending the cloud of hair dancing about her face and shoulders.

Never had she worn anything so fine. Studying her reflection, she could almost believe she was the elegant woman in the mirror.

As if in a dream, Cameron turned and followed the old woman back to William Lampton's bedroom.

Quenton was standing beside the bed. He turned expectantly. She gave him a brilliant smile, then walked toward the bed. The old man's face seemed chiseled from granite. He stared, unblinking, for long moments. Cameron felt a sense of his shared pain. This was his daughter's dress. And he, too, had never accepted her death.

"I'd like you to pose in the sun parlor. The light is best there." Quenton held out his hand, and Cameron accepted it.

She knew without turning around that the old man was still studying her. She could feel his steady gaze boring into her back.

Quenton led Cameron to a sunny, spacious room filled with plants. In front of the window he positioned her on a low chair and fussed over her hair and the skirt of the gown until everything was as he wanted it.

Today he worked quickly, as though driven to paint the woman before him as soon as possible.

Sensing his impatience, Cameron remained quiet, allowing him to concentrate completely on his work. She didn't speak, and she avoided asking him any questions about himself. She was content to watch his hands at the easel and to study the intense expression on his face.

A shadow darkened the doorway, and Cameron's

gaze followed it. A moment later, Colt filled the room with his presence.

Her eyes rounded in surprise. Seeing her expression, Quenton followed her stare.

"Well. Back from your ride?"

Colt nodded.

"What are you doing here?" Cameron's tone hardened.

"I might ask you the same thing."

She glowered at his impudence.

Quenton, seeing the sparks between them, interrupted. "Colt is boarding here, Cameron."

"Boarding?"

He paused. "He pays us well."

She was instantly sorry for her outburst. She should have realized their financial circumstances.

"I see. I hope you lock up your valuables."

"Cameron!"

She bit her lip.

A hint of a smile curled Colt's lips.

Quenton turned to him. "Cameron has agreed to pose for me. What do you think?"

"Why are you allowing him to look at the portrait when you won't let me see it?"

"Because it's bad luck to let the model see it until it's finished."

She watched in silence as Colt walked closer and studied the canvas.

His gaze slid from the picture to her. As he silently studied her, she felt her skin begin to burn. The look was as intimate as a touch. With his eyes, he was undressing her, one by one unfastening the hooks at her back, slipping the satin gown from her shoulders, over her hips, and dropping it with a whisper to the floor.

Quenton had studied her just as carefully, but she had never felt this embarrassment at his look. He had studied her as an artist would, seeking out the contours of her face, the lift of an eyebrow. But Colt's look was intimate, as if already knowing every line and curve of her as well as he knew his own body.

Quenton began once more to work, ignoring Colt, who stood beside him devouring her with his eyes. While he worked, Quenton saw the change in Cameron's expression. Before, she had been simply a beautiful woman. Now, watching Colt beside him, her eyes softened to a dreamy expression. Her lips parted slightly, not in a smile, but in an invitation. The artist saw so much more than others could see. While he painted, he continued to search her expressive face, knowing what she herself might be still denying—that she was in love with the man standing beside him.

Cameron wondered how long she could endure having Colt in the room, those dark eyes pinning her, those lips parted in the most tempting of smiles.

"How much longer?"

Cameron lifted her hair from her damp neck and stretched her cramped muscles. Quenton looked up from the canvas suddenly.

"I'm sorry, Cameron. I've been so immersed in my work, I forgot how long you've been holding that pose." He set down his brush. "I think I've burdened you enough for one day. Can we continue this tomorrow?"

She nodded.

When she again looked up, Colt had left the room, as silently as he had entered.

Quenton began cleaning his brushes. "Would you like Rose to help you change?"

"No. I can manage. Should I stop by your father's room before I leave?"

"Yes, if you don't mind. If he's still awake, I'm sure he'd like to wish you good day."

Cameron climbed the stairs and let herself in to Elizabeth's room. Once again she was struck by the musty odor of disuse.

She walked to the closet and removed a sachet-scented hanger. Placing it on the bed, she straightened and attempted to reach the fasteners at her back. The door opened, then closed softly, and Cameron turned with a smile.

"Oh, Rose, I'm so glad—" She stopped in mid-sentence, at the sight of Colt.

He leaned against the closed door and crossed his arms over his chest. She was reminded of a mountain lion flattened against a rock ledge, about to strike an unsuspecting deer.

Cameron could feel her heartbeat begin to accelerate. This house was so big, no one would hear her if she called for help. She studied Colt's face. His gaze trailed from her delicate features to the pale column of throat, and to the soft swell of breasts exposed beneath the daring neckline.

She felt herself begin to blush at the way he was looking at her. Heat infused her skin and coursed along her veins. She ran a tongue over lips gone suddenly dry.

"Please, Colt. Leave me alone."

His frown turned to a smile. There was no happiness in the smile. There was a thread of danger in the curve to his lips. "At least you're learning some manners, Cammy. This time you said please."

In swift strides he was across the room and caught her by the shoulders. "I only wanted to look at you. And to touch you. To see if you were real or a vision."

She lifted her head proudly, to deny the fear that his presence created. Her nostrils flared. "And what have you decided?"

His hands kneaded her bared shoulders. "Oh, you're real, Cammy. A very real woman." His voice lowered ominously. "Downstairs, did you know what I was thinking?"

She flushed.

"I thought about carrying you away and lying with you, alone, somewhere on a hillside, beneath the stars. I thought about undressing you, gently, and taking the time to look at you, and touch you, and hold you."

She was too paralyzed to speak.

His hand circled her throat and pressed against the back of her neck. "And now, I'm beyond thinking."

She felt a tremor pass through her. His breath was warm where it feathered the hair at her temple. His head dipped lower, drawing her slowly to him, and her eyes widened, anticipating the kiss.

He stared into her eyes, loving the warmth of those green depths. And then her lashes fluttered, and his lips claimed hers.

He wanted the kiss to be gentle. He wanted to taste, to touch lightly. But the moment his lips found hers, the kiss became hot, seething with the passion he fought to control. His hands pressed her tightly to him, and still it wasn't enough.

His mouth was avid, moving over hers, drawing her deeper into his passion. His hands moved along the satin-clad back, sending sparks skittering along her spine. Everywhere he touched her she was infused with heat.

The satin gown, the roughness of his hands, the growing passion she could sense in him, combined to test her control. She felt a searing, blinding heat and flashes of color in her brain as his lips moved over her lips, her eyelids, her cheeks.

"Oh, God, Cammy. How I want you." The words were spoken inside her mouth.

She moaned softly, clutching his shoulders for support. "Colt. Oh, Colt. I feel . . . I feel on fire."

He lifted his head, studying her lovely face. Her lips were moist and swollen from his kisses. Her eyes, round and luminous, seemed too large for her face.

His eyes narrowed. In one swift movement he lifted her in his arms and deposited her on the bed. Then he was beside her, pulling her roughly into his embrace.

His lips roamed her face, then dipped to her throat. She gasped and for a moment stiffened in his arms. His lips continued to nibble at the sensitive skin of her shoulder until he felt her resistance waver. Boldly, he slid the satin from her shoulders and moved his lips lower, until they probed the delicate swell of her breasts.

She moaned softly, unable to stop him, and unwilling to end the pleasure his lips brought. The need for him was becoming almost pain.

Passion was driving him, until he no longer cared if she protested. She wanted him. He could sense it in her response. And he wanted her with all his being.

His fingers slid the satin lower until his lips could claim the breast whose nipple grew taut at his touch. He heard the moan that escaped her lips and felt her arch toward him.

Cameron's heart lodged in her throat. Her body was on fire. Her mind refused to respond to her commands. She felt fear. Yet even the fear was being overruled by a growing passion. She was at Colt's mercy. And she sensed that he had gone beyond all thought.

"Cammy." Her name was breathed against her throat, and then his lips covered hers, taking her deeper, until she writhed and whispered his name.

"Colt." Her hands cradled his head, her fingers twining in his dark hair, while her lips opened to his kiss.

They had slipped over the line of reason into a hard, driving need. They both sensed it. He hovered over her, gripping her shoulders until she nearly cried out.

She was slipping away, losing herself to this man's touch. His lips, his fingertips, his breath mingled with hers, were all that mattered now.

"Miss McCormick?" Rose's muffled voice sounded from beyond the door. "Would you like some help undressing?"

Colt lifted his lips from hers. Her eyes widened. Her mouth opened, but no words came out.

He gave her a wry smile and touched her lips with his fingertip.

"Miss McCormick? Quenton thought you might need a hand."

Cameron swallowed. Even now, Colt's lips brushing her shoulder brought a tremor of delight.

"Thank you, Rose. I can manage." Her own voice sounded strange to her. She hadn't realized how difficult it would be to speak.

"I'll just wait here then. I want to be certain Miss Elizabeth's gown is properly fastened before I put it away."

Reluctantly, Colt and Cameron moved apart, each struggling for breath. It seemed an eternity before their breathing returned to normal.

With a sigh, Colt struggled to his feet. He wore a grim smile as he whispered, "It seems again it wasn't meant to be. Farewell, little Cammy, for now."

He lifted her hand, then allowed his gaze to travel lazily over her one last time. She lay on the bed, her hair a fiery contrast to the green eyes smoldering with newly discovered passion. Her lips pursed in a little pout. The satin gown caught the rays through the gauzy curtains, making her appear like a sun goddess. He pressed his lips to her palm, then curled her fingers over it, as if to hold his kiss.

Without another word, he stalked to an adjoining door and was gone.

Slowly, almost languorously, Cameron stood and studied her reflection in the dressing mirror. Was it this dress that had so changed her, from the prim maiden to a wanton? Was it Elizabeth's ghost, infusing her with a passion that was alien to her? Or was the passion her own, springing to life at Colt's touch, banked now for the moment but simmering just below the surface, ready to leap to life whenever Colt summoned it?

With a long sigh, she removed the velvet ribbon and the fiery emerald and slid the satin gown over her hips. When she had dressed once again in the prim cotton dress, she again studied her reflection. It told her nothing.

She opened the door for the patient servant.

"Thank you, Rose. I'll go now and say my good-byes to Mr. Lampton and Quenton."

"The old man is asleep. But Quenton is waiting downstairs."

Cameron walked slowly down the stairs, puzzling over all that had happened to her this day.

Quenton was waiting on the sagging porch. "Will you come tomorrow, Cameron?"

"Yes. I'll try. Tomorrow."

"Noon. We'll lunch with my father again."

He helped her mount. He studied her face for long moments. She was wearing the same cotton dress, the same bonnet. Yet she seemed somehow different.

Without another word, she wheeled her horse and was gone.

Chapter Thirteen

"Miriam, didn't you tell me the mines had been abandoned years ago?" Kneeling beside Miriam's wheelchair, Cameron's voice was edged with excitement.

"Yes. Most of them were started by prospectors on their way to the gold fields of California. I suppose they took a look at these bleak hills and figured they had to be good for something. Unfortunately, the only thing they found was some awful blue clay that clogged their equipment and made separating the gold impossible."

"Could prospectors be digging on McCormick land without any of us knowing it?"

Miriam shook her head. "I don't see how they could dig right under our noses without being seen. Why? What have you found today?"

Cameron lowered her voice. "I found a fresh mine

shaft on my section of land today. It's very near the border between McCormick land and Lampton land."

Miriam smiled at Cameron's apparent confusion. "It's just another old abandoned mine, Cammy. The landscape is littered with them." She shook her head knowingly. "Fools and their dreams of glory. Now, tell me what else you saw on your ride today."

Putting aside her own doubts, Cameron described the hundred and one things she had seen that she was certain would amuse Miriam. Through her eyes, the young woman confined to the wheelchair watched the flight of a hawk as it circled, then swooped down on an unsuspecting little rabbit, before finally carrying it off into the trees.

Miriam's eyes widened at the description of a herd of wild mustangs loping across the barren hills. Cameron recognized the yearning for that same kind of freedom and found herself wondering, as she had so often, how Miriam had managed to keep her sanity in this house of hatreds. Until recently, a simmering anger seemed to be her only emotion. But lately Cameron sensed other emotions. Miriam was like someone who was awakening from a long slumber.

Ti entered carrying an embroidered lap robe. He placed it over Miriam's knees, then lifted her easily in his arms.

"Nina says you are to have some sunshine." He looked down into her upturned face, and Cameron nearly gasped at the tenderness in his expression.

If Miriam couldn't see the affection Ti felt for her, she must be blind.

Following them outside, Cameron watched as Ti settled Miriam onto a blanket spread on the grass.

"I'll be back in a minute with fresh lemonade." He turned to Cameron. "Shall I bring you some too?"

"No, thank you, Ti. I'm leaving."

When he was gone, she knelt beside Miriam. "How long have Ti and Nina been here?"

Miriam frowned. "Alex left about seven years ago on a ship bound for the Caribbean. When he returned, he brought his bride, Nina, and her brother, Ti." She shook her head. "Poor Nina. Alex had convinced her father that he was a good, Christian man and a wealthy landowner in America and that she would live like a queen." Her voice lowered conspiratorially. "Ti and Nina are a real prince and princess, Cammy. Their family is royalty on a small Caribbean island. When they were here for a while, they realized that they had been brought back only to be used as unpaid servants."

"Why don't they leave?"

Miriam glanced around before speaking. "I don't think Alex would mind if Nina left. There is no love there. But she would never see little Alexander again. Alex would see to that."

"And Ti? Why doesn't he go?"

Miriam frowned. "I've often wondered. There's nothing here to hold him back."

Cameron touched Miriam's hand. "I think there is, Miriam. You."

Miriam's eyes widened in shock. "Me! Don't be silly. Why would he stay for my sake?"

"I can't believe you're so blind. Can't you see the way he looks at you? Ti is in love with you, Miriam."

She watched her half-sister's gaze wander to the dark, handsome figure walking toward them. Standing, Cameron smiled at the look of shock on Miriam's face. She was thunderstruck.

The day after their conversation, Cameron made it a point to ride to the same location where she had spotted the fresh digging. This time when she dismounted she walked to a stick she had pounded into the earth on her previous visit. She stared for long minutes, then mounted and rode in a circular path around the mine entrance, looking for anything that would give her a clue as to who could be digging on her land. She was certain now that there had been fresh work done here. Yesterday, the top of the stick had marked the height of the mound of dirt. Today, the mound was nearly a foot higher than the top of the stick. Someone had managed to haul a lot of dirt from below the ground. She was certain of one thing. This work hadn't been done in the light of day.

As she headed her horse toward home, she came to a decision. She would grab a quick nap before dinner. Tonight she would need to be alert while she concealed herself along a ridge overlooking the fresh mine shaft.

Dinner seemed to go on forever. Alex was in a rare expansive mood. Usually surly and uncommunicative, tonight he seemed almost jolly by comparison.

"I hear old Lampton's failing. Doc says he won't live much longer." He turned to Cameron. "You remember your first introduction to the town drunk, little sister."

Dark eyes flashed her a knowing look, and she found herself flushing as she recalled again that night in the saloon. Alex would never let her forget it.

Alex gave a cruel laugh. "Old Lampton is the town drunk's father. All these years that old man was just too ornery to die. Till now. And his son will soon drink himself to death." He snorted. "Good riddance. To both of them."

For the first time that she could recall, Cameron saw Nina's temper flare.

"Don't call Quenton Lampton the town drunk. It's a disgusting, demeaning title."

Alex rounded on her like an enraged bull. "He hasn't gone to bed sober one night in a hundred. I'd say that makes him the town drunk." His voice lowered ominously. "And I'll remind you to be very careful about whom you stand up for in this house. I don't think that limp-wristed painter is worth it, woman."

Cameron saw a momentary flash of hatred in Nina's dark eyes before she stared down pointedly. Cameron was genuinely surprised. Why would Nina risk Alex's wrath to defend Quenton Lampton? What could he possibly mean to any of them?

Cameron sipped her tea in silent contemplation. Hadn't Miriam suggested that Alex was Nina's prison? Until now, she had given no indication. Cameron felt a surge of sympathy for the beautiful woman. How could she have ever consented to marry a brute like Alex?

As soon as the evening meal ended, the family members drifted away to their rooms. Alex and Jarret rode off, presumably for their night of cards at the Delta Saloon. No one, it seemed, wanted to be in the company of the others. They weren't a family, Cameron concluded, but a motly assortment of loners held together by a mutual distrust.

Alone in her room, Cameron laid out the clothing she had managed to barter from a stable hand earlier in the day. The boy was taller than she, so his faded britches had to be rolled to the ankles. The stiff, homespun shirt was torn at one elbow, but the long sleeves would serve as protection from the night chill. With a handkerchief tied about her nose and mouth and a wide-brimmed hat to hide her fiery curls, she was sure she could ride about the countryside undetected.

A light tap on her door sent her pulse racing. Looking about the room frantically, she scooped up the strange assortment of clothes and crammed them in a dresser drawer. After one last glance to be sure she had hidden all the evidence, she opened the door.

"Nina. I . . . Come in."

The woman paused for long, silent moments. Then, almost reluctantly, she entered.

As Cameron closed the door, Nina whispered, "I'm not sure I was right to come to you." She licked her lips, then met Cameron's eyes.

"Miriam has told me how kind you've been to her. You've made a difference in her life."

Cameron remained silent and indicated a chair. Nina perched on the edge of the seat, staring intently at Cameron's face.

"Have you ever been afraid?"

Cameron smiled gently. "Lots of times, Nina."

"Are you afraid of Alex?"

Her features were so grave, Cameron couldn't resist taking her hand. It was as cold as death.

"I'd be a fool not to have a healthy fear of Alex."

"But you stand up to him."

Cameron replied softly, "So did you this evening at the dinner table."

Nina looked down quickly. A flush stole across her cheeks. "I'll pay for that. But I don't care. I want to learn to be strong like you." More firmly, she added, "But you've stood up to him so often, I fear his hatred for you is building." She sighed. "Oh, Cameron. Watch out for Alex. I'm afraid for all of us. But mostly I'm afraid for you."

Cameron dismissed the chill that rippled through her at Nina's words and said, with more confidence than she felt, "Thank you, Nina. But you needn't worry. I intend to watch out for Alex—very carefully."

When Nina left her room, Cameron wasted no time worrying about Nina's warning. She dressed in the boy's clothing, then lay down on her bed, determined to wait silently until everyone in the house had retired for the night.

* * *

Cameron let herself out the door and picked her way through the darkness to the stable. When the horse was saddled, she led him a distance from the buildings before mounting.

Dark clouds scudded across a full moon, blotting out the light, leaving horse and rider in darkness. The terrain had become more familiar to her each day, and Cameron instinctively followed the contours of the hills toward her destination.

As she drew nearer the spot where she had found the fresh digging, she could hear the murmur of voices and the sound of an occasional horse's whinny. Quickly dismounting, she tied her horse near the edge of a clearing and continued on foot.

Coming up over the ridge, she dropped to her knees and inched closer to the mound of earth. Peering around it, she made out the form of a man standing nearby, calling softly to someone she couldn't see. A muffled reply came from beneath the ground.

The mine shaft. Someone was down there. Straining, she could hear the crunch of shovel and pick scraping against stone and earth.

When the clouds passed, allowing the full moon to drench them in its glow, Cameron ducked quickly behind the mound of earth. She couldn't see from here. And she couldn't step away without being seen. She needed to climb to the ridge above them, where she would be able to see everything without being observed.

By crawling until she was out of sight, she scurried down a rock-strewn slope, then ran until she reached the hill on the opposite side of the mine shaft. It seemed forever before, crawling, her hands and knees scraped and bloody, her breath coming in short spurts, she reached the summit and peered at the scene below.

Bathed in the light of the moon she could make out a man standing at the entrance of the mine, heaving on a wheeled cart filled with sand. The man strained as he pushed it beyond the entrance, dumping the contents, then returning the cart inside. In the darkened mine he spoke softly to someone further down the line.

Across the ridge, Cameron made out a shadowy figure leaping across a narrow gorge. The figure of a man merged with the shadows of a large rock. For long minutes she continued to stare, but the figure never emerged from the darkness. Finally pulling her gaze back to the mine shaft she was perplexed. The man at the entrance was no longer there.

From the corner of her eye, she detected a movement close to her. Leaping to her feet, she started to run. Before she could scream, a hand covered her mouth and a strong arm lifted her off her feet. She kicked and bit, but the burly figure continued carrying her as easily as if she were a rag doll. At the edge of an abandoned mine shaft, she was held immobile for one agonizing instant. Then, as her screams were swallowed by the sheer terror she felt, she was tumbling through space down the darkened shaft.

The long moments she dropped through a curtain

of blackness seemed an eternity. Her whole being was exploding in panic.

There was no way to cushion the fall. With only her hands in front of her face, she crumpled on the rock-hard floor of the mine. Her breath was knocked from her. Dazed, she lay still for long moments before the searing pain began sending out signals, causing her breath to come in short little gasps.

The interior of the mine shaft was so dark she couldn't see her own hands. Moaning softly, she tried to sit up. Pain crashed through her temple, causing her to lose consciousness for long minutes.

From a great distance she could hear the sound of a scuffle. Sitting up in a haze of pain, she realized the sound was coming from somewhere above her. High in the sky, the shimmering light of a star pointed the way to the opening of the mine. So far away.

The sounds above grew louder. A voice cursed. She heard the thud of fists striking flesh. Feet thrashed about. Something blotted out the light of the star. A body hurtled through space and landed with a dull thud beside her.

Frantically she tugged at the still form in the blackness. "Who are you? Answer me."

Her hands found a muscular shoulder, and she began shaking it, demanding a response.

"Oh, please be alive. Answer me. Who are you?"

She ran her hand down the length of the arm, then moved to the head. At the temple, she felt something warm and sticky. On the hard rock she felt the growing pool of blood. She knew, before she felt the lifeless pulse, that he was dead.

A scream of terror bubbled in her throat. She backed away, trying to put some distance between herself and the body on the floor of the mine shaft. With a gasp of pain she came up against the sheer rock wall, bounced backward, and landed in a heap in the pool of slowly congealing blood.

Cameron covered her face with her hands and wept in desperation. No one knew she had slipped out of the house this night. No one would miss her until morning. And then they would have no idea where to begin looking. She and the dead stranger beside her would be left here together forever.

Forever in this deserted mine shaft. Years from now, her flesh gone, her clothing rotted, her bones bleached, she would still be trapped in this hole in the landscape. McCormick land. Her land.

No! She stood on trembling legs and groped along the darkened wall of the mine. Her hands passed over rough timber that supported the roof of the mine. If there was a way in, there had to be a way out. If it took her forever, what did it matter? The time would be better spent searching for an escape than simply settling into gloom and despair and waiting for death's ominous approach.

The time passed slowly. Cameron had no way of knowing whether it was still nighttime or whether the dawn had crept over the land. Deep inside the bowels of the deserted mine shaft she groped about in the blackness, feeling her way along cold damp rock and earth.

Terror was just a heartbeat away. By sheer determination she held it at bay, refusing to give in to the panic that threatened to engulf her.

She rounded a corner and held her two hands up in front of her, groping for the wall that seemed to have disappeared. Without warning, her hands slammed against something warm, something human.

She screamed. Hands gripped her shoulders roughly, nearly knocking her off balance. She clutched at the hands, and her fingertips grazed a wrist. Encircling it like a bracelet was a long forgotten scar, thick and knotted like a cord.

"Michael!" Her voice trembled. "Oh, please Michael. Say it's you."

The voice was rich and warm and flowed over her like honey. "Cammy. Thank God I found you. Are you all right?"

"I don't know about all right. I'm alive."

"Thank God." His hands found her face, tenderly tracing the outline of her eyes, her cheeks, her lips.

"How did you know I was down here?" she asked.

"I was watching the digging. I saw someone come up behind you and throw you down the shaft. I couldn't reach you in time."

"But how did you know it was me?"

She heard the soft, familiar chuckle and felt his warm breath fan her temple. "I may have been fooled by your crazy getup once, back in that other world you inhabited." His hands found her shoulders, and he drew her closer. "But now that I've held you in my arms, little Cammy, there's no way you could ever hide from me. Even in a nun's robes, I would know you."

She shivered at the thread of passion in his voice. Reaching a tentative hand to his face, she whispered, "Do you understand what's going on here, Michael?"

She felt him stiffen. "You're forgetting your lessons. The name's Colt. Remember that."

She sensed the authority in his tone and for a brief moment resented it. Then, grateful that she was no longer alone in the mine shaft, she brushed aside the resentment and touched his lips with her fingertips.

"Yes, Colt. I'll remember."

"Good. Now let's get out of here."

"There's a man back there. He was thrown down the shaft after me. He hit his head on an outcropping of rock. He's—dead."

"Do you know him?"

She shook her head. "I was hoping you'd know who he is."

She felt him shrug in the darkness. "My guess is it's a drifter. There are plenty of them in Virginia City. They use them for this secret digging, then dispose of their bodies in deserted mine shafts. No one's the wiser."

He caught her hand. "Stay close to me. We have to find our way out of here."

"Do you know the way?"

He stopped, and she felt him turn toward her in the blackness. "I hope so. I've been prowling around these mine shafts for quite a while now, and I've found some pretty interesting bits of information."

He moved cautiously forward, keeping her hand firmly in his.

They made several false starts and spent long hours

in the drafty mine shafts before finally crawling along a narrow tunnel and emerging through a wooden door set in an earthen floor.

"My cottage!" Cameron exclaimed.

"Yours?"

She nodded, smiling as she stared around the moon-drenched room. "I found this lovely old place one afternoon while I explored my land."

Seeing his puzzled expression, she explained, "My father left this land to me. Two hundred fifty acres of land that adjoins the Lampton property and any buildings on it. So that makes this cottage mine."

For Colt another piece of the puzzle fell into place. This was hers. She had now become even more—valuable to certain interests.

She held her hands out in the moonlight. "Isn't it a beautiful place, Mi . . . Colt? Can't you feel the love here? I think this cottage is filled with pleasant ghosts."

He studied the tiny figure dressed in the faded clothes of a stableboy and found himself smiling despite the sight of all her bruises. "Yes, little Cammy. I do feel love here." He took her hand. "Now. Sit."

At her look of surprise, he added, "I want to check for broken bones."

Her voice softened. "I—haven't thanked you yet, Colt, for saving my life. If you hadn't found me down there, I would have never made it out alone."

He paused in the act of probing her arm.

"Nothing's broken. I'm only badly bruised. Thank you, Colt."

His eyes, she noted, were almost black. His gaze fastened on her mouth. His voice thickened. "I do feel love in this old cottage. But it isn't from any ghosts."

He drew her up into his arms. His hand beneath her chin, he tilted her face upward and brushed her lips with his. Despite all she had been through this night, splinters of fire and ice began a dance along her spine.

His words sounded strangled in his throat. "You could have been killed tonight. And I couldn't have stopped it." She felt him tremble. "I couldn't have saved you, Cammy."

His hands held her close, as if fearing she might slip away. His lips trembled over hers.

There was danger in his kiss. Cameron tried to steel herself against all feeling. She knew that each time he kissed her he led her further into the unknown. And though she tried with all her will to resist the onslaught, she lacked the strength to fight him. His kiss was practiced, seductive. His touch was one of authority. His mastery was complete.

She knew nothing of the whirlwind that engulfed his emotions. It never occurred to Cameron that he might be as unable to control his passions as she. She knew only that in his embrace she was unable to think, to reason. She could only hang on to his strength while waves of feelings washed over her, dragging her into an undertow that was too powerful to fight.

"Cammy. Little Cammy." The words were thick and muffled against her throat as his lips pressed to the pounding pulsebeat.

Arching her neck, she leaned against him, feeling the familiar warmth begin to drain her strength.

In his arms she felt small and helpless, fragile as a flower bending to the slightest breeze. His hands pressed along the small of her back, drawing her against the length of him, as if measuring her frailty to his strength.

His fingers found the buttons of her rough shirt, and as he unbuttoned first one and then a second button, his lips burned a trail of fire along her collarbone, and then lower still, to the soft roundness of her breast.

The heat and weakness seemed to spread, until she could no longer stand. They dropped to their knees on the earthen floor of the cottage, bathed in rays of moonlight.

Her breath was hotter now, as the darkened head bent lower. She had never believed a man's lips and fingertips could bring such pleasure. The bruises from her fall were forgotten now. All pain had disappeared, to be replaced by a taut contraction somewhere deep inside her that flowed and ebbed like a pulse.

"Cammy. Oh, Cammy." His lips took hers, tasting her deeply, feasting on her, and she gave, needing to give more, not knowing quite how.

Now they were lying together, their legs tangled, their bodies touching.

"Michael . . . Colt. I feel—oh, I feel lost somewhere." She sighed as his lips closed over hers possessively. When his lips moved along her throat, she heard a soft moan and realized it came from her. She was moving in his arms as if in a dream.

"Help me, Michael. Help me stop this. It can't be right."

Through the hazy swirl of emotions, he heard her plea and fought for control. She trusted him. He couldn't let her down. Now, more than ever, he needed her trust.

Battling his own needs, he knelt up and turned stiffly away.

Leaning on one elbow, Cameron's breath was ragged, burning her throat. Beside her she could hear him taking deep breaths in order to steady himself.

For long moments the only sound in the cottage was their breathing, and the pounding of their heartbeats. Two figures huddled on the moon-dappled floor, drawing strength from their shared weakness.

When he could trust his voice, he turned. "Come on, Cammy. We have a long walk ahead of us."

He held out his hand and helped her up. Awkwardly buttoning her shirt, she accepted his hand, then preceded him out the door.

As the two figures made their way down the moonlit ridge, they fell silent, each lost in private thoughts.

How had this—insignificant creature, this—McCormick, managed to tug at his heart? It was impossible to ignore the need for this woman. Despite who she was, he wanted her. More than anything in his life, she had become an all-consuming passion.

The thought of her drifted through his dreams, destroying his sleep. And when he should be alert, and sharp-witted, she disturbed his concentration, dulling his senses. She was definitely dangerous.

Cameron berated herself for this uncontrollable attraction to a gunfighter. How could she allow his touch to bring such excitement, such pleasure? She fought the unfamiliar longings of womanhood. She had no right to feel such things for a villain, even one as compelling as Colt.

Straightening her spine, she unconsciously put some distance between herself and the man beside her. She must not let him get close to her. Only if she stayed away from him would she be able to control this explosive situation. When he was close, she seemed to forget everything except the way she felt in his embrace. He had the power to hurt her. Instinctively, she realized that he could hurt her in a way Jarret never could. Because with Colt she would be a willing partner in her own destruction.

She shivered, and he wrapped his sheepskin jacket around her, engulfing her in its warmth—his warmth, his scent. She snuggled deeply into the lingering heat from his body, oddly touched by this simple gesture of caring.

They stopped on a ridge overlooking the McCormick house.

"I'll wait here until I see you go inside."

She turned and handed him his jacket. "Why were you there tonight, Colt?"

His expression was closed. His eyes narrowed perceptibly. "Let's just say I was following a hunch. Go home now, Cammy. Let me get some sleep."

He leaned against a tree and held a match to a thin cigar. As the smoke curled above his head, he watched the slim shadow cross the wide expanse of open land, then slip silently into the brooding house.

Chapter Fourteen

"You came home very late last night. In fact, it was nearly morning." Miriam's sharp eyes scanned Cameron's face.

"You must have been dreaming. I didn't go out last night." Cameron draped her shawl about her shoulders, avoiding Miriam's gaze.

"Really. Am I dreaming those bruises too?"

Cameron's eyes widened in surprise. Then she sighed in resignation. Her voice lowered. "You don't miss much, do you, Miriam? All right. I did go out." She glanced around before adding, "But I don't want the others to know about it. Do you remember when I told you there was some fresh digging on our land?"

Miriam nodded.

"Well, last night, after everyone was asleep, I went to see for myself."

Miriam's eyes were round with interest. "And?"

Cameron shrugged. "I saw someone digging."

Miriam raised one eyebrow. "And you got those bruises from just hiding in the shadows?"

Cameron laughed. "All right, Miriam. You're very perceptive. I'll tell you the rest. I was thrown down a mine shaft." She ignored the sudden gasp. "But I managed to find my way out." She deliberately avoided mentioning Colt. There was no way to explain his part in all this since she wasn't really sure of him herself.

At the mention of the mine shaft, Miriam seemed to have shrunk back into herself. The pain she had buried all these years was suddenly fresh in her mind.

Cameron caught Miriam's cold hands. "Don't dwell on it, Miriam. The problem now is, who is digging on the land, and why?

"You didn't see who tried to harm you?"

Cameron shook her head. "And they didn't recognize me either. They thought I was a drifter. They think I'm dead and out of their way."

"What will you do now?"

"I don't know. I only know I don't intend to give up on this mystery."

Miriam clutched her sleeve as she stood up. "Be careful, Cammy. Your next fall down a mine shaft could leave you . . ." She couldn't bring herself to finish the sentence.

Cameron nodded somberly. Crippled like Miriam. Or worse. That thought had already crossed her mind.

* * *

"Jarret said he saw you coming out of the Lampton house." Alex stood, his hands on his hips, glowering at Cameron.

"That's right."

"I don't ever want you to go there again."

"I will if I please."

"No, damn you!" He pounded his fist on the table, sending a vase flying. It shattered into a million pieces.

At the sound of breaking glass, Nina and a servant came running. Alex gave them such withering looks, they cringed against the door in silence.

"I swore no self-respecting McCormick would ever set foot in the Lampton house while I'm in charge here."

"Then we can easily remove that simple burden, Alex. You are not in charge of my life. I will do as I please."

As she turned to leave, Alex jerked her by the arm, spinning her around. He caught her by the shoulders, gripping her so tightly she gasped. With his face just inches from hers, he snarled, "You've pushed me to the limit, little nun. Now you listen. Unless you want to be watching over your shoulder every step you take, you'll do exactly as I say. You stay away from the Lamptons. And stop roaming around the countryside like some damned loose woman. Just stay put here in the house and take up needlepoint. It's much healthier, if you know what I mean."

"Healthier for whom?" She pushed his hands away

and straightened her skirts. Meeting his angry stare, she added, "I told you once, Alex. Don't touch me."

He spat a cruel laugh. "Really? What will you do to me, Little Miss Prim? Slap my hands?"

She went very still. "Don't force me to show you, Alex."

Something in her tone stopped him. His eyes narrowed, studying her closely. She didn't look away but simply continued to stare back.

Realizing that Nina and the servant were watching, he laughed mirthlessly. "See that you remember my warning, Cameron." He moved around her and out the door.

"And see that you remember mine." She slammed the door behind him before hurrying up the stairs.

Behind her, the servant watched in stunned silence. Nina's eyes remained rounded with a look of admiration.

"Nina. You look lovely." Cameron stopped in the upper hallway as Alex's wife emerged from her bedroom.

Her thick, ebony hair hung nearly to her waist. Cameron had never seen it loose before. Always Nina wore it pinned in a careful twist at the nape of her neck. Instead of the drab, dark dresses she usually chose, she was dressed in a pale pink confection carefully fitted to accent her bosom and narrow waist, then falling in wide billows about her ankles. It was the perfect contrast to her coffee-colored skin. She carried a pink beribboned parasol, to protect her from the sun.

"Is this a special occasion?"

Nina flushed. Her fingers nervously pleated and unpleated the side of her skirt. "No. I'm just going into town for a few things."

For the first time Cameron realized how young Nina was. Without that prim hairstyle and matronly dark attire, she revealed herself for what she really was—a very striking woman in her early twenties.

"If you can wait awhile, I'll ride along with you to the fork in the road. I'm going to the Lamptons' in an hour."

"Yes. I know. But I can't wait. Goodbye, Cameron."

Cameron watched as the beautiful woman hurried down the stairs and out the door. Beyond, she spotted the horse and rig waiting.

As she turned toward her room, a thought struck. How had Nina known that she was going to the Lamptons' in an hour? Cameron hadn't said a word about it to anyone until now.

She ran a brush through her hair and studied her reflection closely. She knew she was taking great pains with her appearance. But knowing that Colt was at the Lamptons', she wanted to look her best. The last time he saw her, she had been dressed in a stableboy's clothes, her face and hands caked with dirt and blood. This time, she wanted to look like a lady.

Into the pocket of her soft ivory dress, she placed the little Remington. It had served no good purpose the night she was thrown down the mine shaft, she thought ruefully. Still, she took it everywhere. It would do her no good hidden under her mattress.

In the stable, she saddled her horse, then rode off across the hills toward the Lampton house. The day was hot, with a molten sun reflected off the barren hills of sand.

She was still a distance from the Lampton land when she saw Nina, seated in the rig, emerge from a wooded area. Cameron was puzzled. Nina should have been all the way to town by now. Glancing to her right and left, the dark woman scanned the horizon, then flicked the reins and turned onto the road that led to town.

Cameron slowed her horse to watch. Nina had seemed ill at ease, as if worried that she might be seen. A few minutes later, she realized why.

The familiar dark stallion emerged from the same woods, carrying Colt. Even from this distance, Cameron knew him. She felt her heart leap at the sight of him. He, too, scanned the horizon, then headed toward the Lampton house.

Cameron halted her horse. To the right, she watched the small cloud of dust that spewed from the rig's wheels. To the left, the black stallion galloped across the hills, then dropped out of her line of vision.

Nina and Colt had met in the woods. Why? Cameron felt tiny beads of moisture begin to form on her forehead and upper lip. Why not? Nina was so beautiful, so exotic, she could win any man's heart. And Colt was definitely a man, and a handsome one.

There was no denying that. Even if he was a gunfighter.

Cameron felt the sting of tears scald her eyelids. A married woman like Nina would know how to please a man. And Colt. Her heart contracted violently. He would be able to give Nina all the love Alex was incapable of giving.

Nina's life was so austere. She deserved to be loved. Cameron wiped the tear that trickled down her cheek. But why did it have to be Colt?

Suddenly she needed to ride hard, to be free of this terrible, stifling place. She needed to push herself to the limits, to work off the anger, the frustration, the pain.

Giving her gelding his head, she leaned far down over his neck, feeling the hot dry air whistle past them. His hooves flattened the grass as he thundered over the hill. Faster he ran, faster, while she urged him on, until she felt as if she were flying. He mounted the ridge at a run, crested the hill, then flew at breakneck speed down the incline. Trees and boulders sped past her line of vision. Slowly, ever so slowly, she began to rein him in, until, his flank wet with foam, she walked him into the Lampton yard.

"You little fool! You ran this horse until he's ready to drop. Look at that lather. There's no excuse for such treatment."

Colt stood by the barn, his face reflecting the fury of his words.

She supposed a gunfighter would always take good care of his mount, in case he needed to get out of town quickly. Cameron led the horse past him and, reaching for a towel, began methodically wiping down the animal's overheated body.

"What in hell got into you, Cammy? You know better than to treat an animal like this."

She continued to ignore him, intent on toweling the horse.

"Damn it! Talk to me."

She rounded on him, relieved at the opportunity to vent her anger.

"You're the second man who's sworn at me today, Colt, and tried to tell me what to do. I'll give you the same warning I gave him. Don't use that tone with me. I won't be ordered about like a child." Through gritted teeth she added, "And don't ever touch me again."

His eyes narrowed a fraction. Leaning against the door of the barn, he took a slim cigar from his pocket and lit it, watching her through a haze of smoke.

Her emotions were close to the surface. Living with the McCormicks, that was understandable. But her anger seemed directed at him, not at her family.

"Having lunch with Quenton and old Will again?"

She clamped her mouth shut and finished drying the gelding. Leading him to a stall, she closed the gate and strode stiffly past Colt. Without a backward glance, she climbed the front steps and knocked on the door.

When Rose answered her knock, she gave a quick glance over her shoulder in the direction of the barn. Colt leaned against the door in a lazy stance, his hat shoved forward to shield his eyes, his feet crossed at the ankle. Despite his casual attitude, she could feel his dark eyes branding her.

"My father isn't up to a visit," Quenton explained, as he led Cameron through the cool interior of the house. "So I thought we'd take our lunch in the sun parlor. That way I can set up my paints while we talk. I seem to be a little disorganized today."

Cameron followed him to the cheerful porch, where vines and flowers lent their heady fragrance to the oils and paints.

"You seem a little—out of breath yourself, Cameron. Have you been rushing?"

She frowned. "I had the urge to ride hard and fast."

He looked up sharply. "Do you have that urge often?"

"Not so often, I suppose." She shrugged, feeling his intense look. "Well, often enough. Yes, all my life I've had this need to rush headlong about. Especially on a horse. There's a feeling. I can't explain it. But I feel as if I'm flying. The world is easier to bear if I can escape once in a while and be free." She looked up shyly, aware that he was carefully studying her. "Does that sound crazy, Quenton?"

At her question he shook off the strange feeling that engulfed him. "No, Cameron. I don't think it sounds crazy at all." He set aside his paints and brushes and stared into the distance. "My sister Elizabeth used to go tearing about the countryside on our most spirited stallion. I don't think she ever knew fear."

He stood and dug his hands deep into his pockets, still staring at the hills beyond the window. "I was terrified of riding horses when I was about three or four. I remember my father getting into a temper about it. No son of his was going to be a sissy. He threatened to tie me on a horse and keep me there until I could ride." Quenton shook his head, remembering.

"Elizabeth took me out before Father could lay a hand on me. She coaxed me into sitting in the saddle. Before the day had ended, I was riding. Not well, you understand," he said, laughing. "But at least I could sit a horse. And for the moment, she had won my reprieve. My father relented and allowed her to continue to teach me."

His voice grew softer. He was speaking to himself now, having forgotten Cameron completely.

"I'm afraid the pattern was set from the beginning. Nothing I could ever do would please my father. I wasn't the son he wanted."

Rose entered carrying a silver tray laden with steaming soup and tea, along with warm biscuits and jam.

While they ate, Quenton brightened. "I'm sorry, Cameron. There must be more pleasant things to talk about. Why don't you tell me about your childhood in the convent?"

While she sipped her tea, Cameron began describing Allumette Island and the sisters who had been her constant companions in her youth. Before long her unhappiness had disappeared like the morning mist, leaving her laughing and chatting comfortably.

While Rose cleared away the remains of their lunch, Cameron hurried upstairs to change. Quenton again set Cameron's pose, then moved to the easel.

"I think I'll be able to finish this today, Cameron. I hope you don't mind if I don't talk. There are so many little details I want to catch while the light is good."

"All right." She withdrew into her mind, allowing herself to drift back to her beloved island and the women she would always remember with love and gratitude. The softness about her eyes and mouth told Quenton that her thoughts were happy ones.

She watched his hands as he worked. He was so sure of himself. He painted boldly, without hesitation, as if he had already completed the portrait in his mind. As he mixed the colors on his palette, she studied his face. It was a handsome, boyish face, despite the occasional silver strand in his hair. His forehead was wide. She watched it furrow as he studied her face. Then he bent once more to the canvas. His eyes were the only thing he seemed to have inherited from the man in the upper bedroom. They were dark, almost black. But where William's were fierce, hawklike, Quenton's were surrounded by crinkles of smiles, as if everything he saw through them brought him joy. He held one brush in his teeth while he worked with another. She studied his row of even teeth and firm, perfectly etched lips. His skin was ruddy from years spent beneath Nevada's scorching sun.

Cameron found herself wondering, as she always did in his presence, why a man who seemed so at peace would need to drink himself to death. Or was

Alex exaggerating? She thought again about the first time she had ever seen Quenton. His face had gone chalk white. He had stared at her as if he were seeing a ghost. And he had stumbled from the Delta Saloon. Alex had no need of exaggerating Quenton's condition that night.

"Do you need to stretch, Cameron?"

His voice brought her out of her reverie.

"Oh, yes. It would help."

He wiped a brush on a rag. "I'm sorry. I tend to lose myself in my work and forget all about you. Walk around for a while."

On a table, she fingered a sculpture of a mustang, its forelegs reared as if in battle. It reminded her of Colt. "Did you do this, Quenton?"

He glanced up from the canvas. "Yes. I've tried my hand at sculpture. But I prefer painting."

She moved about the room, stopping to study the framed paintings. All of them bore Quenton's signature.

"Tell me about Elizabeth."

His head came up sharply. "Why?"

"Because I sense that you loved her very much. And you still miss her."

He nodded, staring into space. "She was much more than just my older sister. She was mother, confidante, best friend."

"When did your mother die?"

"Just after my birth. I never knew her. My earliest memories are of Elizabeth, holding me when I was afraid, teaching me, laughing with me. Very early on I realized that she was the only buffer between me and my father. His temper was famous. He could go into a black mood for days. Elizabeth said it was because he blamed the whole world for our mother's death. But privately I've always thought he blamed me for it. Then it would be as if he had never been angry. He would bring us gifts, laugh with us. The tension would be gone—until the next time."

Cameron followed Quenton's gaze to the barren hills. This was a harsh land that seemed to breed harsh people.

He turned. "Well, are you ready to pose again?"

She nodded.

He worked in silence, studying her, bending to the canvas, then looking up again to be certain he had captured a perfect image.

When a shadow darkened the doorway, Cameron schooled herself to show no emotion. Her gaze flicked over Colt, walking soundlessly toward the easel. Then she fixed her gaze firmly on Quenton and forced herself not to waver.

Quenton gave Colt a brief smile, then continued painting. "It's going well, don't you think?"

Colt nodded, studying the canvas. "Very well." He lifted his head to study the beautiful woman sitting like a statue. "I didn't think it could be done, Quenton, but you've actually captured her. The essence of her. The vitality, the energy, the inner strength." His voice thickened. "The passion and fire beneath the fragile beauty."

Cameron's gaze locked with Colt's. Quenton raised his head and watched them, but they were unaware of anything except each other.

Her chin lifted in defiance. Why was he trying to charm her after a secret rendezvous with Nina? Did he think her so naive that he could flatter his way into her heart? Was his ego so large that he needed the affection of more than one woman? Little Sister Adele's words echoed again in her mind. "Oh, Cammy, don't ever pin your hopes and dreams on a man. For he'll be a thief and steal your most precious possession of all—your hopes, your dreams, your very future. Remember, Cammy, don't ever trust your life to the whims of a man."

Quenton watched Cameron's eyes darken with anger. Her lips thinned. The hands at her sides clenched into tight little fists. He glanced at Colt. His expression was closed. It was as if a shutter had passed over his eyes, blotting out all sight of her. He turned on his heel and was gone.

Within the hour Quenton stepped back from the easel. "I'm finished, Cameron. If you'd like to see your portrait, you may now."

She stood, stretched her cramped muscles, and hurried to view the canvas. Her mouth dropped open in surprise. No words escaped her lips.

Was this how she looked, or just how Quenton saw her? The red-gold hair cascaded across one shoulder and spilled over a breast. The green of the emerald was reflected in her eyes. Her chin was lifted in a haughty, defiant pose. Her lips were parted in invitation.

She studied the woman on the canvas, feeling her heartbeat quicken. "Is that really me, Quenton?"

He smiled gently. "I told you I had found the most

beautiful model in the country." He lifted her hands to his lips and kissed them. "Thank you, Cameron McCormick. This is my crowning achievement."

She could only stare wordlessly at the stranger in the portrait. There was no trace of the child she had been. In her place was a woman, with all her dignity, her modesty and vanity, and her vulnerability.

Quenton's voice was soft. "Your strength is here." He pointed to the head in the portrait. "There is a certain way you hold yourself. An aloof pose, as if to defy the fates. And here." He pointed to her chin, thrust slightly forward. "And especially here." He touched the eyes of the portrait. "You meet everyone directly, as if in challenge."

She continued staring at the canvas, seeing herself through the artist's eyes.

"There is aristocracy here." He pointed to the high cheekbones. "And here"—he touched the lips—"I see sensuality. The full lower lip. The slightly parted invitation to the one man strong enough to dare."

He turned his full attention to the woman beside him. "Cameron McCormick, you are a challenging, exciting, explosive, passionate woman. And I sense that you are going to give some poor man the most frustrating but rewarding time of his life."

He smiled down at her, and she stood on tiptoe to brush her lips over his cheek.

"Now that the portrait is finished, I'll miss our time together. It's been so good to have someone to talk to, and to listen to as well. I feel a kinship with you, Quenton. May I come over from time to time, just to visit, or maybe to argue with your father?"

He threw back his head and laughed. "I'd like that. And I know my father would relish the chance to lock horns with you. Our door is always open to you, Cameron."

She touched the skirt of the green gown. "I'll take off Elizabeth's dress now." In a swish of satin, she hurried from the room.

Chapter Fifteen

CAMERON WAS ELATED AT THE COMPLETION OF THE portrait. Feeling far too excited to return to the gloom of her family house, she headed her horse toward the crumbling cottage.

Each time she came here, she read another small portion of someone's private life. The girl who had kept that diary had poured out her soul on those pages. And Cameron, lacking anyone in whom she could confide, understood her longings. That girl, probably long since gone from the region, was becoming her best friend.

Tethering her horse in the shade of the cottage, she stepped inside and eagerly reached for the yellowed pages, hidden inside the wall of loose bricks.

She sat in the old rocker and turned the pages until she came to a portion of the diary that she hadn't as yet read.

January 24, 1856

We never meant it to become this obsession. Our first meeting, when my horse reared up and nearly crushed him as we crested a hill, was shocking for us both. I thought I knew everyone in our small village. This man was a stranger. The most handsome stranger I'd ever seen. After his first moment of surprise, he'd caught the reins, nearly unseating me from my mount. In our confusion, we both simply stared. After a long, breathless moment, I jerked the reins from his hands and galloped away.

I began unconsciously to look for him on my daily rides. And I sensed he was looking for me. Each time we came upon one another, we would stare wordlessly, nod, and continue on our way. Until the day my horse threw me in a thicket. He helped me up. The moment he touched me, I was on fire. For a long time, we simply stared. Then, still without a word, he wrapped me in his arms and kissed me. I shall never forget that kiss as long as I live. For the first time in my life, I was truly alive. My blood thundered in my temples. My mind left me. I couldn't think. Could not protest. My heart—sang. After that, he went off to retrieve my horse. We exchanged first names. He told me I had a beautiful, regal name. And diary, before we rode off in separate directions—we agreed to meet again. How could I know what this man would mean in my life? Who would have believed that I would allow myself to get caught in such a web of passion? Only with him did I feel truly—whole.

Many pages later, Cameron gasped as she read:

July 30, 1856

I did not mean to break my father's heart. For he will never forgive me. I have fallen hopelessly in love with his enemy. I did not know. And he did not even dream that my last name would cause such dismay. My child—our child—will forever remind my father of his disgrace.

My lover swears he loves only me. His wife is wife in name only. We plan to leave here and make a new life for ourselves far from my father's long arm of vengeance.

Cameron read long passages telling of the intricate plotting to meet without being seen by the townspeople. When she read the description of the vacant cottage where they held their love trysts, she gasped in recognition. It was this very cottage.

September 2, 1856

I knew about this little cottage. Knew that it stood empty. It was our safe retreat from the world. Here we could pretend, for a little while, that we were truly married, and this place, so filled with love, was ours.

For the next several pages, the neat handwriting became almost a scrawl, as if written in haste. It told of a sudden shift in their plans. The writer had become too ill to travel. And so the lovers agreed to hide her condition and to flee to this cottage when her time was near. After she delivered the baby and regained her strength, they planned to leave to make a fresh start.

The anonymous author wrote long paragraphs, proclaiming her love, and longer passages regarding her terrible fear that she had left her baby brother at the mercy of a domineering, bitter, hate-filled father.

Cameron came to the last page of the diary. With pounding heart, she carefully read the barely legible words, written in a faint scrawl.

> December 12, 1856
>
> Diary, from the moment I first saw him, so handsome and proud, I was lost. When finally I learned who he was, it was too late. I had crossed the line of reason into a passion so intense it consumed me with its fire. I leave this world with but one regret. Never again will I feel the warmth of his strong embrace. The child born of our love will grow to be doubly strong, brave, proud—for the blood of two headstrong fools flows through her veins.
>
> John. Oh, John! I love you so.

Cameron gasped at the signature initials. E.L. Elizabeth Lampton.

She stood, dropping all the pages of the diary. She stared, unseeing, as they spilled on the earthen floor. Frantically she paced the small room. Hadn't she unconsciously known, almost from the beginning?

Baby brother was Quenton, the shy, sweet dreamer who would never be able to please his father. The black-tempered father was William Lampton, a man consumed by a need to avenge losing five hundred acres of his prized land to a gambler. John, the mysterious lover, her father's sworn enemy, was Big John McCormick.

And the child born of that love . . .

Cameron picked up the pages of the diary and stuffed them down into the pocket of her gown. Frantically pushing the gelding to his limits, she urged him across the hills toward the Lampton house.

By the time she reached the front yard, the horse was lathered and flecked with foam from his run. Colt walked down the front steps just as Cameron dropped the reins and ran past him. Seeing the condition of her mount, he was tempted to towel him dry. But noting the look of concern on her face, he whirled and followed her first.

The elderly servant woman was standing at the head of the stairs.

"Where is Quenton?"

The old woman read the determination in Cameron's tightly compressed lips.

She motioned toward the corner bedroom. "With his father."

Without ceremony, she threw open the door of the bedroom and strode across the room. The old man lay in his bed, his eyes glistening with tears. Quenton sat beside him, holding his hand. Standing on easels at the foot of the bed were two portraits. One was the recently completed picture of Cameron. The other could have been her twin.

Cameron could only stare. Except for her heavy breathing from the strenuous ride, she made no sound. She was shocked into silence.

The other woman's hair had more red than gold. Her eyes were the same shade of green. She was wearing the satin gown and the emerald at her throat. The head was lifted in a proud pose, her chin jutting at a challenging angle.

After what seemed an eternity, Cameron turned to face the two men. "This is a portrait of Elizabeth."

Quenton nodded.

"My mother." She saw the old man's face blanch, then crumple.

Cameron remembered the snip of red hair in the little metal box along with her birth records. She directed her words to Quenton. "You knew. You both knew. And you didn't tell me."

He patted his father's hand, then stood. "I knew, Cameron. That first night, in the Delta Saloon, I thought Elizabeth had come back from the grave."

"But why—"

He held up a hand. "Let me finish. When Alex introduced you as a member of the family, Big John McCormick's daughter, I suddenly knew so much more than I wanted to."

"But you never let on. Were you ever going to tell me?"

"I realized there was no easy way to break the news to you. I thought, if I could induce you to meet my father and you could get to know us slowly, you might not regard your heritage with such distaste." He hesitated, and she found some of her anger dissipating. "We have not prospered as the McCormicks have. We have little to offer you—except love."

For the first time, she allowed herself to meet the old man's eyes. "And you, William Lampton? How can you claim to offer love to your daughter's child when I am also the daughter of your enemy, John McCormick?"

With a trembling hand he wiped the tears that brimmed and trickled down his cheek. "I have never forgiven him for taking for himself what was mine. If I could convince myself that he forced himself on her, then I could hate him still. But although I never allowed myself to admit it, I saw how Elizabeth changed. The spring in her step. The flush in her cheeks. The way she rushed on the wind to some secret rendezvous. I suppose I knew even then, in my heart of hearts, that my daughter was in love. Only love can effect such drastic changes in a woman. And such an impulsive, headstrong woman! There was no stopping her." William Lampton sighed from deep within. "No, Cameron. I can no longer hate Big John McCormick. His only sin was in being alive and being so much bigger than life, so strong, so compelling a figure, that he was the only man who could have ever captured my daughter's heart. I suppose I always really knew it. But I was too blinded by hatred to see. I would not accept that. I couldn't even think it in the darkest hour of the night. There was no way I could have said this aloud eighteen years ago. Elizabeth had fallen madly, uncontrollably, wildly in love with the man who had won five hundred acres of my prized land in a card game. The man I had vowed to destroy. Big John McCormick."

With gleaming, tear-bright eyes, he whispered, "Look at her. And just look at you, Cameron. The beautiful product of that love." His finger pointed to the two portraits. "How could I not love you?"

Cameron saw the question in Quenton's eyes. With hesitant steps, she moved toward the bed. The old man held his arms wide. With a burst of emotion, she fell into his embrace.

"Oh," he sighed against her temple. "Cameron, you are so like her."

Her heart caught in her throat. She recalled her own father's similar words when he had first seen her.

"And I loved her so."

"We both did," Quenton sighed, slipping his arms around both his father and Cameron.

Rose and Colt stood in the doorway, watching the reunion.

"Do you know how Elizabeth died?" Cameron asked.

Quenton shook his head. "We don't even know where she was buried. A note was delivered telling us that Elizabeth had died in a faraway place. I'm afraid Father never accepted that."

Rose's voice startled them. "She's buried beside my cottage. Next to the roses she loved."

"Your cottage!" Cameron turned toward the old woman.

"When I was a young bride I lived there with my

husband and infant daughter. He was caretaker to the Lampton estate. When they died, I came to live here in the Lampton house, to take care of his wife, who was with child and failing in health. After she died, I stayed on to help care for the big house and the family. I left the little cottage vacant. I didn't realize Elizabeth and John were meeting there. When Elizabeth discovered it was her time, she sent for me. I did my best for her, but . . ." She spread her hands in a gesture of futility.

William and Quenton were staring at her as if she were mad.

"You knew and you never told us, Rose?"

She flushed. "Miss Elizabeth swore me to secrecy. So did Mr. McCormick. They loved each other more than I've ever seen two people love. And when he gave me the baby and begged me to take her to a convent in Canada, I couldn't refuse."

"You took me, Rose?" Cameron understood now why this old woman had been so fascinated with her on her first visit. She realized just how involved this old woman had been in her life.

Rose nodded. "When I left Mr. McCormick that night, his heart was broken. When I returned from my journey, I wouldn't have been surprised to hear that he had taken his own life." She shrugged. "But instead he decided to live out his hell."

Colt watched all of them without comment. Seeing the deep emotions that had been unlocked, he left them to their privacy and went to see to Cameron's horse. These were very special moments to be savored by a motherless girl who had finally discovered her roots and, in the process, discovered a grandfather and an uncle as well. The last thing he saw before walking away was Cameron wiping a tear from her eye.

William Lampton held out a trembling hand to her. "All these years, I've hated Big John McCormick for cheating me out of my land. I was so blinded by hatred I didn't even see what was happening to my own daughter. Now, knowing she died having his child, I should hate him even more." As Cameron began to interrupt, he added, "But I have no hatred left in me. Look what their love gave me. You."

He drew her into his arms, kissing her tenderly on each cheek.

"You must stay for dinner, Cameron. We have so much to catch up on."

Cameron nodded. Rose hurried down to the kitchen.

Dinner was a family celebration eaten in the big corner bedroom. Quenton and his father told Cameron stories about her mother's childhood, regaling her with tales of Elizabeth's escapades.

"She was absolutely fearless on a horse," William said with fervor. "I used to worry that she would break her neck. Something inside her drove her to dash about the hills, as if searching for some missing part of herself."

Cameron stared at the portrait of her mother. "When she met my father, she found what she was searching for."

Quenton smiled gently. "You talk about her as if you know her, Cameron."

She suddenly remembered the pages of the diary stuffed into her pocket.

"I do know her. Since I first discovered the cottage I've been going there and reading about the person in this diary." She spread the pages on the blanket of the bed beside William. "I grew to care about her. I knew, if she were here today, I would like her very much. I even began to think of her as my best friend." She smiled shyly at her grandfather. "I'll leave this with you. You can read all about Elizabeth's feelings."

The old man held the pages of the diary to his heart, and tears again threatened to spill.

Cameron stood. "I think you've been through enough for one day. I'll leave you now to rest. But I'll come back tomorrow."

He held out his arms. She went to him.

"Elizabeth's daughter. Cameron, my granddaughter."

She kissed him. "Good night—Grandfather."

At the doorway, she turned and blew him a kiss.

Quenton walked with her to the porch. "You've just made him the happiest man in the world. How do you feel about all you've learned?"

Cameron linked her arm through his. "It's such a relief to know who I am, who my mother was. I'm glad you're my uncle, Quenton. I've already grown to like you while you painted my portrait. Now, I know I'm going to love you."

She kissed his cheek, then mounted her horse. "I'd like to come by tomorrow."

"And every tomorrow, Cameron. Our home is yours."

She waved and turned her horse away. Before heading toward the house that loomed on the distant hill, she had a brief pilgrimage to make.

Cameron stepped into the crumbling cottage and looked around her. Now at last she understood why, right from the start, she had been drawn to this place. She had been conceived here, born here. There had been so much love here.

Now she knew why her father had left her this land and any buildings on it. This property formed the border between McCormick and Lampton lands. Had he hoped she would be able to succeed where he and Elizabeth had failed? Was she capable of uniting the families? As a descendant of both the McCormicks and Lamptons, she was the only one with even a slim chance.

A narrow beam of moonlight drifted through the broken window. She stepped into the pool of light and stared up at the stars.

"I hope you're together," she whispered. "You loved against all the odds. Your love will survive in me. Rest now. You've earned your peace."

The scent of roses lay heavy on the night air. Cameron mounted and rode slowly. As they descended, horse and rider were silhouetted against the moonlit hillside.

Chapter Sixteen

STRIDING ACROSS HER ROOM, CAMERON THREW OPEN THE bedroom window, allowing a blast of hot, dry, Nevada air to billow the curtains and ripple across the rumpled covers of the bed.

Cameron dressed quickly, eager for the day. She had decided to pick some roses at the cottage and take them to her grandfather.

Grandfather. She savored the word. A short time ago she had been all alone in the world. Now she had met her father, though briefly, and had discovered through the diary her beautiful mother. There was a half-sister, who was gradually becoming her friend. And now, wonder of wonders, a grandfather and an uncle.

Giving her hair a quick brush, she surveyed her reflection in the dressing mirror. She still couldn't see the woman Quenton had seen as he painted her. The fresh-faced girl staring back at her, her tousle of fiery curls at odds with the pristine white muslin gown, seemed far remote from the haughty beauty on the canvas.

She descended the stairs lightly, intent on eating a quick morning meal before she rode to the cottage.

She entered the dining room, then stopped in mid-stride. Her eyes rounded in shock. Seated at the table between Alex and Jarret was Colt.

"What are you doing here?"

His steely gaze lifted. Colt gave her an impersonal glance before continuing with his meal.

Alex shot her an angry look before saying, "This man is our guest. Keep a civil tongue, little sister."

She hesitated at the table, debating whether or not to stay.

Alex's lips quirked in an imitation of a smile, remembering suddenly why she hated Colt. His gaze swept her insolently. "Cameron, you dress like a nun. Is this what they taught you in that convent? You have a woman's body." He shot the others a meaningful look before adding, "We've all seen it, so why try to hide it? Why not display it?"

She felt the sting of humiliation begin to burn her cheeks. He enjoyed making her uncomfortable. She was reminded once again that Alex loved to make her squirm.

Jarret was staring pointedly at her. His eyes seemed vacant, but his lips widened into a smile.

"I think Cameron has a beautiful body, Alex."

His ignorance was almost as painful to bear as Alex's insolence. She whirled and would have rushed from the room but for the grip of Jarret's hand holding her. She realized that both brothers were putting on a show of their strength for Colt's benefit.

"Sit."

At Alex's command, Jarret pushed her into the chair and motioned to a servant to bring her meal.

"So, it's going to be one of those mornings, is it, Alex?"

He raised one dark eyebrow. "I would enjoy sparring with you some other time. But right now I have more important things to talk about." He turned his attention to Colt, but his words were aimed at Cameron. "In this house, we keep everyone in line." His brooding gaze raked the young woman seated across the table. Then, as if dismissing her, he said, "We have an empty bedroom upstairs." With the barest hint of a leer, his glance flicked over Cameron, before he added, "The last occupant of the room doesn't have a need for it anymore."

She caught her breath. Her father's room. What was going on here?

"Of course, we'll want something in return."

Colt sipped his coffee. "Such as?"

Alex grinned at Jarret. "We'll talk about it later—in private."

Cameron scraped back her chair. All three men turned to stare at her.

"You will excuse me," she hissed through gritted teeth. "I've lost my appetite."

She hurried from the house and saddled her horse. She needed to get away from this place.

As she headed toward the cottage, her mind was in a whirl. Why had Colt deserted the Lamptons? And why was he moving into the McCormick house? The reply sprang unbidden to her mind. Her heart lodged in her throat. To be nearer to Nina, of course.

At the cottage she picked the roses until her arms were laden with the scarlet blooms. Then she mounted and headed toward the Lampton house. Burying her face in the fragrance, she felt the sudden sting of tears. She wiped them away with the back of her hand. She would not cry over Colt. He wasn't worth her tears. Besides, she had known from the beginning that they were not meant to be. He was a gambler and a gunfighter. His kind drifted from one boom town to another, seeking new adventures. He would have toyed with her affection and then left her, more alone than ever, and brokenhearted in the bargain. Nina had better beware. She was risking a great deal. If Alex were to find out what Colt was really up to, there would be an explosion of revenge.

At the Lampton house, she dismounted and hurried inside.

Rose stopped her before she could enter her grandfather's room. Laying a hand on her arm, she whispered, "Old Mr. Lampton's been growing weaker through the night. I don't think he'll linger long."

No! her mind protested. It couldn't happen to her again. First her father. Now her grandfather. He wouldn't die. She wouldn't let him.

Cameron crossed the room and stood looking down at the figure in the bed.

"Look what I've brought you, Grandfather."

She saw the eyelids flutter, then open slightly. A weak smile curved his lips.

"They're roses from the cottage, where Elizabeth is buried. I thought they might help bring her closer to you."

The voice, when he spoke, was not the voice she remembered. It was barely a croak. "I feel close to her now, Cameron. Very close. Soon I'll be with her again."

At his words, her heart plummeted.

His lids fluttered down. She watched him in silence for long moments. Then, convinced he was in a deep sleep, she motioned for Rose to take the flowers.

"Where is Quenton?"

Rose wiped a tear that trickled from the corner of her eye. "He's gone for the doctor. But it won't do any good. The old man is ready to die now. He told us that the only thing that had kept him going was his belief that Elizabeth would return one day. Now he wants to go to her."

For over an hour Cameron sat by his bedside watching the faint rise and fall of his chest. He didn't stir.

Again and again she found her gaze riveted on the two portraits at the foot of the bed. How alike they were.

Elizabeth had been driven to ride across these very hills at breakneck speed, defying the fates. On one such ride she had met the man who would forever change her life. The similarities between their two lives were startling. They were so alike. And yet,

Cameron prayed, so different. Elizabeth threw caution aside and gave in to the passion that tugged at her. Yet, for their brief moments of happiness, both Elizabeth and John had come to an unhappy end. The only good thing that came of their love was their child. Cameron knew that she would have to break the pattern of their lives. She must never allow herself to be alone again with Colt. She must see that the passion that ruled John and Elizabeth would hold no power over her.

She allowed herself to study the old man's sleeping form. With her eyes, she traced the contours of his face, the hollows of his cheeks, the firm chin, the finely chiseled lips. Flesh of my flesh. Bone of my bone.

A fierce protectiveness welled up inside her. She loved this tough old man. She wanted him to live long enough to know that. *Live,* she willed him. *Live, for my sake, and for your own.*

Unable to bear the inactivity any longer, Cameron walked from the house and pulled herself into the saddle. She needed to ride fast and free, to sort out the conflicting thoughts that crowded her mind. She needed to break loose from the spell of this place and these people, who were so much a part of her.

It was early evening when Cameron turned her mount over to a stable hand and walked to the house. She saw the curtain flutter and knew that Miriam watched her return.

She felt a stab of guilt. So much had happened lately, and she hadn't had time to share it with

Miriam. Maybe tonight they would find some quiet time to talk.

Miriam rolled her chair forward as Cameron entered. On her face was an eager, expectant look.

"Cameron." In her excitement, her voice was higher than usual. "Something new has happened." She grasped Cameron's hands, and lowered her voice. "We have a boarder. His name is Colt."

"Yes, I know," Cameron said dryly. "I heard Alex and Jarret discussing the arrangement with him this morning. It seems they've given him our father's room."

Miriam brightened. "You've seen him?"

Cameron nodded.

"He looks . . ." Miriam groped for the proper words. "Dashing, mysterious. And a bit frightening, I think."

"More than a little frightening, Miriam. I don't know what he's up to, but I don't intend to trust him."

Miriam's eyes were bright with anticipation. "I heard them talking in Father's old study. But I couldn't get there soon enough to overhear anything. They left before I could roll my chair close enough to eavesdrop."

Cameron dropped to her knees and covered Miriam's hand with hers. "Miriam, promise me you won't do anything foolish. If they were to catch you spying, there's no telling what they might do. Promise me you'll stay far away from them."

Miriam's chin rose defiantly. In that brief moment there was a flash of recognition. For an instant, she looked like her father. "You aren't the only McCormick with spunk, Cameron. I told you. I intend to be your ears. Trust me. I'll be careful."

Both women looked up suddenly as Alex stood in the doorway.

"What are you two whispering about?"

"It's none of your business, Alex." Miriam's voice shattered the silence.

If Cameron was surprised at Miriam's boldness, she didn't show it.

Alex's mouth dropped. At his sides, his fists clenched.

"Ti," he bellowed.

When the young man hurried down the hall, Alex shouted, "Bring Miriam into the dining room now." Glowering at the two women, he added, "Unless, of course, you've lost your appetite since you had a taste of Cameron's courage." His voice lowered ominously. "Just be careful you don't bite off too big a chunk, little sister. You could choke on it."

Dinner was a strained affair. Alex sat at the head of the long table with Nina at his right. Beside her sat young Alexander. Across from them sat Miriam and Ti. Cameron was seated at the far end of the table, with Jarret on her left and Colt on her right. Often during the meal Cameron found herself silently studying Nina and Colt, as she unconsciously sought to catch them casting some sort of mysterious eye signals. They seemed oblivious to each other.

Alex glowered at Cameron. "Where do you go all day? No matter when I look for you, you always seem to be out."

"I was riding over my land."

"Your land." His lips thinned. "You'd better beware of *your* land, little nun. There are a lot of deserted mines around here. You're liable to find yourself at the bottom of one."

"Is that a threat, Alex?"

He shrugged. "Call it a warning. There are plenty of dangers out there."

She clamped her mouth shut on the retort that sprang to her lips. All the dangers weren't out there. Some were right here at the table.

"Are we going to the saloon tonight, Alex?" Jarret's voice sounded pleading.

"Why not?" Alex seemed in an unusually expansive mood. "I think we should celebrate our new partnership."

Cameron's head came up sharply. She studied the three men. "Partnership?"

Alex ignored her question. "Maybe we can lure some suckers into a card game. What do you say, Colt?"

The gunfighter smiled and said, in a low, easy drawl, "Sounds fine to me."

"Good." Alex grinned at Jarret.

Cameron felt a sudden chill grip her heart.

Dinner had seemed interminable. Now Cameron listened to the silent household. Alex, Jarret, and Colt had gone to the Delta Saloon. Ti and Miriam were in the parlor, where Miriam had offered to teach him a card game. Nina was in Alexander's room, reading to him.

Cameron dressed quickly in the garb of a stableboy. This was the perfect time to ride to the new mine shaft and see what was developing. Slipping out the door, she saddled and rode off in the darkness.

When she reached the site of the fresh digging, she was disappointed. There was no one around. No work was being done this night. With a sigh of disgust, she swung away.

For a moment she was tempted to ride to the Lampton house and inquire about her grandfather's health. Instead she wheeled her horse and headed back to the stable.

As she let herself into the darkened house, Cameron realized the members of the household had retired for the night. Making her way cautiously to the stairs, she stopped abruptly. There were voices coming from her father's study.

As she moved stealthily toward the closed door, she prayed no creaking floorboards would betray her. Pressing her face to the door, she peered through a crack. Alex and Jarret were facing Colt across a desk. Each man had a drink in his hand.

Alex was speaking. ". . . get my hands on all of it. That's where you come in. Think you can handle it?"

Colt had his back to her. She could hear the smirk in his tone. "It should be easy. I'll just ply him with plenty of whiskey. You know that's his weakness. Then I'll lure him into a card game."

"But how can you be certain he'll lose?"

Colt threw back his head with a low rumble of laughter. "Don't forget, I've made it a point to get to know him very well. Quenton Lampton is the worst poker player I've ever met. Don't worry. Once he's drunk enough, the rest will be easy."

Cameron saw Colt drain his glass and set it on the desk. "By the time I'm through with him, you two will have the deed to the Lampton property in your pockets."

"And that fancy artist and his old man will be penniless." Alex slapped Colt on the shoulder. "Here's to us, partner."

He poured another drink for Colt. The three men touched glasses and emptied them in silence.

Cameron's heart was pounding. She covered her face with her hands and fought down the hysteria that bubbled in her throat. They were plotting to destroy the Lamptons. She had to warn Quenton.

The door handle turned. Cameron's heart stopped. Frozen with fear, she forced herself to shrink back and flatten herself against the wall. The doors were thrown open, and the three men strode out and down the hall.

One set of footsteps paused, then returned. Cameron's heart leaped to her throat. She had been discovered. They would have to kill her, to ensure her silence. Pressed against the wall, she closed her eyes tightly, too afraid to open them lest she see Alex's dark eyes looking at her.

The sound of the footsteps halted at the doorway. The silence was so ominous, Cameron stopped breathing. She was certain that the person standing there could hear the rapid pounding of her heart. When she thought she couldn't endure another second of the tense silence, she opened her eyes. Alex swung through the doorway, carrying the half-filled bottle. His footsteps moved away. Still, she continued to stand rigidly until her legs buckled. Trembling, she knelt on the floor, taking in great gulps of air to steady her nerves.

Chapter Seventeen

CAMERON WAS AWAKENED BY A TIMID KNOCK ON HER door. She sat up, trying to clear her sleep-drugged mind.

She had tossed and turned during the long hours of the night before she managed to fall asleep. The conversation she overheard in her father's study had left her reeling. From the beginning, she had sensed the anger and hostility in her stepbrothers. But now, in her mind, Alex and Jarret were the personification of evil. They were the Devil himself. And Colt! He was now much worse than just a gambler and gunfighter. He had used Quenton's hospitality; he had lived in his home, eaten at his table, to get to know him better, to assess his weaknesses. Now he was willing to sell that knowledge to the highest bidder. The man she had once foolishly thought of as a hero was actually going to help her stepbrothers cheat her uncle of his inheritance.

During those long hours of restlessness, she had come to a decision. She would warn Quenton and find a way to help him. Alex and Jarret weren't going to get away with this evil scheme.

Despite her fears, she smiled as she bounded from bed and pushed the heavy dresser away from the door. Her early morning visitor was probably Alexander. The little boy had begun to come often to her room to visit when the household was first coming to life. She loved listening to his childish jabbering while she went through her morning ritual of washing and combing and dressing behind an ornate screen. She enjoyed seeing his animated features while he plunked himself in the middle of her big bed, his dark eyes, so like his mother's, round with excitement. After the terrifying drama of the previous night it would be good to listen to someone sweet, to be reminded that in this world there still existed simple, normal goodness.

On the second knock she threw open the door with a smile. Her smile faded a fraction at the sight of Nina.

Covering her surprise, she invited, "Won't you come in?"

"I—I've disturbed your sleep." Nina hesitated on the threshold, then peered over her shoulder cautiously.

"I don't mind, Nina. Please come in." Cameron wrapped a shawl about her nightdress of cotton lawn.

The woman clasped her hands together nervously, then crossed the room. "I need to talk to someone, Cameron. I hope you don't mind?"

"No." Cameron showed her guest to a chair. "What's wrong, Nina?"

Ignoring the chair, Nina paced. "I—I find myself in an intolerable situation."

Cameron pulled the drapes open to allow the brilliant sunshine to flood the room, then sat and waited, her heart in her throat. Was Nina about to confess her love for Colt?

When the trembling woman continued to pace, Cameron asked gently, "How can I help, Nina?"

"I don't think anyone can help me. But I need to talk to someone. I thought . . . You seem so strong, so fearless. . . ." She knelt down before Cameron and caught her hands. "I am desperately in love with someone—someone other than my husband."

Cameron's throat went dry. She couldn't speak. Her eyes fastened on Nina, as if praying she would say no more. She couldn't bear the pain of the words that were to follow.

"He is the kindest, gentlest, finest man I've ever met. Oh, Cameron. We both know our love is wrong."

Cameron felt a knife slice her heart.

"We've tried not to meet. But we can't stay away from each other." Nina let go of Cameron's hands and covered her face. Her words were muffled. "If Alex finds out, he'll kill us both."

Without realizing it, Cameron began to stroke the

black hair, to comfort the grieving woman. "Nina, how long can you hope to keep a thing like this a secret?"

The woman shook her head. "I don't know. We seem to have gone beyond thinking. I only know that I must see him again."

Cameron's voice was barely a whisper. "Listen to me, Nina. You need to think this out very carefully. There's also Alexander to consider. What will his life be like here with Alex, without you? Or do you intend to spirit him away and go far away with—your lover? If you continue on the course you've begun, without stopping to think, you're all going to be hurt. It can be no other way."

Wiping her tears with the back of her hand, Nina stood, her head bowed. Her words were a cry of pain. "Oh, Cameron. I love him so. But Alexander . . ."

Cameron stood as well. "I know you'll do the right thing, Nina."

Nina nodded her head as if in agreement. Without a word, the two women embraced.

As she reached for the door, Cameron said softly, "Nina."

The dark eyes met hers.

"I—know what you're going through. My heart goes out to you."

A brief smile touched the lips of the beautiful, haunted woman before she turned and walked from the room.

Odd, thought Cameron, that she could feel so much compassion for the woman who loved Colt. Michael, the lover of her dreams, in love with Alex's wife. it tore at her heart to think about the two of them meeting secretly, sharing their love.

As the door closed behind her, Cameron pressed her fists to her pounding temples. Why must love be so complicated? She thought of her mother. Nina. Her own conflicting feelings for Colt. Why must it be so painful? Where was the pleasure in love?

Cameron was suffering through another stiff, uncomfortable breakfast with the entire family as well as their new boarder. Throughout the long ordeal, Cameron's gaze darted from Alex to Jarret to Colt. Several times she felt Colt's dark eyes leveled on her. Knowing what they were plotting against her uncle, she found their company nearly intolerable.

A servant entered to announce that Quenton Lampton was at the front door.

At the announcement Colt's eyes narrowed a fraction. Nina's hand flew to her mouth. Alex pounded the table with his fist.

"By God! What nerve!"

The servant shrank against the door before adding, "He asks to see Miss Cameron."

Everyone at the table turned to study her. Scraping back her chair, she ignored their questioning looks.

In the hallway Quenton was pacing. Seeing her he stopped, then held out his hands to her.

"Cameron, I've come with sad news."

Her heart seemed to stop for a long moment.

"My father has died."

She nodded, as if somehow knowing that was the

only thing that would bring him to the McCormick house. She hung her head for a moment, swallowing back the tears that threatened. Meeting Quenton's sad gaze, she walked into his outstretched arms and embraced him.

Against his chest, she murmured, "Oh, Quenton. First my father. Now my grandfather. I never got a chance to know them."

Quenton continued to hold her close. Stroking her hair, he whispered, "Before he died, my father asked that you not grieve for him, Cameron. He died happy in the knowledge that he had a granddaughter. He told me to tell you that the two most beautiful women in his past, his wife and his daughter, had meant much to him. But now, knowing that they live on in you, the future looks even brighter for the Lamptons."

Quenton's voice continued in that soothing tone. She marveled at his tenderness. "My father's life after my mother died was not a happy one. He's known much sadness. Now he has finally found his rest."

Swallowing back the tears that burned her throat, Cameron nodded and kissed her uncle's cheek.

Touching her arm, Quenton cleared his throat. "One thing more, Cameron."

She tried to smile, for his sake. "Yes?"

"My father wanted you to have an equal share in our estate. You and I are the only heirs. He and I both agreed that you show much promise, much more love for the land than I ever could."

Shock registered on her face. "But Quenton, I can't possibly—"

He touched his fingers to her lips to silence her.

"You must accept my father's will, Cameron. It made him so happy to know that his daughter's child would continue to care about and share this land."

She stiffened, suddenly aware that their conversation was being overheard by the others in the dining room.

Quenton bent and kissed her lightly on the cheek. "I must leave now, Cameron. The funeral will be in the morning. I'll come by for you."

"No." That wouldn't be safe. She must keep Quenton from her stepbrothers. "I—I'll ride over alone. You have enough to think about." She clutched his arm at the door and whispered, "Quenton, we have something important to talk about. There are terrible things going on here—"

He bent and kissed her cheek. "We'll talk later, Cameron. For now, I have much to see to."

Cameron stood in the doorway and watched as he mounted and rode away. Then, reluctantly, she returned to the dining room. Seeing the curious stares of those around the table, she steeled herself for the expected onslaught of questions.

For a moment the silence was ominous. Then Alex boomed, "So. We have a traitor in our midst. You're a damned Lampton bastard."

As she pushed back her chair to stand, he thundered, "A gambler like Big John and the high and mighty Elizabeth Lampton. Who would have ever believed it?"

He threw back his head in a roar of laughter. "I would have loved to have seen old Lampton's face when he discovered there was a McCormick who claimed kinship with him. I'll bet he did his best to deny it."

Colt was watching Cameron. He studied the proud spirit that stiffened her spine and infused her with fire.

Her head lifted, the jeweled eyes blazed. "He was no more shocked than I. But he accepted the fact with dignity. And we managed to have a loving reunion before his death. For that, I will be eternally grateful."

Alex's eyes narrowed suddenly. "Did I hear Quenton Lampton say you were sharing his inheritance?"

"You seem to have a great deal of interest in my business, Alex." Cameron stood and walked to the door.

Alex's words hit her with the force of a blow. "Since you're going to marry my brother, I intend to make it my business."

She turned on him. "Marry your brother!" Her glance left him to dart across the table, to the vacant, bland eyes that stared back. "Marry Jarret! What are you saying?"

The sweetness of his tone mocked her. "Did I forget to tell you? Jarret has expressed an interest in marrying you, Cameron. And I think it's a match made in heaven. After all, who else but a simple man like Jarret would have a bastard for a wife?"

A hint of a smile curled his lips at her shocked reaction to his words. "There won't be too many men standing in line to marry a mongrel. So I've just this minute decided to give my approval. That way, all your land will remain within the family. And now, of course, we'll have the Lampton land as well. You'll need us to oversee the operation of such vast holdings." He chuckled. "Jarret will make a good husband. As for you, I'm sure my brother can teach you to be an obedient little wife."

Cameron stared at Alex as if really seeing him for the first time. He would stop at nothing to have it all. Her voice felt strangled in her throat. "We're family, Alex. I can't possibly marry my own brother."

"Stepbrother, little nun. And it can be arranged."

"Never!"

She whirled and ran up the stairs to her room. The sound of Alex's laughter seemed to follow her. The slamming of her door reverberated throughout the house.

Cameron stood at the window staring out over the land. Her land. A jumble of conflicting thoughts whirled through her mind. Even without her conscious commitment, she seemed to become more and more wedded to this harsh country. The strong people who had come here to tame the land had forged a bond with the next generation. The same people who had given her life had left her a legacy. In their lifetime it may have been a legacy of hope and dreams. For her, it was becoming a legacy of terror.

Jarret. She clenched her fists. Never in her most frightening nightmare could she see herself married to that cruel, mindless tormentor. They must all be mad.

The funeral was simple. A mere handful of people stood on the hill beside the house. Most of them were strangers to Cameron, old men and women who had known William Lampton and his wife in younger, happier times.

While a priest uttered the words of final parting, Rose wept openly. Hearing the old woman's sobs, Cameron and Quenton clasped hands as if to offer each other strength and comfort.

As the dirt was being shoveled over the plain wood box, Cameron's gaze drifted to the windswept hill that stood facing this land. Even in death, Big John McCormick and William Lampton staked out their claims. Each man rested now in the land that divided them. Each man lay beside a brooding house meant to show the other how much wealth and power he possessed. And despite their bitter struggle, each man shared a special place in her heart.

Quenton kept his arm about her shoulder as he accepted the condolences of his neighbors. When they were alone, his words interrupted her sad reverie.

"Come, Cameron. Rose has prepared a lunch."

For the first time they ate in the once lavish dining room. An ornate table of cherry wood surrounded by a dozen matching chairs dominated the room.

At Cameron's admiring look, Quenton explained, "My father had it shipped from England. It traveled by rail and by stage, clear across the country from Boston. All of our furniture came from the East, or from Europe. As well as our clothes. There was a time, my dear, when your grandfather was the wealthiest landowner in all of Nevada."

"What happened?" she asked as he held her chair.

"I suppose it all began to crumble when my mother

died. My father began drinking heavily. He started going to town and staying away for days at a time. We weren't aware of his gambling losses until he lost to John McCormick. That was when he seemed to lose heart. From then on, my father lost all interest in everything, except revenge."

As Rose served the lunch, Cameron studied Quenton's haggard features.

"You've been through so much. Yet you have so much love and compassion for everyone—your sister, her lover. You don't seem to harbor any hatred for the rejection by your father or for his less than admirable life."

"Cameron," he said softly, "I've seen what bitterness can do to a person. It destroyed my father. I learned years ago to channel my energy into other things. There's no room for hatred in my life."

To change the subject he brightened and pointed to the wall over the fireplace.

"I think I'll hang your portrait here, Cameron. It will bring warmth and light to this room. And I'll put Elizabeth's in the living room. What do you think?"

"I'd like that."

The fireplace, she noted, was handcrafted of native rock, each piece perfectly fitted to the next. The hearth was a solid slab of white granite.

The wood moldings at the ceiling and walls were intricately carved, bearing the marks of fine woodworkers. The hardwood floor, now dull with age, was covered with a beautiful woven rug.

She tried to imagine this room as it had once been, with a fire crackling in the fireplace, the floor and furniture polished to a rich luster. The table covered by fine linen and gleaming crystal. And most of all, the people, laughing, smiling, loving. How fine it must have all seemed to Elizabeth and Quenton in their innocence.

Sipping her tea, Cameron waited until Rose left the room, then lowered her voice. "Quenton, we must talk about something important."

"All right." He smiled gently.

"I overheard my stepbrothers and Colt last night in my father's study. They're plotting to steal your inheritance."

"Really. And just how do they propose to do that?"

"By—getting you drunk and luring you into a card game."

Quenton patted her hand, as if dealing with a child's bad dream. "Come now, Cameron. Do I really appear so easy to dupe?"

"But they're scheming—"

Rose entered carrying a plate of tea cakes. She refilled their teacups before once more leaving the room.

In exasperation Cameron hissed, "You're not taking this seriously enough, Quenton. Don't you understand? My stepbrothers are evil men. For some reason they've decided to continue the vendetta between our families. And they've enlisted the aid of a gunfighter. Now you must be careful."

Quenton studied her grim expression. Taking her hand in his, he smiled gently. "All right, little niece. Now you've seen that I'm properly warned. And I will be careful."

Cameron let out a long sigh. "Do you know how to shoot a gun, Quenton?"

His smile grew. Laughing, he said, "No self-respecting Texas Ranger would admit to not being able to handle a gun."

She joined his laughter. "I'd forgotten. I still think of you as an artist instead of a Texas lawman. All right. I'll feel better knowing you have some protection."

Quenton was relieved to hear her laugh. Her life, he realized, was becoming one long, grim experience. She deserved better. A woman like Cameron deserved to be pampered and cherished. If this nightmare ever ended, he would see to it.

As she was leaving, Cameron kissed his cheek and murmured, "Remember what I've told you, Quenton. Promise me you'll be careful?"

"I promise." He squeezed her hand. "But I still think you're imagining troubles where none exist."

As she rode away, Cameron turned back to stare at the two people on the crumbling porch. Her uncle, Quenton, the sweet, dreamy artist, and the old servant woman, Rose, who had carried her as an infant to distant shores. They looked so alone. So helpless. She pressed her lips together. Alex and Jarret were not going to be allowed to hurt her uncle. And not even a gunfighter like Colt would be strong enough to help them succeed in their evil undertaking. She would see to that.

Chapter Eighteen

ALTHOUGH THE DAYLIGHT WAS FADING AND TWILIGHT was drifting over the land, Cameron resisted the urge to go back to the McCormick house for what she knew would be another tense gathering at the dinner table. She felt a need to go to the crumbling cottage where she had first discovered her mother's diary. There, she hoped, she would find the sense of love and peace for which her heart yearned. This day, more than ever, her spirit needed some special healing.

A crimson sky bled into the barren hills. The flaming disk of the sun sank behind the tallest peak, trailing ribbons of mauve and pink across the horizon. Behind a rose-tipped cloud, the pale amber light of day disappeared and the dusk of evening spread its cloak.

The door swung easily at her touch. Attached to the

door frame by a loose hinge, it tilted at a lopsided angle.

She stared at the heap of straw covered by the faded quilt. Running her hand along the rough brick of the fireplace, she imagined her parents here, warm and happy. Touching the broken pitcher, she realized that her mother had probably brought this from her own house. She had noticed a similar pattern on several objects in Elizabeth's room. It was a little thing, but it pleased Cameron to think that her mother had tried to make this vacant cottage a home.

Leaning her arms on the windowsill, she inhaled the rich fragrance of roses and stared at the twinkling stars that were just beginning to dot the heavens.

What is Your plan for me in all of this? she prayed. *Should I have heeded Colt's warning in the beginning and returned to the convent?*

No sooner were the thoughts formed in her mind than the response sounded firmly on her lips.

"No. I have a right to be here. My father and grandfather nurtured a dream for this land. And I intend to stay and, if necessary, fight, for what is mine. I don't know what my destiny is yet, but I believe it will be here in this wild, beautiful, savage place. I belong here. This land, and everything on it, is mine."

Her words echoed in the tiny room.

"It won't be yours long if your stepbrothers have their way."

She whirled at the sound of Colt's deep voice behind her.

"What are you doing here?"

Her eyes, he noted, were dark and stormy. "I followed you. I needed to find some place where we could be alone, to talk privately."

"I have nothing to say to you, Colt." She turned her back on him.

She jumped as his voice sounded closer. "But I have plenty to say to you, Cammy."

He saw her go rigid, the fists clenching suddenly at her sides.

With deliberate calm, he said, "I came here to warn you. As William Lampton's newly proclaimed heir, you are now in the gravest danger."

"From you, Colt?"

He watched her head lift defiantly. In one step he was directly behind her.

"No, little fool. From your stepbrothers. Now that Alex knows about your latest inheritance, he is determined to have it."

"But I have no intention of giving it to him."

"Cammy." Colt touched her shoulder and felt her flinch. Swearing, he immediately dropped his hand to his side. His voice lowered. "You will only be hurt if you stay in that house."

She turned, her eyes blazing. "Thank you for that kind warning. And where would you have me go?"

He shrugged. "Go to Quenton. Now that you've established your kinship, he would welcome you. At least you'd be safer than you are now."

"You'd like to get me out of my house, wouldn't you, Colt?"

His voice raised in anger. "Damn it, Cameron. Why can't I make you understand? You can't stay in that house. You're marked for death."

"By you?"

He let out an exasperated sigh. His fists clenched at his sides. "You are the most infuriating woman I've ever met. You would try the patience of a saint."

"The saints!" Her eyes rounded. "Are you hinting that you're one, Colt? I don't think even you could have the nerve to put yourself in the same category as the saints."

She stood with her feet wide apart, her hands on her hips, her eyes flaming with fury.

He remembered the little wildcat who had once attacked him when he was trying to help. His blood began to pound in his temple. The surge of desire was so swift, it shocked him.

Colt's eyes narrowed dangerously. One hand snaked out to grasp her by the shoulder. His hot breath fanned her temple, feathering little wisps of hair. "At least you understand that much, Cammy. I'm no saint. I'm a mere man." His voice dropped to a husky whisper. "With a man's weakness. A man's hunger. A man's passions."

There was no time for fear. As her mouth opened to protest, his mouth covered hers. She felt the tension of the tightly leashed fury he sought to control. His hands gripped her shoulders, drawing her firmly to him.

She closed her eyes, trying to shut out all feeling. With all her might she tried to steel herself against giving anything at all to the man whose punishing kiss was threatening to draw all the breath from her lungs.

His control was slipping. She could feel it in the painful way his fingers dug into the soft flesh of her arms. His mouth moved over hers, his tongue plundering, demanding a response from her.

Her heartbeat was hammering in her temples. Her blood thundered in her veins.

"Colt, stop. Oh, stop this."

He lifted his head, and for a moment she thought he would heed her plea. His eyes were black in the dim light, with a shining brightness that signaled desire. As he studied her, his hands trailed along her arms, her shoulders, then moved up to grasp a tangle of hair. His eyes narrowed as he lifted a fiery handful and allowed the strands to sift through his fingers. Abruptly he crushed her to him, and again his lips covered hers.

The kiss was hot, searing her with its fire.

The rage that engulfed him swept her up as well, carrying them both along in a helpless tide.

He was no longer content with just her mouth. His lips began a journey across her cheek to her ear, then to her eyelid.

The touch of his lips on her skin brought on a new onslaught of feelings.

"I don't want you, Colt," she said.

The words echoed in her mind.

He continued raining kisses on her lips, her ear, her throat. And always, his lips came back to claim hers, tasting deeply their sweetness. He couldn't get enough of her. There would never be enough of her.

She was slowly becoming caught up in his passion. Her mind refused to function. Had she really spoken or only dreamed it?

As his lips covered hers, she whispered again. "I don't love you, Colt. I won't. I won't."

The words were swallowed up in a kiss so passionate, she felt on fire.

What was there about this damnably independent little creature that drove him to the brink of insanity? She was like no other woman he'd ever known. His mouth moved over hers, drinking of her and wanting more. How many nights had he lain awake, tasting her on his lips, dreaming of lying under the stars with this bewitching woman in his arms. The need for her drove him. His hands, his kisses, could not be restrained. He knew he was acting like a savage, but his feelings were out of control.

He lifted his head. His hands roamed her tangle of hair. With his fingertip he traced her lips, moist and swollen from his kisses. Their eyes locked. He slipped a rough finger inside her lower lip, tracing it gently.

A thread of primitive longing took over her control. Damn him! What was he doing to her? He had to know the effect his touch had. She felt a violent tremor rock her.

"Oh God, Colt! I can't stand it. Hold me. Hold me."

Her hands, which she had balled into fists and held firmly between them as a barrier, now clutched at his shirt. Feeling her trembling response, his hands roamed her sides, pulling her hips firmly against him.

Her hands slowly grasped his shoulders, needing to cling to his strength. She stood on tiptoe to reach his lips. She heard his slight intake of breath before he crushed her to him. As he deepened the kiss, she twined her arms about his neck, allowing her fingers to luxuriate in the dark silk of his hair that curled above the collar of his shirt.

He caught her face between his hands and slowly kissed her eyelids, her temple, her cheeks, the corner of her mouth. With a little moan, she opened her lips to his kiss, wanting more, wanting all.

Her arousal only enflamed him further.

"Cammy. Oh, Cammy," he breathed as he brought his lips to her throat.

She arched herself in his arms, loving the feel of his lips on her skin. With fumbling fingers he unbuttoned the tiny pearl buttons, then bent his lips lower still, to the soft swell of her breast.

There was no tenderness in his touch. The rage within him fueled his passion, and his arousal only fanned the flames in her as well.

She felt too weak to stand. Her legs could no longer support her. Weakly, she clung to him, needing to feel his strength. He sensed her vulnerability. Sweeping her into his arms, Colt deposited her on the faded quilt and lay beside her. His ragged breathing told her just how far they both had come.

"I don't give a damn about land and family and right or wrong. I only know I want you, Cammy. I want you more than I've ever wanted anything in my life."

His lips plundered hers. His hands roamed her body, feeling the softness of her, the delicate bones. His fingertips explored her narrow waist, the flare of her hips. She was so tiny, so helpless. He could break her in two if he chose, and she would be defenseless. His fingers circled her wrist. So fragile. It would snap like a twig if he bent it. Why was it, with her, feelings surfaced that he had never even known he possessed? He couldn't bear to see her hurt. If anyone inflicted pain on her, he would kill. A fierce protectiveness welled inside him. And all the while the touch of her, the smell and taste of her, drove him further into insanity. He wanted to possess her. All of her.

With one last burst of reason, Cameron pushed herself from him and rolled away. For long moments she sat fighting for breath. On legs that felt as if they were part of a rag doll, she forced herself to stand. Her hands trembled as she sought to clutch the gaping bodice of her dress across her heaving breasts.

What was it in his touch that made her forget everything except the passion that raged between them, like a fire that could never be extinguished? A feeling of shame swept her as she recalled the scene she had witnessed between Colt and her stepbrothers in her father's study. How could she have forgotten so easily what he really was?

"I know why you want me out of the McCormick house, Colt. And even this—this display of lust won't make me forget what you really are."

With a strangled sound of rage, he turned away from her and took in deep gulps of air before sitting up. Pulling a thin cigar from his pocket, he made a bid for time by holding a match to it and inhaling deeply. She watched the sudden flare of light, the circle of smoke that curled above his head.

"And what is it you think I am?" The sound of that deep, honeyed voice slid over her, causing her to tremble.

"Not think. I know. You're a gunfighter. A gambler. And worse, you're a cheat. You don't want me around because you don't want any witnesses to what you're going to do to Quenton."

His eyes narrowed. Through a blur of smoke he watched her closely. For long moments there was no sound in the cottage.

One hand reached out to catch her wrist. "What are you talking about?"

She snatched her hand away and backed up a step. "I know you're helping Alex and Jarret. I know you're planning to cheat Quenton out of his inheritance. I overheard everything the other night."

He let out a long sigh. "I wish you hadn't."

"I bet you do." She backed up another step as he straightened and with catlike grace moved closer. "Don't come near me, Colt. Don't touch me again. I tried to warn Quenton. I don't think he really believes me yet. He thinks I'm exaggerating the danger. But he will. I'll make him believe me."

"Now, Cammy, you listen to me." As he took a step nearer, she felt herself backed up against the rough brick wall.

"I told you, Colt. Don't touch me."

"You little fool."

Feeling trapped, she reached into the pocket of her gown and pulled out the Remington.

Colt's lips thinned. "I think you'd better know the rules out here, Cammy. Don't ever pull a gun on a man unless you intend to use it."

"Then be warned, Colt. I'll use it on you if you take another step toward me."

In one swift motion the gun was knocked from her hand and swept across the dirt floor. Stunned, she could only stare at the man whose eyes had narrowed to tiny slits of fury.

"The second rule is, if you don't succeed, be prepared to accept the consequences." He grasped her roughly by the shoulders and pulled her against him. With his face just inches from hers, his breath blew hot against her cheek.

Through gritted teeth he rasped, "I want you out of the McCormick house. Do you understand me?"

He saw the hard glitter of hatred before her lashes fluttered down to veil her eyes from his scrutiny. With a fury that astounded him, he pushed her from him, sending her reeling. He bent and picked up the gun. Emptying the chamber, he pocketed the bullets, then, with a mock bow, handed it back to her.

"I'm warning you now. You leave me little choice. The next time you choose to draw on me, Cammy, I may not be able to use my hand. Don't force me to do something we'll both regret." He touched the gun at his waist, then stalked from the cottage.

Watching him, she seethed with impotent anger. He

was not going to be allowed to hurt Quenton. She would see to that. Even if it meant killing him.

Her heart lurched as she thought of Nina's tears in her bedroom. That lovely woman had called him the sweetest, gentlest man she had ever known. But Cameron knew better. Behind the ardent kisses and disarming seductiveness lay the cunning of a rattlesnake.

She realized suddenly that she hadn't mentioned to him that she knew all about him and Nina and their secret meetings. As she pocketed the gun, she shrugged. It was just as well. He probably would have denied that just as smoothly as he denied everything else.

She paused. Come to think of it, he hadn't denied her charges. He hadn't denied being partners with her stepbrothers. He hadn't denied scheming to destroy her uncle. He had simply ordered her to move out of the McCormick house. Her house. Her hand clenched at the unfairness of it. What right did that—gunfighter have to give orders? She had more right to be there than he.

The sky was a curtain of black velvet as she mounted her horse. The twinkling diamonds of a million stars made a deceptively serene background as she turned her mount toward home. While her mind was awhirl with tormenting thoughts, the horse picked his way carefully over the rock-strewn hillside. What a deceptive country this was. On a perfect night such as this, who would believe any evil could befall her?

Chapter Nineteen

FOR DAYS, CAMERON MANAGED TO AVOID COLT AND HER stepbrothers, except for the inevitable evening meal. In the mornings, she stayed in her room until she was certain they had left the house. During the day, she spent long hours with Rose and Quenton, listening happily to their stories about her mother and grandfather and going through her mother's roomful of clothes and personal articles, which had been meticulously preserved.

With Quenton by her side, Cameron rode over much of the neglected Lampton land, seeking out deserted buildings that had once housed caretakers and their families and deserted mines that had once fueled the dreams of the men who worked them.

"I love this land," Cameron breathed as they rested their horses on a ridge that gave them a view for miles.

Dust swirled in little eddies and blew across the hill. Their horses lifted their heads to the wind, shifting nervously as they caught the scent of wild mustangs moving in a long trail to the east.

"I can't imagine why. It's impossible to raise crops in this barren soil. There's little grass to graze cattle. And all the recent mining ventures have proved fruitless. This land is worthless, Cameron."

"Then why are my stepbrothers so determined to have it all?"

He shook his head sadly. "I think they're just driven to continue the feud between the families. What Big John won isn't enough for their appetites. They want to see the Lamptons destroyed."

Cameron brushed the hair from her eyes and continued to study the sand and rock that stretched as far as she could see. "I don't believe that, Quenton."

"You sound like—"

She turned. "Like who?"

He shrugged. "It doesn't matter." He leaned across the saddle and gently touched her arm. "You just don't want to believe that so much hatred, and even threats of death, can all be over something worthless. I still think this land is nothing more than an evil temptress that makes men go a little mad, and even kill, only to discover she's an undeserving beauty, an empty shell with no soul."

She shook her head. "I simply can't accept that."

"When you've lived here as long as I, you'll be ready to believe the worst about this place." He glanced up at the sun high above them and gave her a smile. "I have to leave you now, Cameron. I—have an appointment."

Cameron stared pointedly at her uncle's waist. "Why aren't you carrying your gun?"

"I have no use for them, Cameron. I had my fill of killing when I was a Texas Ranger. I want no more of it."

"What will it take to make you understand that Alex's threats are real?"

"If they're really determined to kill me, one paltry gun won't deter them."

She reached into the pocket of her gown and drew out the Remington. "Two guns, Quenton."

He smiled gently. "I fear even two guns won't be enough against a determined killer."

"Two guns are better than none."

He stared at the flashing eyes, and for a moment he was that little boy again, listening to his sister Elizabeth. "Cameron, you're the most wonderful surprise. I adore you every bit as much as I adored your mother."

He leaned far over the saddle and kissed her cheek. Then Quenton urged his horse forward. With a hopeless shake of her head, Cameron turned her horse back toward the McCormick land. She glanced back. In his haste, Quenton had already crested the hill and was gone from sight. She rode home at a slower pace.

"Miriam! Just look at you. You look—radiant."

Cameron paused at the front door to stare at the lovely figure in the chair.

Her half-sister gave her a brilliant smile. "Thank you."

Dressed in a pale yellow gown and matching bonnet, she resembled the buttercups that dotted the hillsides of Cameron's beloved island. Spotting the parasol in Miriam's hand, Cameron's eyebrow rose. "Are you actually going out?"

Miriam's laugh was as tinkling and clear as a bell. "Yes. Isn't it amazing? Ti has persuaded me to take a ride in the rig."

"That's wonderful. Where will you go?"

"Anywhere." She sighed. "As long as it isn't into town. I don't want the townspeople staring at me. I'm sure they've whispered about me through the years. I'm something of a freak, you know."

Cameron touched her arm. "You have to stop thinking like that. You're a beautiful woman. You'll turn all their heads with that cornsilk hair and those blue eyes. They're bound to stare at you."

Miriam's brows shot up. Her hand flew to her cheek. "Beautiful?" Her eyes took on a dreamy, faraway look. "That's just what Ti told me. But I didn't believe him."

"Well, it's time you listened to him. He's right, you know. You are a beautiful woman. Even I can see that." Cameron grinned. "And I'm not a man in love."

"Oh!" Miriam gasped at Cameron's words.

Cameron's smile widened. With an impish light to her eyes, she added, "You may as well get used to it, Miriam. Ti is in love with you. And I think you've begun to realize you share those feelings."

Miriam blushed. Cameron watched her features soften at the sight of the tall, dark-skinned man who walked up the front steps.

He smiled down at her as he lifted her easily in his arms. "Your carriage awaits, my lady."

She shot Cameron a radiant smile. "We'll be home by dinner time."

"Don't rush. I'm sure everyone around her will manage without you."

The house, she noticed after they left, was unusually quiet. A search of the upstairs revealed only little Alexander playing under the watchful eyes of a servant woman. Nina was nowhere to be found.

Peering cautiously around the stable, Cameron discovered that Alex, Jarret, and Colt were gone as well. She let out a sigh of relief. For a little while she could relax.

The digging had begun again. Cameron was certain of it. Although the mound of fresh dirt had disappeared, Cameron could see that the mine shaft was long and deep. There were rutted marks of wagon wheels in the ground, and Cameron followed them across the hills to an old deserted mine shaft. The residue of fresh dirt on the ground near the entrance was evidence that the earth from the new mine was being dumped in here. Whoever was doing the digging would be able to dig forever, and no one would be the wiser. As long as they had found a hiding place for the dirt they were hauling from the new dig, they could continue their work in secret.

As she rode home for dinner, a plan began forming

in her mind. Tonight she would have to keep her wits about her. No matter how long it took, she was going to find out who was digging on her land, and why.

As the family assembled in the dining room, Cameron studied their faces. Ti and Miriam were flushed and happy. The feelings they had discovered for each other colored all their movements. Ti, always gentle and patient with Miriam, was now even more attentive. And Miriam's eyes danced with a light that even Alex's biting words could not dim.

"Where were you two today?" he demanded.

Miriam and Ti sat side by side. Cameron wondered if they were holding hands under the table.

"Ti took me for a ride."

"Why?"

Miriam shot Alex a look of complete surprise. "I don't need to explain to you, Alex."

"I don't want you riding over this land."

"I will if I please. Need I remind you that this is my house?"

His voice lowered. "Need I remind you where Jarret and I found you the last time you decided to go exploring? You were lying at the bottom of a deserted mine shaft, and your exploring days were over."

Her face drained of all color. Instantly, Ti's arm went around her shoulder, drawing her close.

"Take me to my room, please Ti. I've lost my interest in food now."

Without a word, he lifted her in his arms and carried her through the doorway. The family sat in silence, listening to the sound of his footsteps as he made his way down the hallway.

"That was uncalled for," Nina snapped.

"Was it? I rather enjoyed watching the young lovers come up for air and smell the stench of reality." Alex was just warming up. Next, with a sneer, he turned on his wife. "And where were you today, Nina? Out taking in the view of the countryside, too?"

She stared at her plate. "I went to town."

"You seem to have a great need to go to town lately. Is there someone there who interests you?"

She shook her head.

"Speak up, woman."

"Well." She seemed to be searching for something, anything to say. "There's a"—she swallowed, then lifted her head to meet his eyes—"new seamstress."

"Ah." Sarcasm colored his tone. "A new seamstress. Is she good?"

"Yes. She's—very good."

"What's her name—this seamstress. Maybe I'll drop by and compliment her on the lovely dresses she's been making for my wife. Though I've seen them in your closet, you've never bothered to wear them for me."

Cameron glanced at Colt. He was staring at the scene with absolutely no emotion showing on his features. She marveled at his ability to remain aloof while Alex was humiliating the woman he loved.

"I—didn't think you'd like me in bright, pretty colors."

"Then why did you have the dresses made?"

She shrugged. "I liked them. The colors made me think of my sunny island. I was feeling terribly homesick. So I bought them, even though I knew you would disapprove."

"Well, my dear wife, you were wrong." With an evil grin, he added, "After dinner, put on your prettiest gown, Nina. That might please me. If it does, I'll show you just how much it pleases me."

Cameron saw the shudder that passed through Nina's slender frame at his words. How much longer, she wondered, would this beautiful young woman have to submit to his brutish demands?

Alex had been just warming up until now. Turning to Cameron, he hissed, "And you. You spend entirely too much time at the Lampton house. From now on, I want you to stay close to home, where we can keep an eye on you."

Cameron carefully folded her napkin and placed it on the table. She met his look with an icy stare.

"I have no intention of doing as you say, Alex. I will continue to do exactly as I please."

"No!" He pounded the table and half rose from his chair. Nina touched his sleeve, but he shook her hand away.

Sitting back down, he pointed a finger at Cameron. "From now on, as Jarret's betrothed, you will do exactly as you're told."

Jarret lowered his cup and grinned foolishly at her.

Cameron warned herself to remain calm. Alex enjoyed these little scenes. She was determined to deny him the pleasure of seeing her lose her temper yet again.

"I'm terribly sorry, Jarret," she said sweetly, determined to exclude Alex from her conversation. "I can't marry you."

"Cameron, I'll be a good husband. Alex says you need a man to tame you. You'll like being married. I'll show you things—all kinds of things. I'll be good to you."

His voice, so like a child's, frightened her. The scene in the Delta Saloon flashed through her mind. She remembered his surprising strength. And his determination to have her. Despite her attempt at control, her temper flared.

"No. You don't understand. I have no intention of marrying you, Jarret. No matter what Alex says."

She pushed back her chair and faced Alex across the table. "You can't force me into a loveless marriage, Alex."

The smile he gave her chilled her. "Can't I? What a child you are, little sister. Oh, I think you'll be—persuaded, all right."

Cameron stood at the window of her room, once more dressed in the clothes of the stableboy. Before this night was over she intended to know who was digging on her land, and why. She would conceal herself in the shadows and watch and listen.

The sun had long since dropped behind the mountains. She had watched the sky darken from deepest blue to midnight blackness. Tonight no stars were visible through the swirling clouds. The air in the room was oppressive. There was an electric, expectant feeling in the air. Far on the horizon, flashes of lightning lit the inky sky, then flashed off, leaving the night even darker. A storm threatened, but this was more potent than any storm she had ever witnessed on her sleepy island.

Despite the sticky heat of the room, Cameron shivered.

Was Ti holding Miriam now, offering her the comfort of his tender embrace? She hoped so. No one deserved love more than Miriam. She had been alone too long. It was wonderful to see her opening up to the world around her.

And what of Nina? Would she and Colt arrange to meet later, when Alex was out of the way? Now that Colt was living in the same house, it was easy for them to make their secret arrangements.

Cameron pressed her feverish forehead to the windowpane. Today, even Quenton had to hurry off to meet someone. Everyone, it seemed, had someone.

Except me. The words echoed in her mind. *All I have is a dream lover. Michael Gray.* She closed her eyes, and instantly she could see him astride the black stallion, so sure of himself as he urged her to ride harder. Michael handing her his shirt to tend to Sister Leona's wounds. Michael kissing her hands before riding away.

Now he was here in Virginia City, in the person of Colt. But they weren't the same person. Colt looked like Michael, and when he held her in his arms and kissed her, her heart responded to Michael. But Colt was in partnership with her stepbrothers. Colt had agreed to destroy her uncle. Colt had to be stopped. And if, in the process, Michael was hurt as well, it couldn't be helped. Her heartbeat raced for a moment, but she paced the floor until it settled back to its natural rhythm. Colt or Michael Gray. It mattered not to Cameron. She would fight either one to protect Quenton.

She glanced at the billowing dark clouds. It was time. Stealthily she made her way from the house to the stable. Under cover of darkness she rode across the hills toward the new mine.

Cameron crouched on the ridge above the entrance to the mine. This time there must be no mistakes. She couldn't afford to get caught here a second time. She might not survive another fall down a deserted shaft. Shivering, she remembered the body that had hurtled through space to land beside her. Had that drifter been killed in the scuffle or in the fall? Not that it mattered. He was still dead.

Lightning sliced the blackness. A distant cannon burst of thunder rumbled, echoing and re-echoing across the hills. The storm that threatened drew closer. Cameron hoped it would hold off until she was able to reach the safety of home.

The sound of voices drew her attention to the mine below. Two men spoke in hushed tones, then disappeared inside the shaft. She needed to get closer. There was no way she could see or hear anything from this distance.

Slowly, she inched her way down the ridge toward the opening in the ground. Voices drifted and echoed from deep inside. Carefully glancing around, Cameron gauged the distance from where she huddled to the entrance. Fifty feet. No more. There was no movement from the surrounding ridges. And the night was so black, no one would be able to see her. Unless someone from the mine chose that moment to come out.

She took a deep breath, stood, then made a run for the mine. When she reached the entrance, her hands encountered the rough planking that shored up the mine. With her breath coming in hard spurts, she ducked inside and felt around for a place to hide. Inching along the wall of the mine shaft, she could feel the timbers set nearly every twenty feet to shore up the earth around the dig.

She was completely enveloped in blackness. Even when she held her hand to her face, she couldn't see it. Cameron experienced a strange sense of dislocation. She had to keep touching her hands to her face to assure herself that they were still attached.

One part of her wanted to flee in horror. This was a terrifying place to be. Without light, without companionship, this tunnel, deep in the bowels of the earth, was like a tomb. She wondered if a cough or a scream would echo and reverberate throughout the tunnels, unleashing similar coughs or screams from those working down here.

Despite the terror, Cameron forced herself to keep moving. She had to know who was down here and why.

She stopped. To her right she could hear the rumble of voices. Feeling in the blackness, she discovered that the tunnel intersected with another, forming a fork that moved east and west. Choosing the westerly direction, she heard the murmur of voices growing louder. Dropping to her knees, she crawled closer until she could make out the words.

". . . shore up this section before we move on. I'm going back to the other end, to make sure they keep working. Mind you, Jarret, don't let them slack off. We're too close now to start slowing down."

It was Alex's voice. Cameron stared at the soft glow of lights from the torch in his hand. Beside him, Jarret held a similar torch.

Alex was turning to make his way back along the same route she had just taken. If she didn't find a hiding place immediately, he would spot her.

Scrambling along the tunnel, she glanced over her shoulder and saw the eerie light of a torch bouncing off the walls of earth and rock behind her. Feeling her way, she began to move even faster. Her breath came in short gasps. Her hands encountered sharp edges of rock, splintered wood, hard-packed earth and mud. Several times she had to bite her lower lip to keep from crying out in pain. Still she hurried on, hoping to find either an end to the tunnel or a small indentation in the wall where she could safely hide from the man behind her.

A light flashed to her left, then she was once more engulfed in darkness. The sharp crack of thunder signaled the entrance to the tunnel. Unless she made it outside before the next flash of lightning, Alex would see her illuminated in its glare.

She began running. The sound of her footsteps echoed through the shaft. Behind her, she heard a muffled exclamation. Alex had heard her footsteps.

She was certain of it. Instinctively, she ran harder, praying she wouldn't miss the mine entrance.

She slammed into a wall of solid rock and fell back, stunned by the impact. With her heart racing, her brain flashing stars from the pain, she got to her feet and began blindly feeling her way along the wall of the tunnel.

Another flash of lightning showed her that she was only feet from the mine entrance. Running, her breath nearly choking her, she darted into the fresh air and kept running.

Behind her she saw the light of Alex's torch. Scrambling along a ridge, she dropped to the other side, then peered cautiously over the edge. Below her she could see the torch flitting around the mine entrance. After what seemed an eternity, it disappeared once more inside.

She was safe now. She could go back home and forget this nightmare. She had part of her answer. She had probably known this much from the start. Alex and Jarret were responsible for the digging. But knowing this wasn't enough. She needed to know why. Why, in this land pocked with deserted mines, would they go to all the trouble of digging yet another? What was it they were searching for?

Cameron took a deep breath and ran across the open expanse from the ridge to the mine entrance. Afraid or not, she was determined to have all her answers.

She again followed the black tunnel, feeling along the wall with her hands. When she came to the fork, she took the turn which she hoped would lead her to the area where Alex had gone. Knowing Alex, he would leave the dirty work to Jarret while he took the important job.

Far ahead she could see the flickering light of torches casting eerie shadows leaping along the walls of the tunnel. Although she heard an occasional man's voice cursing, there was no conversation. Inching closer, she watched as four men worked with picks and shovels. Alex was standing beside a huge metal box or bin, into which they tossed dull, blue, mud-coated rock.

Flattening herself behind a plank, she peered cautiously at the scene. She needed to get one of those rocks from Alex. But how?

One of the men stopped to mop his brow with a filthy bandanna. "The pay better be as good as you promised. I thought there'd be a lot more workers than just us."

"What are you complaining about? It's work, isn't it?" Alex tossed the rock he was examining into the bin and glowered at the man. "What were you doing when I found you? Sitting in the dust of Virginia City, hoping to get up enough grubstake to head over to San Francisco and hunt for gold. Well, you're never going to get that grubstake unless you finish tonight. So get back to work."

The man seemed to hesitate for a moment, then bent to his work. The others hadn't even bothered to look up at the exchange. All four of the men were gaunt, unshaven. Drifters. Cameron had seen hundreds of men like them in Virginia City. Miners, dreamers, men down on their luck, hoping to find gold. Miriam had said the town was filled with losers hoping to find their pot of gold at the end of the rainbow.

Cameron glanced at the growing pile of rocks in the metal bin. By no stretch of the imagination could this be called gold. What, then, was driving Alex and Jarret to work this mine?

Alex picked up his torch and headed toward Cameron. Squeezing herself into the corner of the plank, she flattened herself against the damp earth and prayed he would pass her quickly, without turning back. If he turned, even for a moment, he would have to see her.

"No stopping," he ordered the four. "Just keep digging. I'll be back in a few minutes."

Cameron didn't move, didn't even breathe, until the light from the torch had moved far down the tunnel. Taking several deep breaths, she peered around the wood plank to watch the workers. As soon as they were certain Alex was gone, they dropped their picks and shovels and wearily sprawled on the ground. Grumbling among themselves, they were oblivious to the slender figure that crawled toward the metal box. Keeping it as a barrier between herself and them, Cameron made it easily without being spotted. Raising to her knees, she inched her hand over the top, felt around until she located a stone, then began crawling back to the shelter of the timber.

She leaned against the wall of the tunnel, taking deep breaths. Now she must make it to the entrance of the mine before Alex returned.

She jammed the rock into the bulging pocket of the baggy pants she wore. Slowly, she began feeling her way along the blackness. How many precious minutes had she wasted? Alex would be returning. She began to move faster. Did she hear footsteps? No, she was letting her imagination get the better of her. Remain calm. Soon she would breathe the fresh night air. She fought the feelings of disorientation. There was nothing here but rock and sand.

Something grabbed her shoulder so roughly she was spun around. A hand covered her mouth before she could scream. A terrified scream rose to her throat, then threatened to choke her.

"What are you doing here?" The gruff voice belonged to a stranger.

Still pinned against the wall by his rough hand at her shoulder, she could feel him bend. Straightening, he let go of her and lit a torch. Holding it up to her face, he stared at the slender figure in faded britches and torn shirt, a handkerchief tied about the lower half of her face, a wide-brimmed cowboy hat covering her head.

She dared not speak. Her voice would give her away.

"Did Alex send you from the other tunnel?"

Blinking at the light of the torch, she nodded her head.

He backed up a pace, then spotted the bulge in her pocket. "Helping yourself to a sample, sonny?"

Wrenching the rock from her pocket, he tossed it behind him, then snorted. "Hell, you're just a kid. Too damn skinny to keep up with us. Go back and tell

Alex we want one of the bigger ones. You can work with the crazy brother."

When she didn't speak, he shoved her. "Go on now. Tell him we need a man, not some kid still wet behind the ears. Get. And keep your pockets empty, or Alex will nail your hide to the wall."

Nearly running, Cameron escaped the faded light of the torch and plunged into the blackness of the tunnel. There was no time to waste. Alex would be returning any minute now, and when he discovered a stranger had been in the mine, he wouldn't stop until he had searched every inch of these tunnels.

There was no time to lament the lost rock. She would be lucky to escape with her life.

When at last she smelled the cool fresh rain at the entrance to the mine, she nearly cried with relief. Lightning tore the heavens; thunder crashed and rumbled across the mountains, echoing and reverberating its fury.

Mindless of the rain that pelted her, Cameron clawed her way up the ridge of the mountain and down the other side, determined to put as much distance between herself and the mine as possible. Reaching the place where she had tethered her horse, she sank to her knees, too exhausted to go another step. She needed all the rest she could manage because, now that she had reached safety, she had come to a decision. She had gone through too much to back down now. She would wait here until her stepbrothers and their workers left. Then she was going back for that rock.

Chapter Twenty

THE SOUND OF MUFFLED GUNSHOTS STARTLED CAMeron. Getting stiffly to her feet, she pulled on the buckskin jacket she had been using as a blanket.

The storm had blown eastward, the thunder now just an occasional rumble in the distance. The rain had gentled to a fine mist. By daylight the parched, dry earth would show no signs of this infrequent rainfall.

Climbing to the ridge, Cameron strained to see where the gunshots might have come from. There was no sign of life at the mine entrance.

She guessed that it would be several hours before dawn. The storm clouds had passed, but the sky was still midnight blue. A sliver of moon cast only a pale light.

Taking her chances, she crawled down the ridge, then, crouching in the shadow of some rocks, debated whether or not to try running the distance to the mine entrance.

A horse approached. She shrank back into the shadows.

Alex emerged from the mine carrying a torch. Plunging it into a mound of dirt to extinguish it, he called out, "Did you pay them off like I told you?"

Jarret, astride the horse, laughed. "Just like you said."

"Where'd you dump 'em?"

"Down the shaft."

"Good. Let's go."

Alex mounted his horse, and the two of them rode off in the direction of the McCormick house.

Cameron waited long minutes, until the sound of their horses' hoofbeats faded. Then, running across the open space, she picked up the torch Alex had discarded, lit it, and hurried inside the mine. Even though she had light to show her the way, she had to fight back the feelings of terror that threatened to engulf her. Moving quickly, she found the metal bin, loaded with rocks and stones. Choosing a small rock that would fit in her saddlebag, she hurried back outside. Extinguishing the torch, she ran to her horse and, elated by the success of her mission, headed toward home.

On the way, she puzzled the words she had heard spoken by her stepbrothers. What had Jarret dumped down a shaft? And what were the gunshots that had disturbed her sleep? She hadn't actually been asleep; just dozing. But awake or asleep, she knew the sound of gunshots. It hadn't been thunder. Colt had told her that they were using drifters to dig in the mine, then disposing of their bodies in deserted mine shafts. She shivered, then dismissed the thought as too horrible. Even monsters like Alex and Jarret couldn't do such a brutal thing. But what else would explain the shots she had heard? Had someone been shooting at Jarret? He hadn't seemed upset by anything. In fact, he had laughed. Cameron shivered. The sound of Jarret's laughter always set her teeth on edge.

At the house, she dismounted and walked her horse to the stable. Removing the rock from the saddlebag, she dropped it into a hole beside the barn and covered it lightly with straw. Tomorrow she would find out what was being mined on her property.

As she made her way to the house, Cameron stretched happily. Despite the sleep she had missed this night and the terror of that darkened mine, she had managed to accomplish a great deal. A smile curved her lips. She deserved to sleep late and relax in a warm bath.

"Out enjoying a moonlight ride, little sister?"

Her head shot up. Alex leaned against the side of the house. His arms were folded across his chest. One foot was crossed over the other. He seemed inordinately pleased with himself.

"Yes. I—couldn't sleep."

"That's too bad. What you need is a good man in your bed."

Her throat went dry. Something in Alex's tone sent ice along her spine.

"I've got just the thing for you." He grinned. "My brother, Jarret."

Cameron swung her head in time to see Jarret's hand reaching out for her. He caught at the lapel of the buckskin jacket, ripping it open. She twisted away from him, leaving him holding an empty wrap.

He tossed it angrily to the ground, then watched, laughing, as she nearly ran into Alex's arms. Dodging at the last second, her hat flew from her head, allowing the wild tangle of hair to drift down about her face and shoulders.

With an agility that astounded them, she broke into a run. The front door. If she made it that far, someone might hear her.

She was halfway there when a hand shot out, catching a handful of hair, snapping her head back. Tears sprang to her eyes at the searing pain.

Jarret's fingers grabbed at the collar of her shirt, nearly choking her.

"Whose clothes are these, Cameron? Did you steal them off some poor old drifter?"

With a chuckle, he ripped the shirt from her, leaving it hanging in tatters from her sleeves. With no effort, he pulled it from her wrists and dropped it to the ground. Beneath the boy's shirt, she wore a chemise of softest cotton lawn. With narrow straps over her shoulders, an insert of white lace barely covered her breasts.

Jarret caught her by the arms, his rough fingers pressing painfully into the soft flesh. "There now, that's better. You're starting to look like a woman."

Behind her, Alex laughed.

"Hold her while I get these off her," Jarret called to his brother.

Alex's hands were rough as he pinned her against him. One hand fondled her breast, sending a spasm of shock through her.

Jarret's fingers fumbled with the waist of the faded britches. With a tug, they slipped to the ground, revealing brief lace bloomers.

Jarret sucked in his breath as he stood back to stare at her. Even in the semi-darkness, her creamy skin and the delicate white undergarments were a vision of loveliness.

"Now, little nun, my brother is going to show you what you've been missing all these years." Alex's voice dropped to a menacing whisper. "And when he's through, you're going to agree to marry him." He caught her chin in his hand and lowered his face to hers. "Do you know why you're going to marry him?"

Her eyes narrowed. She tried to jerk her face away, but he tightened his grip until she nearly cried out from the pain.

"Because he'll leave his brand on you, little nun. You won't be a high and mighty, holier-than-thou little virgin any more." His eyes stared into hers, seeing the fear lurking there. "You'll have a choice. You can be his wife, or you can be Jarret's little slut. Either way, no good man will want to have anything to do with you after this."

He shoved her backward, into his brother's waiting arms. "Show her what a woman's good for, Jarret."

Two muscular arms came around her, pinning her firmly to him. He lowered his head and pressed his moist mouth over hers. Cameron tried to cry out, but his mouth covered her cries.

She struggled and managed to get a hand free. Frantically she pounded on his shoulder, then his head and face. With no effort, he caught the offending hand and pinned it between them, then drew her against him and again bent his mouth to hers.

As he raised his head, she cried out, hoping someone in the house would hear. Instantly, his hand covered her mouth to stifle any more attempts to cry for help. Lifting her as easily as if she were a child, he began carrying her to a dry spot beneath the tree.

In the darkness, she heard Alex's jeering laughter. "Have fun, you two. I'd stay and watch, but I've put in a long night. I think I'll turn in."

Jarret dropped Cameron roughly in a mound of grass, then knelt, straddling her. Her flailing arms and legs seemed to do no more damage to him than the wings of a bird. Laughing, he tossed back his head, as if enjoying her useless battle.

She tried a new tactic. Going completely limp, Cameron waited until Jarret bent to touch a hand to her face. With all her strength, she brought both fists to his nose. With a roar of pain, he straightened for a moment, covering his nose with his hand. When the hand came away warm with blood, he slapped her so hard it snapped her head to one side.

With a cry of pain, Cameron writhed and twisted, trying desperately to break free from the brute who held her fast.

Grabbing both sides of her face, he brought his mouth down hard on hers. Rough hands caught the delicate straps of her chemise and tore it in two. Then his hands were at her bared breasts, fondling, pressing, hurting as she had never been hurt before.

Through a haze of pain, she heard the muted sounds of a scuffle. Turning, Jarret saw two men silhouetted in the near-darkness. Leaping from Cameron, he ran to help his brother.

Scurrying to the barn, Cameron picked up a shovel and ran back to join in the fight. Spotting Jarret's muscular frame about to attack the man holding Alex, she swung the shovel as hard as she could. Caught off guard, Jarret fell to one knee with a grunt of pain.

Alex went reeling from a blow, and her rescuer turned his attention to Jarret, who was beginning to stand.

Before the man could hit him, Jarret was lunging forward, knocking him into the trunk of a tree. Realizing the man was stunned, Cameron came to his rescue, swinging the shovel at Jarret's head. He ducked, but she swung a second time, hitting him squarely in the stomach. He doubled over, trying to catch his breath.

Alex, springing to Jarret's side, made a grab for the offending shovel, barely missing it. Cameron stepped back, ready to swing again. Just then, at the base of the tree, Jarret made a dive for the man, who was coming to his feet.

"Watch out!" she called.

The man turned, ducked, then landed a solid blow to Jarret's face. Hearing a low moan, Cameron glanced toward the scuffle. In that split second, Alex caught the shovel in her hand and pulled it viciously away. Unarmed, Cameron faced him.

"You little bitch!" Alex swung his hand, catching her on the side of the head, sending her reeling. As she fell, her head hit a rock. Pain skyrocketed through her brain. Little splinters of brilliant light flashed before her eyes. Then there was only darkness.

Cameron drifted on a haze of pain. Keeping her eyes tightly closed, she lay still, wondering if she had died.

Was this what death felt like? Was it always so painful? She shifted slightly, and a fire raged through her brain. She seemed to hurt everywhere.

She knew she must be somewhere in the grass, but her mind couldn't grasp just where. Instead, it was playing tricks on her. She felt as if she were lying between cool sheets. With the fingers of her right hand, she touched her thigh. Her skin felt hot, feverish. Moving slowly, her fingers brushed her waist, her rib, her breast. All were intact. Inching higher beneath the covers, she felt her collarbone, then her throat. As her fingers poked from the blanket to touch her face, something caught and held them.

A hand. With a little sob of terror, she jerked away, recalling Jarret's rough hands on her. She felt the sudden stab of pain. Wincing, she felt something cool on her fevered forehead. A cool cloth. For a brief moment, she tensed. Then, against her will, she began to drift again. It was better this way. The throbbing in her head seemed less torturous. She let go and drifted further.

Something, or someone, was trying to bring her

back. She resisted. "Let me go. Let me alone. I want to sleep. I don't want to wake up."

Someone was talking. It seemed to be her voice. The words were slurred, mumbled, nearly incoherent. It didn't matter. She had no intention of waiting for a response. She wanted to sleep.

Something cool was held to her lips. She sipped, murmured, drifted.

Jarret! His hands were on her. Hurting her. Soiling her. Degrading her. She pushed them away, kicking, biting, moaning. But he was stronger. He pinned her arms at her sides and held her fast. He was tearing her clothes from her. She had to fight him. Had to. Jarret's wife. No! Jarret's little slut. She cried out. A hand pressed softly over her lips, stilling her cries. Her breath came faster, nearly choking her. She would fight him with the last ounce of strength left in her. She would never submit. Never. She suffered the cool touch of his hands, too exhausted to fight him further. Her hands stilled. The agonized expression on her face disappeared, replaced by fitful sleep.

A raw, gnawing pain woke her. She cried out. Instantly, a warm hand touched her cheek. She flinched, turning her face away. The hand remained, stroking her forehead, her cheek, her throat.

Tensing, she allowed the touch to continue. Although she kept her eyes tightly shut, she knew this wasn't Jarret's hand. The touch was too gentle.

She sighed. A hand lifted her head slightly. Pain, sharp, white hot, shot through her brain. Cool water touched her lips. She sipped, paused, sipped again, then closed her lips tightly against more. Her head was gently replaced on the soft pillow.

She was in a bed. She felt cool and clean. There was the aroma of soap and water and the sharper tang of disinfectant.

Clouds seemed to drift through her mind. Layers of soft, murky clouds. She thought about opening her eyes, but it was too much effort. It was simpler to lie here, her eyes tightly shut, listening to the sound of crickets. It must still be nighttime. The room was dark. She sensed that without opening her eyes. Someone moved soundlessly about from time to time. A cool hand touched her forehead often.

With her hand, she again explored her body. Hesitantly, she moved along her thigh, her waist, her rib, her breast, as if to assure they were still there. They hadn't been violated. They hadn't been amputated. Then her hand went motionless as a new awareness pierced her sleep-drugged mind. She was naked. She hadn't dreamed it. Her clothes had been ripped from her.

Slowly, tentatively, her hand poked from beneath the covers. She touched her face, then moved to the back of her head. A sudden twinge caused her to gasp. Immediately, a hand grasped hers. She began to jerk away, but another hand closed over hers, pressing it between two large hands.

With her other hand, she caught at it. Her fingertips traced a wrist. Encircling it, like a bracelet, was a large, knotted scar. She sighed and breathed a name.

"Michael. Oh, Michael. You've come to me." Blissfully, dreamlessly, she slept.

Chapter Twenty-one

SUNLIGHT STREAMED THROUGH THE OPEN WINDOW, bathing the figure in the bed with warmth. The sheer curtains billowed inward on a current of hot, dry air.

For long moments Cameron lay stiffly, listening for some sound of activity. The room was quiet. Even the house seemed strangely silent this day.

Her lashes fluttered, and she glanced uneasily about. She was alone. She sat up slowly, feeling a twinge at the movement. A dull ache throbbed at her temples and the back of her head. Touching a finger to her head, she winced at the tenderness of the swollen mass the size of an egg. Below it, at the base of her skull, she could feel the gash, clean and no longer bleeding, though still painful.

She swung her feet to the floor and paused until the sudden weakness passed. She felt as if she had been through a war.

I have, she thought ruefully. *Last night I was fighting for my life.*

She glanced down at her nakedness. There was no sign of blood or dirt. She had been bathed; her wound carefully disinfected. Her torn, muddied undergarments were gone. Gone, too, was all sign of Michael. Had she only dreamed him?

Her heavy dresser had been shoved in front of the bedroom door to keep out intruders. Cameron knew she had been knocked unconscious last night. Even if she had revived, she would have been too weak to do all this. She hadn't dreamed Michael. He had been with her. Her gaze swung to the open window. He must have gone out there and crossed over the roof to the balcony at the front of the house.

With great effort she dressed. When at last she managed to move the barrier from her door, she opened it. Outside, in a chair in the hallway, Miriam gave a long broken sign of relief.

"Oh, Cameron. I'm so glad to see you up and about. Colt told me to keep all the servants away from your room today. He said you were not to be disturbed. And he ordered that hot soup be kept ready for you when you awoke." Her eyes were wide with anxiety. "What's happened? And what does Colt have to do with this?"

Cameron caught Miriam's hands and smiled. "Dear Miriam. How long have you been sitting here?"

"Since breakfast. It's past noon now. Are you all right?"

"I'm fine." Cameron touched the tender spot beneath her hair. "Just a little bruised. I—had an accident last night. I hit my head. But I'm feeling much stronger now."

"Are you feeling up to taking your meal in the dining room? Or would you prefer to eat in your room?"

Cameron hesitated, feeling a shiver of apprehension. "Where is everyone?"

"Nina has gone to town. Colt left right after he talked to me. I haven't seen Alex or Jarret at all today. They never showed up for breakfast." With a smile Miriam added, "And Ti is pacing about downstairs, waiting for me to leave your door."

"Then, as long as the house is nearly empty, I'll eat downstairs."

Pushing the wooden chair to the head of the stairs, Cameron bent her lips to her half-sister's cheek. "Thank you, Miriam, for your concern. I'm really touched that you would guard my privacy so diligently."

Miriam's voice lowered as Ti, glancing up, began to ascend the stairs. "Cameron, quickly now. Colt is so handsome and mysterious. What is he to you?"

Cameron blinked. She didn't really have an answer. "He's just someone who helped me."

"Well, he looked very stern when he warned me to stay close to you today until you were feeling strong enough to take care of yourself."

Ti greeted Cameron with a smile, then lifted Miriam from her chair and began to carry her downstairs. When he had settled her in a chair in the dining room, he left to find a servant to bring Cameron her meal.

Alone once more, Miriam said softly, "Colt left you a message."

Cameron's head came up.

Miriam smiled knowingly. "He said when you were strong enough, he would meet you at the cottage." She studied Cameron's face. "When are you going to tell me?"

"Tell you what?"

"What's going on between you and Colt. Oh, Cameron, it's so romantic and mysterious. You two have been meeting at a cottage. Where? Why?"

Cameron burst into laughter. "Miriam, it isn't what you think. We're not lovers."

"Why not?"

"Because"—Cameron was unaware of the pain that was evident on her face as she spoke—"he loves someone else."

"I don't believe that." Miriam waited until the servant had brought Cameron's soup and poured tea. When they were once more alone, she continued. "You should have seen Colt this morning as I saw him. He looked so fierce when he said that you weren't to be disturbed. He looked"—she paused, then brightened—"possessive. As if you were his responsibility."

"He was just concerned because I'd been hurt. You're making too much of this Miriam."

Miriam studied her across the table. "Maybe. Are you going to meet him?"

Cameron shrugged. "I haven't decided."

As Ti entered the room, Miriam shot Cameron a

look. "Yes you have. You'll go. If it were Ti, I would."

"You would what?" Ti asked as he touched her shoulder.

"Marry you if you asked me," Miriam said boldly.

He threw back his head and laughed. "I don't know what's come over you, love, but I like it."

Once again Cameron was struck by the lovely musical lilt to his cultured English voice.

With a ripple of muscle, he smoothly scooped Miriam up into his arms and turned to Cameron. "Miriam hasn't left your door since early this morning. If you don't object, I'm going to whisk her away now to myself."

Cameron laughed. "I understand. And Miriam, thank you."

Cameron studied her reflection in the dressing mirror. The gown was pale green watered silk with a prim high collar and long sleeves. A row of mother-of-pearl buttons ran from collar to waist. A darker green sash circled her slender waist. Despite the heat of the day, she left her long hair down, to cover the gash at the back of her head. Into her pocket she shoved the little Remington.

In the barn she saddled her horse, then set out for the cottage. As she rode, she fretted over her decision to see Colt alone.

Part of her was afraid of him. He brought out primitive, almost savage feelings in her that frightened her. But she owed him her life. Besides, although she was loathe to admit it, he excited her. She liked the way he looked at her, and she couldn't define why. If Jarret looked at her that way, it would make her skin crawl. But despite all she knew about Colt—his partnership with her stepbrothers, his betrayal of her uncle, the fact that he was a gunfighter and gambler—she was drawn to him.

The sun had already made its arc across the sky. Light, feathery clouds softened the horizon. A gentle breeze blew clean, fresh scents from pine forests across the hills.

Her horse circled the stand of evergreens that hid the cottage from view. Beside the crumbling wall stood the black stallion. Cameron tied her horse, then pushed the door open.

He was standing by the window. He turned to watch her as she entered. She paused, bathed in a pool of light from the open door.

"Hello, Colt."

He inclined his head. "Cammy."

He was a stunning, virile animal. Her pulse quickened at the sight of him.

"It was nice to wake up in my own bed this morning." She was amazed that her voice sounded so normal. "I could have awakened in Jarret's bed this morning, too humiliated, too beaten down, to go on fighting him and Alex and their ugly scheme."

He didn't move. His arm still rested along the chipped windowsill. His voice was deep, rich, warm. "You would have been stronger than that, Cammy. Jarret just didn't know who he was dealing with."

"I'm not sure. I know that what he had in mind for me was worse than death." She shuddered. In a stronger voice, she taunted, "Why didn't you take advantage of—my weakness last night?"

"I wasn't sure myself until I was confronted with it, and I found there was no decision to make. The idea of taking advantage of an unconscious woman, even one as desirable as you, doesn't appeal to me. I think you know why, Cammy. I want you strong and willing in my bed. I want the fearless little wildcat who attacked me on her island. I want the warm and beautiful woman you've become. And understand—I do want you in my bed."

"Even though you love Nina?"

He blinked at this sudden shift in the conversation. "Nina. I don't understand."

She felt her old anger returning. All those smooth words of his meant nothing. This was what she needed. A dash of cold water, to remind herself what he really was.

"Don't try to deny it, Colt. She told me herself."

His hand dropped to his side. He took a step nearer, then halted. "Nina told you that she loves me?"

"Well, she didn't say it in so many words. She—said she loves someone other than her husband. But you can't deny it, Colt. I saw her riding away after meeting you in the woods."

"When was this, Cammy?"

His eyes, she noted, seemed even darker in sunlight. His mouth wasn't hard. It was soft—almost laughing.

"The last time I sat for Quenton's portrait. I saw Nina drive the rig from the woods and then head toward town. Then I saw you ride in the opposite direction."

"And being the clever little thing you are, you decided that Nina and I are lovers."

"Yes."

She was jealous. He could see it in the darkening of her eyes. He savored the feeling. After all, how many nights had he lain awake dreaming of her satin skin warming to his touch, her lips softening under the pressure of his mouth? The insatiable desire for her drove sleep from him. The anxiety that she would give her love to another ate at his soul, driving him to a fierce restlessness. And now it was her turn to squirm.

"And what is that to you?" His tone was cold, impersonal.

He saw the pain, sharp, swift, before she composed herself. She straightened, her jaw jutting defiantly.

"What you do, whom you choose to love, is none of my concern, Colt. I'm certain gunfighters manage to find pleasant diversions in every town."

His tone softened. "And sometimes they find more than they bargain for, especially on quaint, sleepy little islands." Weary of the game, he sharpened his tone. "If you had ridden up a few minutes sooner, you would have seen Quenton ride away first."

"Quenton. I don't understand."

"I rode to the woods to remind Quenton that you would soon be at his house for a sitting." Colt chuckled. "Artists have a way of forgetting time. Then I waited while he rode away first. Then Nina left. When I thought they were both a safe distance, I rode away."

Cameron was thunderstruck. "Nina and . . ."

"Your uncle. Poor fools. They're miserably in love."

Her hand flew to her mouth. That explained so much. The day of her sitting, Quenton had seemed so disorganized. And the other day he nearly flew across the hills to keep an appointment. He loved Nina. And Nina loved him. And Colt . . .

Her heart soared. Colt didn't love Nina. There was a chance, just a chance, that he could love . . .

How long had she battled these conflicting feelings for this man? Thinking that he had loved Nina, she had experienced her first stab of jealousy. Knowing now that he didn't, she felt a sigh of relief shudder through her.

"Well." She felt the flush begin to creep from her neck to her cheeks. "I'll go now. I just wanted you to know that I'm fine."

"One of these times, you may not be so lucky. I always seem to be picking up the pieces after you've made a mess of things. That's how we met, in case you've forgotten."

She hadn't forgotten a single thing about their meeting. She would never forget that earth-shattering experience.

"Thank you, Colt," she said primly. "For saving my honor, and probably my life."

"You're welcome." A hint of a smile touched his lips. "Of course, if you really wanted to thank me properly . . ."

Her head came up.

"I just thought an innocent kiss . . ."

She licked her dry lips. He watched the movement of her tongue.

"How do I know it won't lead to something more?"

"You don't."

As her mouth opened to protest, his smile grew. "I won't even hold you, if you'd like. I'll just stand here and let you kiss me."

"Why Colt, I believe you're flirting with me."

His smile deepened. "Me flirt! Why, Miss McCormick. What a fine idea. How am I doing?"

"I think you've had some experience in this," she said dryly. She stepped back, torn between being sensible and the growing temptation to feel his lips on hers. "I suppose one quick kiss." She studied him from beneath lowered lashes, then took a tentative step forward. "All right."

He stood, his hands at his sides, his eyes staring straight ahead. On tiptoe she could barely reach his mouth. She moved closer. He wasn't going to make this easy for her.

"Now?"

His gaze flicked over her, then stared over her head. "Whenever you're ready."

She moistened her lips and took a deep breath. Touching her hands to his shoulders, she reached up and touched her lips to his. She kept her eyes wide open, and stared into his. The kiss was as soft as a whisper.

He didn't move, didn't even seem to breathe.

With her lips against his, she murmured, "Thank you, Colt. From the bottom of my heart, thank you for saving me last night."

"You're welcome."

She pressed her lips over his again, then hesitated, with her lips just a fraction away. The kiss was very unsatisfactory. She needed his participation. She needed his response. Still, he stood rigid, unmoving.

Couldn't he see that she wanted something more? Didn't he understand that for the first time in her life, she wanted a man? She wanted him.

"Oh, Colt," she sighed. Her breath was warm against his cheek. "It's so cold like this. Hold me, please, and kiss me back."

"I can't."

She blinked.

His voice deepened, sending a tiny thrill of alarm through her. "I'm not some farm lad, hungering for his first taste of a maiden's lips. I'm a man, with a hunger far greater than that. I can't go on just holding you, and kissing you, without being allowed to love you the way I want. You ask too much of me, Cammy."

Stepping back a pace, she studied him. His hair gleamed blue-black in the sunlight. There was a light in his eyes. Humor, amusement, she wasn't certain. And beneath the humor, passion, carefully banked. But there was a gleam, of mischief perhaps. He was enjoying teasing her. And he was not going to cooperate until she coaxed him.

Now she understood what he had been going through. All those times that he had held her, and kissed her, and wanted more than she had been willing to give, came rushing back to her.

Ever so slowly she pressed herself close to him and

ran her hands up his arms, letting her fingers play along the taut muscles of his upper arms. She ran her fingertips lightly over his shoulders, then twined her hands around his neck, brushing the dark hair that curled at his collar. With a little sigh, she brought her lips to his.

She heard his sudden intake of breath. Without warning, his arms came around her in a fierce embrace, crushing her to him. At once the kiss was hot, hungry. His mouth moved over hers, needing to taste the sweetness of her, needing to draw on the goodness that surrounded her.

She clung to him, feeling the flood of emotions that washed over them both. This was how a kiss should be, she realized. Both of them wanting, needing, sharing, willing to give.

His lips traced the curve of her eyebrow, her soft lid, then grazed her cheek on the way to her ear. He took her lobe gently between his teeth and nipped. She gasped, and his lips eagerly returned to hers.

Her mouth was eager, avid. Her lips parted, inviting his tongue into the intimate recesses of her mouth. He kissed her deeply, their breath mingling, their sighs escaping as he turned his head to change the angle of their kiss.

With a finger, he traced the curve of her lips. She moved against his touch, unwilling to break contact.

His hands moved to the buttons at her throat. He heard her quick intake of breath and glanced at her eyes, searching for a signal.

"Tell me you want this too, Cammy. I want you warm and willing."

In acknowledgment, her eyes softened. "Yes. Oh yes, Colt." Her words were a whispered sigh. "I want you to teach me how to love you."

He felt his heart nearly burst with the pain of wanting. "There's nothing to teach. You'll know."

He unbuttoned first the top button, then the next, all the while watching her eyes. With a whisper, the silk dress slid from her shoulders as he bent his lips to her throat. His hands slid down her hips, easing the dress from her, leaving it to drift to the floor.

She arched in his arms, loving the feel of his lips on her skin. He nibbled at the sensitive little hollow of her shoulder and chuckled when she sighed in delight.

"How many nights have I tortured myself thinking of the softness of your skin," he murmured against her throat.

His lips covered hers.

"And how many times have I tasted you on my lips. Oh, Cammy. How long I've waited to love you."

He kissed her deeply, feeling her fingers clutch at his shoulders.

A strange feeling of languor invaded her body. Her limbs felt heavy. Soon, she knew, her legs would no longer be able to support her. She would have to cling to his strength.

He lifted her in his arms and carried her to the straw mat covered with the quilt. As he settled his long length beside her, she boldly reached for the buttons of his shirt, longing to feel his skin against hers.

He laughed at her sudden boldness and helped her as she fumbled with the first button. He unbuckled his gunbelt and tossed it aside, then shrugged out of his boots and pants.

Cameron tentatively touched the dark hair that curled on his chest and tapered to below his waist. Recognizing her hesitation, he fought his growing need and forced himself to be slow and gentle.

They were bathed in a pool of dappled sunlight. He lifted her hair, watching the fiery strands sift through his fingers. She saw his eyes narrow slightly before he bent to her lips. With his tongue, he traced the outline of her lips. Her lips parted in invitation, but still he only traced their fullness with his tongue. She trembled, aching for his kiss. When she could wait no longer, she caught his shoulders, drawing him to her.

His arms came around her, crushing her to him. The dark mat of hair on his chest tickled her breasts.

"Hold me, Cammy. Put your arms around me."

She allowed her fingertips to roam his naked back, loving the feel of hard, corded muscles.

He pressed his lips to her throat, feeling the little pulse that throbbed. With soft, feathery kisses, he roamed her shoulder, her collarbone, then dipped lower, to the soft swell of her breast. He heard her little gasp as his tongue circled her nipple, feeling it grow taut at his touch. Slowly his tongue moved, ever so slowly, until she thought she would die from the waiting, the wanting. He closed his lips over her breast. Deep inside her something contracted. He moved his lips to her other breast and she moaned, soft and low in her throat.

She had never known such feelings. With soft little sighs she moved in his arms, needing more, needing to give in a way she had never known before. Pressing her lips to his throat, she heard his low, gutteral growl.

He moved over her, his lips, his fingertips roaming her body at will, taking her higher than she had ever been. She seemed to have lost all control. There was only this room, this man, and the pleasure his touch brought. Each time he held her, her heartbeat quickened. Each new touch made her blood sing in her veins. His fingers and lips and tongue probed all the secret places of her body, bringing her to a level of desire she had never even imagined. A slow fire was building inside her until, fanned by his passion, it raged out of control.

Like a flower, she opened to him, and he to her. They closed around each other, their breath mingled, their bodies moving as one.

He cautioned himself to take her gently, slowly, aware that for her everything was fresh and new. They moved together in a soft cadence, a rhythm as old as time itself. And Cameron knew, as she had somehow always known, that this man in her arms was the only man meant to be her mate. She had been born for him alone.

Suddenly, she was beyond thinking. A searing, blinding passion took hold, driving her to match his strength, his rhythm.

Tenderness fled. He took her almost savagely then, crushing her to him, taking her with him to places they had never been before. Higher they soared, and higher still, until Cameron thought she would explode into a million shattering feelings. He felt the shudders that tumbled through her. For long moments she felt lost, drifting, absorbing him, bits and pieces of him, blinded by a white-hot light that blotted out all reason.

They lay, still locked together as one, his face pressed to a damp tangle of her hair. She could feel his unsteady breathing, the wonderful musky scent of him. Her heart was nearly bursting with the love she felt for him.

While his breathing grew more even, she clung to him. This strong, obstinate, tough-talking, surprisingly gentle man was the only one who would ever own her heart. For all those years that she had waited in a kind of limbo, she had been preparing to travel back to this place, this tiny cottage, and this man. In his arms she knew she finally had come home.

Her tears began to flow freely, washing away all that had gone before. Jarret and Alex no longer mattered. The pain and humiliation were forgotten. She was reborn this moment. Her life began now, with this man's love. She made no move to stop the tears.

Colt touched her cheek, then, rolling to his side, he leaned on one elbow and wiped her tears with his thumb.

"Cammy. Oh, God! Did I hurt you?"

She smiled through her tears. "No, Colt. You could never hurt me. I know that now." She caught his hand and kissed it. "I love you."

He was watching her eyes. Suddenly, she realized, he had gone very still.

"What's wrong?" She touched his arm.

For long moments he was silent.

Her heart nearly stopped beating. What if she had spoiled everything by declaring her love? She should have kept her feelings a secret, locked safely in her heart.

He took a deep breath. "Cammy, you're so open, so good. You've just given me the most special gift in the world. And I've kept so much from you."

She watched his face as he absently traced a finger along the curve of her cheek.

"You deserve to know who I am and what's going on here." He glanced at the scar on his wrist. "I suppose it all begins with this."

She touched the scar, then pressed his hand to her cheek. "It begins with a scar?"

He nodded. "In the world beyond Virginia City, my name really is Michael Gray. I'm a Texas Ranger. I served in Texas with your uncle, Quenton."

Her eyes rounded. "Quenton told me he'd served for a year. He said he needed to prove something to himself."

"He wasn't cut out for that kind of life, but he served his year admirably. He was only an adequate lawman, but as a friend he has no equal. One time, while we were hunting a band of outlaws, I nearly lost my life. Quenton and I were crawling toward a cabin where they were holed up, and a buried animal trap snapped over my wrist. It was old and rusted, and it chewed through the flesh clear to the bone. There was no way I could pry it open. We were caught in a crossfire between the bandits and my own men. I ordered Quenton to pull back, out of the range of fire." His voice thickened with emotion. "I was prepared to take out my hunting knife and cut my damned hand off. But Quenton crawled to me, used his knife and rifle to pry the trap open, and hauled me, unconscious, to safety. And all the while, we were under heavy fire."

Cameron traced the scar. "How it must have hurt."

"I barely remember. It was so badly infected I was out of my mind for days. Quenton stayed behind with me in the cabin while the rest of our company took the outlaws back to town. He nursed me back to health and managed to save my hand. I vowed then that if I could ever repay the favor I would."

He drew her close, murmuring against her temple. "When Quenton wrote to tell me that accidents were beginning to happen and that he suspected that someone was out to steal his father's land, I came running."

She pushed away to stare at him. "You mean, you're here to help Quenton, not hurt him?"

He nodded. "Cammy, this was all part of our plan." He ruffled her hair playfully. "But you came along and, being the little hellcat you are, managed to change things."

He could see the relief in her eyes.

"And my uncle isn't really the town drunk?"

Colt smiled. "I'm afraid he's had to do more than his share of drinking at the Delta Saloon lately, but it's all in the line of duty."

"If you're here to help Quenton, why did you move in with my stepbrothers?"

His voice deepened. "To keep an eye on you, little

wildcat. Now that Alex and Jarret know you share Quenton's inheritance, you're marked for the same fate they plan for him."

"Michael." She raised an eyebrow. "What were you doing on Allumette Island?"

"Visiting friends. My family lives in Ottawa. They're—wealthy and rather influential. My father is a magistrate. There's talk of a political future for my brother." He smiled wryly. "My father had always hoped I would follow him into law. But I'm afraid this wasn't quite what he had in mind."

"Do you get back to Canada often?" She found herself wondering if he would have ever returned to her island.

"Not as often as my family would like. But occasionally I show up just to assure them I'm still alive."

She sighed. "I'm so glad you told me the truth. And I'm so relieved to know that you're on the side of the law. You're just pretending to be partners with my stepbrothers. I should have known. I couldn't possibly love someone as evil as them." At the mention of their names, she felt him grow tense. She looked at his face, dark with rage. "Miriam said they didn't come down to breakfast. Did you . . . ?"

"Kill them?" His eyes narrowed. "I should have. I would have, except I was so worried about you I didn't take the time to finish them off. As soon as I was able to knock them out, I carried you upstairs to your room."

He pulled her close again, pressing her tightly to him. "When I saw what they were doing, I went crazy. I don't even remember the fight. I only remember seeing you being held down by that animal and then hearing Alex and seeing you sprawled on the ground, unmoving. I was terrified that they'd killed you. Oh God, Cammy. I've never known such fury. Or such fear."

His lips closed over hers. She could feel the tremors of emotion that rocked him. Her heart soared. The man she loved, the man who had saved her honor, and her life, wasn't a gunfighter or a gambler. He was an honorable man, on a mission of friendship.

When he lifted his head, he studied the tousle of hair that fanned out around her head. Her eyes were wide, luminous, glowing with love. Her lips were moist and eager for his kiss. It didn't seem possible that he could want her again. What had this little creature in his arms done to him? He was bewitched. He felt the driving need grow even as he bent to her.

She matched his need with a wild, primitive joy that surprised him. Kissing his eyelids, his mouth, his throat, she drove him nearly mad with desire. Boldly, she touched him as she had never dreamed she would touch a man. And when he thought he could wait no longer, he took her with even greater passion than before.

Dusk was settling over the land. Colt shifted so that he could study the beautiful woman who lay in his arms.

What had she done to him? Every time they came together, sparks flew. She could make him angrier than anyone he had ever met. She could make him laugh with a simple word or gesture. And he desired her. Even now, sated from their hours of lovemaking, he wanted her.

He had never known such feelings for a woman before. It was more than her beautiful body that sent his blood pounding in his temple. It was more than her impulsive nature that made him want to throttle her one minute and admire her the next. There were out of control passions here—deep feelings that he had never before experienced. He wanted to protect her. In fact, he wanted to kill anyone or anything that threatened her.

He swore in frustration and, slipping his arms from around her, stood and dressed. He had been away from his men, his duties, too long. He was getting soft. His prolonged absence only sharpened his appetite for adventure. Thankfully, this would soon be over, and he could get back to a way of life he had come to enjoy.

By the time she came fully awake, he was standing by the window, staring at the gathering darkness.

She sat up and reached for her dress. As she slipped it on, she sensed his tension, as he kept his back to her.

"Colt."

He turned.

Her voice reminded him of lush velvet. "You said you're a lawman. But Texas Rangers travel far from home. Sometimes, I understand, you even cross into Mexico in search of outlaws. Do you like that rough life?"

He watched the way her hair flamed even in the

shadows. His voice was toneless. "I'm good at what I do."

She paused. "And when you've—paid back your debt of friendship to Quenton, will you go back to—doing what you do so well?"

In the long silence he turned and stared out the window.

He didn't need to reply. She knew. He was an adventurer who loved his life. Fences, walls, ties would stifle a man like Michael. And so would a wife, and a home and family.

And if our child was conceived today, she thought, *my life will have come full circle. Colt will go away, even out of the country if he has to, and never know his own. A Texas Ranger. Constantly on the move, chasing outlaws. And I'll stay here, chasing a legacy of my own. The McCormick's desire for more—always more. And the Lampton legacy of faded riches and shattered dreams of glory. We are alike, but our lives will always be at cross purposes. And we may never meet again.*

She forced herself out of her gloomy thoughts. "Since you're working for my uncle, I think you might like to see what I have." She hurried out to her horse and returned with the rock from the saddlebag.

His eyes narrowed as she handed it to him. "Where did you get this?"

"From the new mine. Last night, after Alex and Jarret left, I sneaked in and stole it."

"My God, Cammy! Don't you even have enough sense to know when to be afraid? They would have killed you if they had caught you in there."

"They're digging on my land. I have a right to know what they've found." She studied him. "Do you know what this is, Colt?"

He nodded. "I think so. I sent a sample to the assayer's office. The report should be back soon."

"So. You've been sneaking around the mine, too."

He gave her a bleak smile. "There may as well be two fools in this together."

He caught her shoulders. "Now, Cammy, you have to promise me you won't go back to that mine or that house. I can't stand worrying about you, and I can't keep on protecting you every minute of the day and night. Sometimes, believe it or not, I have to sleep."

She stiffened. "I'm not asking you to protect me. I can take care of myself. I'm not a fool, Colt. Last night convinced me. Alex and Jarret are far too dangerous. I have no intention of facing them again. I'll go to Quenton's. But first, I want to hurry back and get a few of my things together. And I intend to tell Miriam I'm leaving."

"Yes." He gave his grudging consent. "She'll know enough to keep your secret. I don't want Alex and Jarret even to guess where you are. Tonight Quenton and I will spring our trap. Within the next few days we should be able to have all the evidence we need to bring them to trial. We're planning to set them up in the saloon, with witnesses." He glanced out the window. "If you're determined to go back, you'd better hurry before it gets any darker. I'm riding to Quenton's to finalize our plans. I'll tell him you're coming. Rose can prepare a room." He looked up.

"Would you like her to put you up in Elizabeth's room?"

She nodded. "Yes, I'd like that." She turned.

He caught her hand and pulled her back into his arms. The instant surge of passion reminded him once again of her effect on him.

"Be careful." His lips closed over hers.

"I will."

He took her face in his hands and studied her, as if memorizing her features. "If anything ever happened to you . . ."

"What could happen to me now?" Seeing his stern expression, she grinned. "Colt, I'll be careful." She blew him a kiss and danced out the door.

Chapter Twenty-two

AS CAMERON MADE HER WAY FROM THE BARN TO THE house, she felt a sudden prickle of fear. She had put on such a brave front in Colt's presence. Now she began to regret her impulsive decision to return to this place. The hairs on the back of her neck bristled at the thought of Alex and Jarret and what they had said and done the night before.

She was too close to them here. Just walking the same path from barn to house caused her alarm. It was too soon. The wounds were too fresh. Her skin grew clammy. She wiped her sweating palms on the skirt of her gown.

She must avoid them at all cost. They were both crazed with hatred and jealousy. They had become dangerous opponents.

Inside the front door, Cameron paused to listen for voices. The parlor and dining rooms were empty.

She could smell the rich, biting fragrance of wood smoke. The night had turned cool. The servants had kindled fires in the upstairs fireplaces.

Stealthily she made her way up the stairs to her room. Staring around, she recalled her first impression of the musty suite of rooms Alex had assigned her. It was cheerier now, with her bed linens freshened, the walls and floor scrubbed until they shone. But it had never felt like home.

She thought of her mother's bedroom in the house across the hills. Tonight, she would be surrounded by all the lovely things of her mother's childhood. If she wanted, she could sleep in one of her mother's old nightgowns, lie in luxury in fragrant linens, hang her clothes in sachet-scented closets.

It would be a haven from this house of hatreds. But it, too, would not feel like home. There was only one place where she could completely relax. One place where her soul felt truly refreshed. In the tiny, crumbling cottage of her birth, safe in Michael's embrace, she had found peace.

Into a valise she stuffed a change of clothes. Peering down the deserted hallway, she scurried to Miriam's door, knocked, and hurriedly entered.

Miriam and Ti were seated on a loveseat pulled up before an open window. Locked in an embrace, they seemed oblivious to the world and their intruder.

Embarrassed, Cameron cleared her throat. When they looked up, she flushed.

"I'm sorry to have barged in on you this way."

Miriam's eyes widened. "Cameron, where have you been? I've been so worried about you."

Evading the question, Cameron muttered, "That doesn't matter now. Miriam, I've come to say good-bye."

Ti stood suddenly and turned toward her.

Miriam's face crumpled. "Goodbye! Oh, Cameron, you can't leave us. You're the first real friend I've ever had." She caught Ti's hand and looked up at him. "Except for Ti. And I wasn't even aware of his friendship and—love—until you took the time to point it out to me." Her eyes were pleading. "Where would you go?"

Glancing at Ti, Cameron hesitated, then decided to trust him. "I'm going to my uncle's, Miriam. I'll be safer there for now. And later, when the danger is gone, I'll come back."

"Danger?"

"Yes. I am no longer safe here."

Miriam nodded. Cameron had anticipated Miriam's unhappiness at her decision. What she hadn't expected was Miriam's cool acceptance of the solution, despite her lack of knowledge about what had transpired between Cameron and her stepbrothers.

As Cameron crossed the room and took her half-sister's hands, Miriam said in a monotone, "You'll never live in this house again."

Cameron knelt and hugged her. "Don't be silly, Miriam. I'm only going away for a little while. Then I'll come back here, and you and I can get to really know each other as sisters should."

Miriam shook her head firmly. "No, Cameron. I feel it. All my life, I've been able to sense events in the future. Ti can attest to my nervousness today. Something terrible is about to happen here. And you and I will never live here again."

"Miriam, I must leave. But I give you my word, I'll return. We're family. We'll always care about each other. Nothing will divide us again." Cameron cast a worried glance at Ti. "Promise me you'll stay close to her tonight."

"You know I will." He watched as she embraced Miriam, then squeezed her hand before she walked from the room.

As she made her way along the hallway she froze. Outside the closed door of Alex's suite of rooms she could hear voices raised in anger. As she began to hurry past, the words being shouted stopped her in her tracks.

". . . saw you coming out of the Lampton house. Knowing how much I hate that family, and especially the artist son, you went to him, holding me up to ridicule for the whole town to see. You'll pay for this, you little whore."

Cameron dropped her valise at the sharp sound of a slap and Nina's cries.

"Stop it, Alex. Don't hit me again."

Remembering his cruel hands on her, the viciousness of his attack, Cameron shrugged aside her fears for her own safety and flung open the bedroom door, shrieking, "Take your hands off her, Alex. She's your wife, not your enemy."

"You!"

Enraged, he turned from the crumpled form of

Nina, cowering in the corner of the room, and vented his fury on the fiery-haired woman who was the real object of his hatred.

"You're some kind of a devil. Ever since you came here, everyone has been changing. My wife openly goes to lay with my enemy. My spineless stepsister starts skulking about in her wheelchair, spying on my every move. And my own brother blames me because he can't have you."

Cameron stood in the doorway, her hands on her hips. At those last words, her eyes narrowed in hatred. "It was you who planted that idea in his mind, wasn't it Alex? You told Jarret that if he forced himself on me I would somehow be grateful for his pitiful attempts at love."

"Right now, little nun, you should be grateful that you had one more day to live. I hate you. I hate what you stand for. You, and Big John, and the Lamptons. All of you think you're better than me. Even in death those old men tried to cheat me of the land. But I'll show them. You're not stronger than me, Cameron McCormick. When you're dead, all this will be mine."

Cameron turned, hoping to run. Hearing the argument, Ti and Miriam had rushed to the hallway. Seeing Nina cowering in the corner of the room, Ti attempted to rush to his sister's defense. But Jarret, coming up the stairs, grabbed Ti by the throat, tossing him aside as if he were an annoying puppy. Stunned, Ti slumped to the floor.

Alex's hand closed over Cameron's shoulder. His other hand grabbed a tangle of hair, pulling her head back sharply.

Her eyes wide with terror, she pleaded with the only one left who might be willing to intercede. "Help me, Jarret. Alex will kill me."

Jarret hesitated, watching his brother. His gray eyes were without emotion. "You won't kill Cameron, will you, Alex? You know I want her first."

"Don't be a fool. Can't you see she'll never be yours? We have to get rid of her."

The child's voice inside the man grew louder. "No, Alex. You promised I could have her. I don't want you to kill her." The vacant eyes widened. "At least not until I've grown tired of her."

Cameron felt her stomach lurch. He was absolutely mad.

"Fool! She's in the way. Don't you see? Once she's dead, we'll have her land. Then, when Quenton is disposed of, we'll have the Lampton land as well. We'll have it all." Alex's eyes glittered dangerously.

"No. Kill the others." Jarret shrugged. Their lives meant nothing at all to him.

Cameron's eyes widened at the bland statement. It was as if he were talking about crushing an insect.

"But Cameron lives until I say otherwise."

Still holding Cameron in a viselike grip, Alex backed up to the fireplace and grabbed a flaming torch. Brandishing it like a sword, he faced his brother. "Even you, Jarret? Even you want to start giving orders?"

They faced each other with Cameron between them. "I've always made the decisions. Always given the orders. And now, because of this witch, you want to defy me."

Jarret pouted. "I want her, Alex. That's all. Just give her to me. I don't care what you do with the others."

As he made a move to touch Cameron, Alex poked the flaming stick at his brother. "No. I say she has to die."

Jarret hesitated.

At that moment, Miriam rolled her wooden chair behind Jarret and shoved him with all her might, pushing him into the flaming torch. With a shriek of rage, he beat at his chest and stomach to extinguish the flame that ignited his clothes.

Shocked, Alex dropped the torch and brought his hand across Cameron's face, sending her reeling against the sharp edge of a table. Stunned, she leaned heavily, her palms flat down on the table's surface, trying to clear her mind.

With a fury, Jarret lifted Miriam from her wheelchair and rushed to the head of the stairs. Helplessly locked in his arms, she whimpered, wide-eyed, as he held her aloft.

"Alex should have found a deeper mine shaft the first time. But when we saw you lying down there, we thought you were dead. So we figured it was safe to send Big John down to fetch your body out. If we'd known you were still alive, we'd have left you there to rot."

"You—you pushed her down that shaft all those years ago?" Cameron stared at Jarret in horror.

He turned and grinned at her. "Alex said she was in the way. She was Big John's own kin. So we figured if we got rid of her we'd inherit everything." He looked at the figure cradled in his arms like a helpless kitten. "Alex picked the place. I was the one who threw you down." He laughed. "Later on, I was going to finish you off. But Alex said you didn't matter anymore. You still don't matter, Miriam." With that, he flung her down the stairs.

Cameron screamed, drowning out the shrieks of terror from Miriam as she fell, rolled, then lay motionless, slumped at the bottom of the stairs.

The torch, forgotten for the moment, had ignited the rug. Flames licked across the floor, catching the bottom of the draperies at the window, then surrounding the window with a ball of flame.

Dazed from her beating, Nina crawled toward the doorway. With a cruel laugh, Alex kicked her, sending her backward, writhing in pain.

Cameron's mind raced. They had to get out of here before the entire house went up in flames. The door to the outer balcony was opened slightly. The breeze fanned the flames, sending them leaping across the ceiling. Soon, the entire room would be engulfed.

"Alex. Let Nina go to little Alexander's room. He's asleep. You don't want your son to die, do you?"

Nina cast her a grateful look.

"Jarret," Alex commanded. "Get my son."

Like a spiteful child, Jarret rebelled. "No. I want Cameron. You get your own son."

Alex lost all control. Nothing, not even his own child, mattered now. Nothing except revenge against the woman who had caused all this.

"You." He rounded on her. "You're going to die for this."

From the corner of her eye, Cameron saw Ti begin to sit up. In order to draw attention away from him, she deliberately began to bait Alex.

"You mean, you'd rather kill me than allow Jarret to have what he wants."

Both men stared at her.

She turned to Jarret. "Do you always let Alex tell you what to do?"

Jarret thought about that for a moment. "He's smarter than I am. But I'm stronger than Alex. He always said we made a good team. Mostly, I like it when Alex tells me what to do. But not always." He turned to his brother. "Why can't I have Cameron for a little while, Alex? After that, we can kill her."

"Because she's too smart. She knows too much. She's just trying to trick you, Jarret. She wants you to turn against me."

"Is that what you're trying to do, Cameron?"

Before she could reply, Ti stood weakly, grabbed a heavy silver vase, and brought it down as hard as he could on Jarret's head. Jarret staggered, then went down on one knee. In a rage, Alex rushed at Ti with such a force they both crashed into the wall.

In the confusion, Cameron pulled Nina to her feet and pushed her roughly through the doorway. "Find Alexander. Save him and yourself." When Nina turned as if to protest, Cameron flung her away. "Go."

Jarret's hand snaked out, catching the hem of Cameron's gown. With a ripping sound, she pulled away. With a lunge, he caught her foot, sending her sprawling across the floor.

Instantly, he was upon her, catching her hands above her head, pinning her with his weight. Her breath came in short little sobs.

With a great hiss, the drapes fell from the charred windows, igniting little fires wherever they fell. A spark fell on the bed. Within minutes the quilt, the feather mattress, the down pillows, were a roaring inferno.

"Jarret," Alex cried. "Help me."

Looking up from the floor, Jarret realized that his brother was being overcome by Ti. Fighting for his life, the smaller man was discovering a strength he never knew he possessed.

Within minutes, both Alex and Jarret were engaged in a bitter fight with Ti. Grabbing a flaming dresser scarf, Ti flung it across Alex's face. With a roar of pain, he dropped to his knees. In a rage, Jarret picked up the smaller man and carried him to the head of the stairs, where he flung him down head first.

In those few confused minutes, Cameron rushed out to the balcony. It was her only hope of escape.

She stared around in horror. It was too far to jump. Flames were leaping through windows on the lower floors. The fire had spread throughout the dry wooden house. Flames several feet high, fanned by the breeze, licked across the roof. At any minute, the wooden balcony might collapse.

Alex and Jarret rushed through the door and faced her on the balcony.

Below her, in the darkness, she heard the clatter of horses' hooves and the babble of confused voices.

"She has to die, Jarret." Alex's voice rang with authority.

Jarret nodded blankly. "I'm sorry, Cameron. I wanted you to have some fun with me first. But he's right. It's the only way."

She felt a shudder of revulsion. Her eyes were wide with fright. Backing away from them, she took several steps until she felt the railing of the balcony press against the small of her back.

"Alex. Jarret." Colt's voice was sharp and clear in the night air.

Cameron stiffened at the sound of his voice. Just knowing that Colt was so near, and unable to get to her, caused her unbearable pain.

The two men peered over the balcony to see the figures of their family and servants huddled below.

"You've got to come down from there before the balcony collapses," Colt shouted.

Alex threw back his head with a roar of laughter. "Where've you been, partner? We're about to inherit some more land."

"Alex." Colt's voice grew sterner. "Quenton Lampton is down here with me. He wants to talk to you about giving you and Jarret his land."

Jarret's head came up sharply. Alex gave him a narrow look. "You're lying, Colt. The Lamptons never gave away a thing in their lives. And especially not to a McCormick."

"But that's just it, Alex. You and your brother aren't McCormicks. That's why Quenton wants to talk to you. His feud was with Big John."

Alex seemed to consider this for a moment.

Jarret waited for his brother's decision. A tongue of flame licked at the floor near his feet. "Maybe we should go down, Alex."

Alex's dark eyes glittered feverishly. "It's a trick. Lampton will never part with that land. And that one has to die." His finger pointed at Cameron pressed against the railing. Seeing the unhappy look on his brother's face, Alex snapped, "Are we brothers?"

Jarret nodded.

"Haven't I taken care of you all your life? Didn't I tell you we'd make Big John pay for not loving our mother?"

Jarret nodded again.

Alex's voice lowered. "And he did pay. Wasn't it fun, watching Big John McCormick getting weaker and sicklier by the day? Wasn't it exciting, keeping our little secret?"

"What secret?" Cameron moistened her lips, gone suddenly dry at his words.

Alex's head swiveled, as if seeing her for the first time. Then his mouth split into a sneer.

"I think we should tell her, Jarret, before she dies. It will be fun to see her face when she hears the truth."

Jarret grinned at his brother. "You tell her, Alex."

"We killed Big John," Alex said triumphantly.

She clasped her hands together tightly. "That's impossible. You were at the Delta Saloon when my father died."

"But we started killing him months before that." Alex slapped his brother on the shoulder. "We poisoned him. Slowly. So slowly, he never caught on.

Every day, when he took his medicine, we poisoned him a little more."

A picture of her handsome father lying weakly in his bed flashed through her mind. He had still been a young man, strong, eager for life. Yet he had been so weak he hadn't even been able to grip her hand. And then she remembered. The strange odor at his death-bed. She had thought it medicine. He had been poisoned.

"Why?" The word was no more than a whisper.

"Because he discovered something as important as gold on the land." Alex's satanic eyes glittered. "Silver. The biggest silver vein that's ever been found. We're sitting on millions of dollars worth of the world's richest silver mine. And we got tired of waiting around for him to die. That thieving gambler would have never given up. He would have lived forever, and robbed us of our chance. So we just"—he laughed, and the sound of it rang through Cameron's brain—"helped him along."

The first time she had ever seen Alex Bannion, she had thought he looked like Satan. Now she was certain. He was the devil incarnate. Feeling the tears welling up, she covered her face with her hands. With an anguished cry, she allowed the tears to flow freely. Her mother and father. Her grandfather. And now she was going to die as well. These two monsters wouldn't be satisfied until everyone was eliminated. And all because of this land. This barren, hateful land.

Through clenched teeth, she hissed, "You can have my share of the land, Alex. I don't want it. Even if it is worth millions. Knowing it took everyone I love, I hate it. I don't care if I never see this place again."

"That's good, little nun. 'Cause you're not going to live long enough to see anything again." Alex turned to his brother. "Grab her, Jarret."

As a strong hand clutched at her shoulder, Cameron saw the flames begin to lick along the balcony. A breeze fanned a shower of sparks from the roof, sending a fireworks display of red hot cinders cascading over the three people outlined in the darkness.

Colt stood on the ground, fighting the helpless rage that tore at him. He stared at the bleak scene around him. Beneath the spreading branches of a tree, Quenton held Nina and her child, comforting them. Ti had carried a sobbing Miriam to a soft mound of grass, where he sat rocking her in his arms. At first, the servants had frantically tried to quench the flames with buckets of water. Now, defeated, they milled about, watching the carnage with terror-glazed eyes.

There was no time left. He had to stop those madmen before they were allowed to carry out their threat. If they hurt her . . . A blinding fury gripped him.

"Ti."

The young man spread a blanket around Miriam and hurried to Colt's side.

"Quenton."

Handing Alexander over to a trembling Nina, Quenton kissed her cheek, then ran to Colt.

"I'm going through the house. I've got to reach Cameron. Climb those trees and string a rope between them. I don't know if we can jump that far, but if that balcony goes, it's our only hope."

Both men stood a moment, frozen, as Colt dampened a handkerchief at the pump, then pulled it over his face and dashed through the smoking doorway. Immediately, he was engulfed in flames. Knowing it was a desperate gamble, Ti and Quenton hurried off to find a rope.

The inside of the house was a raging inferno. Colt fought his way through dense smoke, his eyes streaming tears, his lungs burning. When he reached the top of the stairs, they collapsed beneath him. Grabbing for a railing that gave way at his touch, he leaped and landed in the upstairs hallway on his hands and knees. At the end of the hallway, beyond the flaming bedroom, he could see the silhouette of Cameron being held firmly by Jarret.

Inching closer, Colt realized that Alex was moving toward the far side of the balcony, intent on putting some distance between himself and the other two. As he drew nearer, Colt understood why. The balcony was now entirely in flame, and the weight of too many bodies at one spot would cause it to collapse.

With his gun drawn, Colt sprang through the doorway, facing Alex. When he saw the moving figure, Alex took aim. Above the roar of the fire, the gunshot, fired so near, could be clearly heard. Cameron and Jarret turned. With a look of horror, Cameron saw blood spurt from Colt's shoulder.

"Oh my God! No! Colt! No!" She tried to reach out to him, but Jarret held her fast, his beefy hands tearing at her flesh.

Turning her head, Cameron suddenly realized that Alex had been shot as well. Falling backward, he slumped heavily against the railing. For a moment, the only sound she was aware of was the splintering of the balcony railing. A moment later, Alex tumbled through space. She and Jarret stared at the body as it landed with a dull thud.

In the same instant, Jarret grabbed Cameron and spun her around with her back to Colt. Using her body as a shield, he shouted, "Take one more step, Colt, and I'll throw her over this balcony."

"Let her go, Jarret." Colt's voice was low, demanding. "We'll all get down safely and talk about this."

The sound of Jarret's childish laughter rippled on the night air. "You don't understand, do you, Colt?" He shook Cameron like a rag doll.

Her hair fanned out, matching the flames that danced on the breeze.

"I have to kill Cameron. Alex told me to. And I always do what Alex tells me."

"Your brother is dead now, Jarret. You're free to make up your own mind. You don't want to kill a beautiful woman like Cameron, do you?"

Jarret stared at her, then looked beyond her, to the man pointing the gun, who was trying to inch his way closer. "Don't move, Colt. Stay there."

"You don't want to hurt her, Jarret."

Jarret caught her chin and forced her head up. "Yes I do. I can't help it, Cameron. I like being strong. I like hurting things. Alex said it was just something I was born with. Like our mother. Everyone called her crazy."

His vacant eyes glittered for a moment, then became bland.

"Even Big John decided she was dangerous. That's probably why he hid you away, Cameron. He figured our mother would find out about you, and hurt you. If she hadn't, I probably would. Look at your pretty red hair and green eyes. I just love having pretty things and hurting them. I like crushing butterflies. I like strangling kittens. And I'm going to enjoy killing you."

His voice, the strangely childlike whine, grew higher in his excitement.

"I'm going to toss you over this balcony now, Cameron. And I'm going to watch you, just like I watched Miriam all those years ago." His voice lowered, coaxing. "Now I want you to scream, pretty Cameron. Scream as loudly as you can. That makes it more fun."

His grasp tightened on her arm until she could feel nothing. It had gone numb from his painful grip. With his other hand, he clutched her chin firmly and lifted it for his kiss. His wet lips covered hers, drooling in mounting excitement.

For long moments, her heart seemed to stop. She felt frozen in time.

The gunshot was muffled. Jarret's eyes widened. A look of surprise crossed his face. He dropped his hand to his chest. It came away sticky with blood. His surprise turned to horror. For the first time, he glanced down at Cameron's hand holding the little Remington. His lips pursed, as if to speak. A gurgling sounded in his throat and bubbled on his lips. And then, in slow motion, he seemed to hover a moment in space before hurtling to the ground below.

In quick strides, Colt was at her side. Gently he touched her cheek. It was ashen. Her eyes had widened until they seemed too big for her face. He grasped Cameron's arm. She seemed dazed by what had happened.

His voice was low, demanding. "Look at me, Cammy. There's no time left. We have to jump."

She stared at him, unable to speak.

"Trust me, Cammy. See that rope?" He pointed to the lariat outlined against the darkness. "Quenton and Ti secured it between two trees. It's our only hope. We have to leap into the dark air and catch that rope. Come on."

She stood, rooted to the spot. Recognizing her shock, Colt caught her arm and shook her roughly. Through gritted teeth, he hissed, "Don't you dare give up on me now. We've come too far. We've been to hell and back. And we're getting out of this now, together. We're going to make it. Do you hear me, Cammy?"

She blinked. Her voice was strangled in her throat. "Yes. I'll try."

"Good." He slapped at the flames that licked at the hem of her torn gown. "At the count of three, jump."

His words were nearly drowned out by the roar of the fire as it claimed another section of roof. "One. Two. Three."

Everyone on the ground held their breath as two figures leaped through space toward an impossibly fragile-looking lifeline. For a moment it looked as if the flimsy strand of rope had failed. They were falling. The rope sagged under their weight, then held. Bouncing slightly, they dangled precariously. Then one figure dropped to the ground. A moment later, Cameron dropped into his waiting arms. Clinging together, they fell to their knees and watched as the balcony and ceiling timbers crashed through the burning hulk of the once elegant house.

Chapter Twenty-three

THE WAGON HALTED AT THE CHARRED REMAINS. THE weary band of travelers stepped out to gaze wordlessly at the ruins. They had washed and taken a meal at the Lampton house. Colt's wound had been cleansed and bound. There had been little rest. After the terror of this night, they had seemed eager to return at first light, as if to assure themselves that it was really over.

While Rose tended little Alexander, who slept peacefully in the back of the wagon, Nina clung to Quenton. After a quick survey of the smoldering remnants of her unhappy life with Alex, she turned her head away.

"Where will you go?" Cameron asked Quenton.

"I'm taking Nina home. Back to her beloved Caribbean island."

"But what of your land?"

"I don't want it, Cameron. I never wanted it. It's yours now."

"But if Alex was right about my father's discovery, this land is worth a fortune. If the assayer's report confirms it, we could be sitting on the biggest silver mine in the country. Quenton, we could be millionaires."

"Send my portion to the Caribbean, Cameron." He smiled gently, then gazed into Nina's dark eyes. "I want nothing more than to sit in the sun with my love and spend the rest of my days painting her and her beautiful land. Nothing on earth could keep me from her."

Cameron brushed Nina's dark cheek with her lips. "I'm so glad you love my uncle, Nina. Be happy."

Cameron hugged him fiercely, then lifted her lips for a quick kiss.

"Your share of the land will always belong to you and your heirs, Quenton. Whatever feud there was between the McCormicks and the Lamptons is ended. We're one family now. I'll see that you get your share of the mine profits."

Quenton gave Colt a fierce bear hug, then solemnly shook his friend's hand.

After a brief look at the smoky scene, Ti carried Miriam back to the wagon and tenderly settled her on a folded blanket in the back of the wagon.

"We'll rebuild your home, Miriam," Cameron murmured to her weeping sister.

"No." Her head came up, and she clutched Cameron's hand. "I told you I sensed the end of this place. I don't ever want to live here again. I was never happy here, Cameron. For so long I blocked all my childhood pain and terror from my mind. Finally, I began to believe my fall down that mine shaft had really been an accident. But Jarret's words brought it all back to me. The threats, the nightmares, and finally, the crippling fall."

She brushed the tears with the back of her hand, and smiled weakly.

"Ti has asked me to go to his home. His and Nina's. I want to. I want to feel the warm sunlight of his tropical paradise. I want to see bright-colored flowers and lush foliage. I want to hear music and laughter." Her voice thickened. "I need to feel safe. I want to be loved."

Cameron nodded and kissed her cheek. "Then that's what I wish for you as well. I know you'll be happy with Ti, Miriam. But I do hope you'll come back here someday."

Miriam's eyes widened. "Do you intend to stay here alone, Cameron?"

She studied Colt standing off by himself, staring intently at the ashes.

She stood straighter. "Yes. All my life I've been alone. I'll manage."

Her uncle shook his head. "I can't believe you are actually willing to stay here."

His lovely young niece smiled up at him as he settled himself beside Nina. "Too many people paid too high a price for this land, Quenton. I have no intention of leaving. This is my home. I intend to stay and work the mine."

"You can stay in the Lampton house. It's not in a very good state of repair, but it's shelter."

Cameron smiled. "Thank you, Quenton, but there's only one place where I can be truly happy."

At his questioning glance, she added, "There's a tiny crumbling cottage, that stands on the border of McCormick land and Lampton land. Part of the roof is sagging, and I'll be able to look up and see the stars. The same stars you and Nina and Miriam and Ti will be seeing." She gave them a dreamy smile. "That will be a bond between us. Whenever you look up at the night sky, know that I'm seeing the same sky, the same moon and stars. And think of me."

Amid tears and laughter, the wagon rolled across the hills, in the direction of San Francisco, where a ship would be in dock, soon to be heading for the Caribbean.

When they were alone, Cameron turned to study Colt. He stood rigid, tense. He was staring at the distant horizon. Her heart felt wrenched from her. There was a look of longing on his face. That look told her that he was eager to be off, to join his friends in the excitement of the hunt once more.

"I suppose you're eager to get back to your home?"

His head came up, but he didn't speak.

"What are you thinking about, Colt?"

"I'm thinking that I've been away a long time. It's best that I go, Cammy."

He caught the reins and led his horse toward her.

His husky voice washed over her. "You're a very special woman, Cameron McCormick. You're everything a man could want. If I were any other man, I'd stay with you." He reached out a finger, to trace the curve of her cheek.

She forced herself to remain perfectly still, though she longed to move against his touch like a kitten. When he pulled himself into the saddle, he faced her. "I have a job to do. You understand."

She nodded, lifting her head higher. Her eyes were dry as she met his dark gaze. "As you said, Colt. You're very good at what you do."

"Yes." He allowed his gaze to travel the length of her and back, for a moment lingering on the soft auburn halo that drifted about her face and shoulders.

"Thank you for understanding." His voice grew thick with emotion. "In the border towns around Texas we have a saying. Vaya con Dios. It means go with God." He touched the brim of his hat. "Vaya con Dios, Cameron McCormick."

She swallowed. Her throat was so tight, it hurt to speak. "Go with God, Michael Gray."

He wheeled his horse and rode away, without a backward glance.

Cameron stood watching until horse and rider disappeared over the crest of a hill.

Her eyes brimmed. The words of little Sister Adele pierced her mind with blazing intensity. "Oh, Cammy, don't ever pin your hopes and dreams on a man. For he'll be a thief and steal your most precious possession of all."

When would she learn? When would she ever learn?

She brushed the tears with the back of her hand in an angry gesture, then turned to the smoldering ruins. There would be much to do before nightfall.

She glanced toward the hill, for a moment hoping to see the black stallion returning. The horizon stretched empty for as far as she could see. She turned away and bent to her task. There would be no tears, she reminded herself sternly. She had always known that Michael Gray was a man of duty, a man meant for the wider world, beyond her narrow border.

He had touched her life. She had loved him. And now, she must see to the job of surviving.

Cameron stood back, surveying the clutter of the tiny cottage. She had made a bed of clean hay and quilts carried from Quenton's house. A lovely pitcher and basin stood on a small dresser. Beside it, the dressing mirror from her mother's room reflected the mass of scarlet roses that framed the open window.

She had swept the dirt floor and covered it with a braided rug. A cozy fire crackled in the fireplace. On the raised hearth stood a basket laden with kindling.

She had tackled a backbreaking job this day. The endless miles from Quenton's house up the hill to this cottage had taken their toll. But she was grateful. There had been no time to dwell on what might have been; no time to weep.

Cameron removed her dirt-stained britches and rough homespun shirt and poured water into the basin. After washing thoroughly and brushing her hair until it shone, she slipped the elegant nightdress over her head and smoothed down the long skirt. This had been her mother's. It still bore the delicate scent of sachet from the closet. Tonight, she decided, she had earned the luxury of a special garment.

Turning down the quilt, she crossed the room and stared at the midnight sky, watching shadows drift across the hills, listening to the sigh of the night wind. Was Colt lying somewhere in a bedroll, gazing up at the same sky? She swallowed the lump that threatened to choke her. She had promised herself she wouldn't torture herself with thoughts of him. But the night silence brought him rushing back to her mind. She would forever be able to recall the musky scent of him, the rich, deep timbre of his voice, his strength, his tenderness. She could fill her days with work. But her nights, she feared, would be endlessly painful.

With a determined shake of her head, she bent to blow out the candle. Hearing a sound at the door, she looked up fearfully, expectantly.

Moonlight streamed through the open door. Silhouetted in the amber rays was a figure that caused her heart to stop. She forced herself to remain still, even though she longed to rush to his arms.

Michael stared at the figure illuminated by the candlelight. Her eyes rounded, then softened. Her hair, freshly brushed, cascaded in soft waves down her back. Through the delicate, opaque gown, he could see the soft swell of her breasts, the narrow waist, the flare of her hips.

He studied her through narrowed eyes. "I should have been halfway to Texas by now."

"What stopped you?"

"A damn fool headstrong girl who'll probably have me talking to myself next."

He watched her spine straighten, her chin jut at an imperial angle.

"I didn't want to stand in your way, Michael. I know you have important work to do. I can take care of myself."

"Yes. I know you can." He took a step forward. "Except when a dozen evil drifters get wind of your silver mine. I suppose you'll have to hold them off with a couple of hired guns. The more I thought about it, the more I decided you'd probably have need of a trusted gunfighter."

She nodded, feeling the first tiny trickle of hope. "I hadn't thought of that. You could be right."

"My work in Texas is important, Cammy. I don't just do it because it's exciting. I've helped catch some of the West's most vicious killers."

"I'm sure you have. You can be proud of your work, Michael."

He nodded. "But I think you need me here even more than Texas does."

She inclined her head slightly. "I suppose I could use some help."

"Then I'm hired?"

She frowned. "Not yet. You haven't told me how much this will cost me."

He swore in frustration. "It's going to cost you plenty, lady. I'm the best. I'm worth three of any other men."

"How much?"

He paused, calculating. "A percentage of the take from the mine."

She shook her head. "No deal."

Michael stiffened. "What! Why not?"

"The only ones who get a share of this mine are kin. I don't recall hearing of any Grays in the family."

"We could change that."

She went very still. Her heart was hammering so loudly, she was certain he could hear it. "And how do you propose to change it?"

His words tumbled out in a rush. "You could marry me."

"Do you know what you're saying?" She studied him, noting the lines of tension on his face. "It would mean giving up the danger, the excitement, of the Texas Rangers."

Michael moved a step closer to touch her arm, and the shockwave that trembled through her jolted him as well.

"While I was riding, Cameron, I was thinking about something Sister Leona said the day we rescued her. She asked me if I believed that the hand of God touches all our lives."

Cameron nodded, remembering.

A smile curved the corners of his lips. "Isn't it strange how plans have a way of changing, without any warning, when the fates step in?"

Cameron watched him, thrilling to his words.

"All my life I've wanted danger, excitement. That's

why I left my comfortable home in Canada. That's why I joined the Texas Rangers."

She felt the tremor of eagerness, of breathless anxiety coursing along her spine.

He allowed his gaze to trail slowly from her bare feet, planted firmly on the rag rug, to her hands, held stiffly against her sides, to her heaving breasts, impatient to hear all he had to say. He stared at her lovely face turned up to study him. Finally his gaze rested on her mane of burnished hair.

"Cameron McCormick, let's stop playing with words. I can't imagine anything more dangerous or more exciting than you. And I can't think of a greater challenge. There is nothing in this whole world I'd rather do than spend the rest of my life with you."

Her breath caught in her throat. He had just spoken all the words her heart had been longing for. She had feared she would never hear him say them.

"Oh, Colt. Do you really mean it?"

He gathered her into his arms and pressed his lips to a tangle of hair at her temple. Against the pounding pulse beat, he murmured, "I love you, Cameron McCormick. More than anything in this world. When I heard you telling the others to look up at the stars and think of you, I realized I could never again look at the stars without feeling a stab of pain. I could never again enjoy a full moon in a night sky without missing you. What would my life be like without you? Oh, Cameron, you little wildcat. I want to stay with you. I want us to tame this wild savage land together."

He brought his lips to hers, feeling the instant surge of passion. "You've already tamed this wild savage heart, my love."

"Don't ever go away again, Michael. Don't ever leave me alone." She stood there, locked in his embrace, overwhelmed by the scent of horse and leather and by the quiet strength of him. The tears she had fought all through this long day burned in her throat. "I love you so much. When you left me, it was the worst hurt I've ever known."

His voice was a whispered caress. "I'll never leave you again, little Cammy. I know the pain you went through. Today, leaving you was worse than the time I faced cutting off my hand. This time, I had tried to cut out my heart."

"Oh, Colt. I love you so."

He raised his head. His dark eyes sparkled with mischief. "I can see that you're going to have to battle a love for two men."

When she raised an eyebrow, he added, "Colt, and Michael Gray."

She chuckled, then murmured against his lips, "I love both of you. Forever. For a lifetime, and beyond."

Her words were swallowed up in a kiss so powerful, she clung to him.

Once she had thought this harsh land bred harsh people. Now she knew that a certain toughness was necessary to survive this land. She and Michael were two of a kind. Neither would tame the other. But they would love with a passion. And that would be enough.

They had both traveled across a continent to a primitive, distant land, seeking their heart's desire.

"Welcome home, Michael." Her lips opened in invitation.

In this man's arms, Cameron McCormick knew she had also come home. And secure in his love, she was home to stay.

Epilogue

1879

CAMERON BENT AND PLACED FRESHLY PICKED roses on the graves of her father and mother, then moved to the grave of her grandfather, William Lampton, and wiped a speck of dirt from the headstone.

Surveying the land with satisfaction, her glance rested on the magnificent mansion which towered above the stand of trees where the McCormick land had once joined the Lampton land. Now, they were one. When their house had been completed, she had instructed the workmen to move the graves to their present site, alongside the fragrant rose garden.

Kneeling beside the headstones, she took the faded newspaper clipping from her pocket and read it for the millionth time.

August 16, 1874. The largest silver mine in the world has been discovered just outside the town of Virginia City, Nevada. Experts disagree on the value, but estimates are in the millions of dollars. The discovery is a bonanza.

Cameron smiled suddenly, recalling the letter that had arrived the week before. Quenton wrote that he and Nina had presented Alexander with a baby brother. The boy, named William, was pink and plump and so far had a fine growth of dark fuzz on his perfectly shaped little head. A portrait of Nina and the children, painted by the proud Quenton, would follow.

Ti, he added, was teaching Miriam to swim, and although she was still confined to her wheelchair, she was content, and blissfully in love.

At the top of the hill, a black stallion appeared with his tall, dark rider. Cameron's heart stopped, and for a moment she was seventeen again on a tiny, crescent-shaped island, riding alongside a stranger toward her destiny.

She blinked, and over the hill came a pony bearing a small, dark miniature of the man. Behind the boy, her plump arms clinging tenaciously to his waist, sat a barefoot urchin, her red-gold curls bouncing about her shoulders.

Cameron stood and brushed the grass from her skirts. Michael reined in his horse and lifted Cameron easily in his powerful arms, planting a kiss soundly on her lips. The children whooped in glee.

Setting her back down, he said, "A letter came

today. From the Convent of the Sisters of Divine Charity."

He glanced at the children astride their pony. "I've been thinking. Jameson is a very capable mine foreman. We've sent the latest accounting to Quenton and Miriam. The house is complete. Everything is going smoothly. This would be a fine time to visit my family in Ottawa. Maybe we could make a stop first at Allumette Island."

He watched the smile of pleasure on her beautiful face.

"The dear old sisters are probably just about recovered from all those years with you, Cammy. I think they might be up to entertaining a couple of ragamuffins. Especially that one with her mother's green eyes and fiery hair."

"Oh, Michael. Could we?" Her eyes lit with pleasure.

He lifted her gently to the horse's back and wrapped his arms about her waist, burying his face in the wild tangle of hair.

"Together, we can do anything in the world, Cammy. Anything."

She laughed. Her eyes sparkled with mischief. She tossed her head and spurred the horse past the children's pony. Her girlish voice rippled on the breeze. "Come on," she called. "We'll race you home."